Five houses so far, and Jay hadn't liked any of them

"I really think an apartment would be your best bet," Gail said.

Frowning, Jay glanced at her. "I want a house. With a yard for my dogs."

"I didn't know you had dogs."

He lifted a shoulder, aware he was being unreasonable. "I don't have any. Yet. But I'm getting them, as soon as I have a place."

"You're buying a house because of dogs you don't even have?" Gail gazed at him a moment, then heaved a deep sigh and muttered to herself. Jerking her head at the car, she said, "Get in. There's one house we haven't looked at yet."

A short time later she pulled up in front of the perfect house. "Nice," he said. "Why didn't you show me this one first?"

"Notice the location?"

He grinned. "Two doors down from yours. Trying to keep the riffraff out of the neighborhood?"

"No. But if I'd showed you this one first, you would've thought I was making a move on you."

Dear Reader,

The Texas coast is one of my favorite places to be. It's also a favorite of Jay Kincaid's, whom I first met when he showed up in his brother Mark's book, *Trouble in Texas*. I was a goner from the moment Jay stepped off that Harley and onto the page. I knew I wanted to write his story. What writer wouldn't want to get to know a charming young doctor with a heart of gold…who also happens to be totally hot?

I wasn't the only one who fell for Jay. Gail Summers, the heroine of this book, liked him a lot when they first met. But their story wouldn't begin until five years later, when Jay decided to move his medical practice to Arkansas City. Pretty soon Jay's a goner, too, not only for Gail, but for her two little girls, as well.

Naturally, the path to true love doesn't run smoothly. Gail and Jay are in for a few surprises along the way….

Sincerely,

Eve Gaddy

P.S. I love to hear from readers. You can reach me at P.O. Box 131704, Tyler, TX 75713-1704, e-mail eve@evegaddy.com or visit my Web site at www.evegaddy.com.

Books by Eve Gaddy

HARLEQUIN SUPERROMANCE
903—COWBOY COME HOME
962—FULLY ENGAGED
990—A MAN OF HIS WORD

Don't miss any of our special offers. Write to us at the following address for information on our newest releases.

Harlequin Reader Service
U.S.: 3010 Walden Ave., P.O. Box 1325, Buffalo, NY 14269
Canadian: P.O. Box 609, Fort Erie, Ont. L2A 5X3

A Marriage Made in Texas
Eve Gaddy

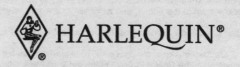

HARLEQUIN®

TORONTO • NEW YORK • LONDON
AMSTERDAM • PARIS • SYDNEY • HAMBURG
STOCKHOLM • ATHENS • TOKYO • MILAN • MADRID
PRAGUE • WARSAW • BUDAPEST • AUCKLAND

ISBN 0-373-71090-9

A MARRIAGE MADE IN TEXAS

Copyright © 2002 by Eve Gaddy.

This edition published by arrangement with Harlequin Books S.A.

® and TM are trademarks of the publisher. Trademarks indicated with ® are registered in the United States Patent and Trademark Office, the Canadian Trade Marks Office and in other countries.

Visit us at www.eHarlequin.com

Printed in U.S.A.

I'd like to thank Sharon Knoell, R.N.,
for answering my questions about childbirth.
And my thanks to Dr. Nancy Lieb, for answering my
medical questions for this and other books. Also, many
thanks to Millard Countryman, for answering all my
questions about real estate.

This book is for my writing buddies
who don't find it at all strange that I hear in my head
the voices of people who don't exist.

CHAPTER ONE

ARANSAS CITY, a tiny Texas town snuggled up to the blue waters of the Gulf of Mexico, boasted three restaurants. Gail Summers was intimately acquainted with all of them. A bar and grill owned by her brother, Cameron Randolph, a burger joint and a Mexican food restaurant. Today, she'd chosen Mexican for her weekly lunch with her sister Cat. Who, surprise, surprise, hadn't arrived.

Working on her second basket of chips, Gail glanced at her surroundings. Though you couldn't tell it from the decor, the place did a booming business. People overlooked the slightly depressing atmosphere for the food—mouthwatering, spicy hot Tex-Mex. Still, ancient chrome and Formica tables and equally old vinyl-covered chairs, along with a couple of velvet paintings of Elvis and a bullfight just didn't inspire you to linger. Which was fine with the management, who wanted to move as many people in and out as possible.

A few minutes later, Cat blew in. "Guess who's moving to Aransas City?" she said breathlessly, before she even greeted Gail.

"How can you look so good at nearly eight months

pregnant?'' Gail demanded as Cat pulled out a chair and sank gratefully into it. "I looked like death warmed over with both my girls.'' Her unlamented ex, Barry, had always rubbed that in, too. "You just...glow or something. It's disgusting. You were like that with Max, too," she added, referring to her three-year-old nephew. "I think I hate you.''

"It's from living a virtuous lifestyle," Cat said, dimples dancing in her cheeks, dark brown eyes gleaming with humor.

They both laughed. "Okay, I'll bite," Gail said, pushing her hair back out of her face. "Who's moving to town and why should I care?''

Cat leaned forward and grinned. "I'm about to tell you some delicious gossip. Show a little respect.''

Gail tapped her fingers on the table, lifted an eyebrow and waited.

"Think tall, blond and gorgeous.''

"That could describe a lot of people. Male or female?''

"Male." Cat's lips curved upward. "Definitely male.''

The waitress came just then and took their orders. As soon as she left, Gail said impatiently, "You know I'm no good at guessing games. Spill it.''

Cat looked around the room, lowered her voice and said, "Jay.''

Gail stared at her for a minute. "Jay Kincaid? Your brother-in-law?'' Six foot two of pure male temptation. And the last time Gail had seen him, six months before, he'd been living with an equally tall, blond and gorgeous lady lawyer.

Cat nodded vigorously. "That's right." She grabbed a chip and bit down with satisfaction. "He's joining Dr. Kramer at the new clinic."

That got her attention. "What? How? He works in California."

"How do you think? He's moving here. He'll be in tomorrow night."

Jay Kincaid, moving to Aransas City? Living in the same town, instead of fifteen hundred miles away? She'd always imagined him as firmly entrenched in California.

"That's not all," Cat continued. "Remember Carla?"

The twinge of pleasure and anticipation she'd felt faded quickly. "Who could forget?" Gail said irritably. "The woman was draped all over him like a cheap fur coat at that family picnic you had last summer."

Carla had spent the occasion making it crystal clear that Jay was off-limits to other women. Especially Gail. Why the woman had felt threatened by her, Gail couldn't imagine, but she obviously had. Carla was smart, successful and beautiful. Gail was a struggling single mother five years older than Jay. And while she certainly wasn't dog ugly, she was no beauty queen, either.

"That's her," Cat said. "I was surprised she didn't leave claw marks on his arm. I never could figure out what he sees in her, but when I said that to Mark, he just laughed at me.''

Gail snorted. "I don't blame him. Get real, Cat. She looks like a men's magazine model.''

"Oh, that," Cat said, waving a hand. "But it's so obvious.''

"Yeah." Gail sighed and looked at her own much smaller chest. Cat had inherited most of the curves in the family. Gail was slighter, not voluptuous at all. On the bright side, though, she ate what she wanted and didn't gain weight. "Let me guess. They're getting married, right?" A shame, really. Besides being to-die-for good-looking, Jay was a really nice man. Sometimes a little too nice, Gail thought darkly.

"Au contraire." Cat's eyes sparkled as she leaned forward. "They're over. *Finito. Kaput.* Jay said he moved out three months ago.''

The waitress set their drinks down, promising to return with the food. Playing for a little time, Gail put sugar in her tea and stirred it before she spoke. "And I should care, why?''

Cat smirked. "Come on, Gail. Every time you and Jay are together there are vibes. Very sexy vibes.''

Gail laughed. "Right. Pregnancy has addled your imagination.''

Their food arrived, steaming hot and smelling like heaven. Gail thought she'd deflected Cat's interest, but no such luck. After a few bites, Cat laid her fork down and said, "You know, you can be as closed-mouthed as you want, but I know for a fact something happened between you two during Mark's and my wedding.''

''Do you?'' Gail shrugged. ''That was five years ago, Cat. Even if something had gone on, what would it matter now?''

''So you admit something happened.''

''Nothing happened,'' Gail said flatly, pushing her suddenly tasteless enchilada aside. But not from lack of trying on her part. She still winced whenever she thought of the reception that evening, at their mother's stunning waterfront home. She and Jay had spent most of it together. Dancing. Talking. And late in the evening, in the darkened shadows of the terrace, kissing. She resisted the urge to fan herself as memories bombarded her. Oh, the man could kiss.

So when Gail's mother had offered to keep the girls at her house, Gail had asked Jay to come home with her. They'd driven to her house and then…nothing. Jay had very nicely and very gently, turned her down.

I'VE GOT TO GET A PLACE OF MY OWN, Jay Kincaid thought at six-thirty on a Saturday morning.

Peace and quiet did not exist at his brother's house. Not at any time of day, but particularly not in the morning. Medical residents kept better hours than parents of toddlers—or their houseguests.

Groaning, Jay rolled over. Max, his sticky-faced nephew, had just landed knees first in the middle of Jay's back. It wasn't broken…quite, but twenty-five pounds of pint-sized terror could do a lot more damage than seemed possible. "Hey, Max, where are your mom and dad?"

"Mommy's frowing up," the dark-haired little boy told his uncle, sliding off the bed to face Jay squarely in one sleep-deprived eye. "Daddy's cooking. Lots of smoke comed out of the pan and then Daddy said a bad word." Max grinned, looking remarkably like his father. "I'm not 'sposed to say it, or Mommy will tan both our—"

"Hides," Jay finished for him. He couldn't help smiling. Mark usually left the cooking to Cat, who loved to cook. But her pregnancy kept her out of the kitchen in the morning these days.

Jay dragged himself from the bed, pulled on his jeans and a white T-shirt and went to the kitchen, his nephew perched on his hip. Sure enough, Mark stood at the stove, a blackened mess in the pan before him and a scowl on his face that would frighten armed convicts. And had.

"Yum," Jay said. "Max said you were cooking. What do you call that, baked charcoal?" He set the child in his booster seat, pulled out a box of cereal from the pantry and milk from the refrigerator. "Here, kid, if you wait for your old man to feed you, you'll starve to death."

"Microwave's broken," Mark said, throwing him a grateful glance, a bit of a desperate look in his eyes. "Max wanted bacon. No one can cook bacon on the stove top without burning it."

"Want bacon, want bacon," Max chanted, devilment sparkling in his big, brown eyes.

"Sorry, kid, you're out of luck," Jay told him. He finished fixing Max's cereal and gave the little boy a spoon. "Your dad's hopeless at the stove. Take it from me, I remember."

"As I recall, you didn't starve. So I'm no good at breakfast. I make up for it in other areas." Mark threw out the charred bacon, then left the pan to soak in the sink. "Cat told me this morning she's off breakfast duty for the duration," he added glumly.

"Cheer up, bro, it's only five more weeks. Go buy a new microwave." He poured himself a cup of coffee—Mark could make that with no problem—and sat at the table. "Which reminds me, I'd better get moving on house-hunting."

"What's your hurry? You know you're welcome to stay with us as long as you need to," Mark said, dark hair falling over his forehead as he reached down to pick up the newspaper that littered the floor.

"I figure since I'm staying in what's going to be the baby's room, the sooner I get out of the way the better." And the sooner he left the bedlam of his brother's house behind, the better for his sanity. Not that he'd tell Mark that, of course. He loved his brother and his family, he just didn't want to live with them.

Judging from Mark's smile, though, he had a pretty good idea of Jay's true motives. Mark's attention went back to his son, absorbed in flinging soggy corn pops to all corners of the kitchen, and he sighed. "Eat the food, don't launch it, Max." Obediently, Max spooned cereal into his mouth. Mark ruffled the child's hair. "Good boy."

After pouring himself a cup of coffee, Mark took another chair, flicked cereal off the back and dragged it up to the table. "Look, I know you say that helping Tim Kramer start this clinic is what you want, but you've been living in California the past what, twelve years? This is the Texas coast. It's a hell of a long way from California."

"You can say that again, brother." He smiled at Mark. "Relax. The decision isn't as sudden as it seems. I've been unhappy with practicing emergency room medicine for a long time now. I'm looking for a different lifestyle." One that didn't include ulcers, insomnia and life in the fast lane. Family practice in this sleepy little town was going to suit him just fine.

Mark started to say something, then closed his mouth. After a moment, he shook his head and asked, "Are you sure the move doesn't have more to do with Carla than your job?"

Carla. The woman Jay had been living with until a few months ago. Jay shrugged. "That was over before I found out about Tim Kramer needing a partner."

Mark merely lifted an eyebrow and waited.

Jay sighed, and rubbed a hand over the back of his neck. "Okay, I'll admit, getting away from Carla seemed like a good idea." Carla hadn't taken their breakup well. In fact, she seemed certain it was only a matter of time before they'd be back together. Jay, on the other hand, had never felt as relieved as he had on the day he moved out. "But I didn't have to come to Texas to accomplish that. I want to live here, Mark. I want a practice where I know my patients, and they know me. I want time to do something besides work. For the first time in twelve years, I'll have weekends free. Hell, I may take up fishing. And windsurfing."

Mark still looked skeptical. "Fishing and windsurfing aside, you've visited us enough to know it's not the most exciting place on the planet."

"I like Aransas City." Jay sipped coffee, savoring it. "I always have."

"Yeah, you like to visit, but living here's a different story."

Knowing his brother meant well, Jay curbed his exasperation. "I know what I'm doing. I'm thirty years old, not Max's age." Which Mark sometimes forgot. Not surprising, since he'd raised Jay and their youngest brother Brian from the time they were twelve and thirteen.

Mark looked chagrined. "Sorry, I know you're not, I just worry about you. It's a hard habit to break, that's all."

Max chose that moment to dump his bowl of milk and cereal on the floor. "Oopsy."

"Oh, man, Max, did it have to be the whole bowl?" Mark said, hastily grabbing a towel.

"I'd say you have plenty to worry about without adding me to your list," Jay said, laughing.

"Everybody's a smartass." Mark knelt on the floor and began mopping up the mess.

"Smartass," Max repeated, clear as a bell.

"Now you've done it," Jay said, pushing back his chair and rising. "I'm out of here before Cat comes in and lets all of us have it."

"Before you go, I need a favor." Mark scooped the mess back into the bowl and blotted the floor with the damp towel.

Jay grinned at the image of his big, bad brother, scourge of animal smugglers everywhere, on his hands and knees cleaning up after his son. Domesticity suited Mark, Jay decided. But then, Mark had always been the responsible one. No shock that the marriage and family thing worked for him. Too bad Jay wasn't cut out for it.

"Depends on the favor. Am I going to regret it if I say yes?"

Mark laughed and got to his feet, dumping the cereal in the sink. "Nope. I need you to take Mel's birthday cake over to Gail's house. The party's today and Cat wants to make sure it gets there in plenty of time." He glanced at his son with a wry smile. "And safely. She's afraid she'll run late since she's bringing Max, and I have to go into work this morning. So, how about it?"

Gail Summers. Pretty. Blond. Smart. Sassy mouth. He hadn't seen her since the last time he'd visited Mark, several months ago. Carla had been with him then, he remembered, and she hadn't liked Gail at all. Possibly because she'd sensed his attraction to her. But Carla was no longer in the picture. The thought of seeing Gail again brought a smile to his lips. "Not a problem."

"I didn't think you'd consider it a hardship," Mark said dryly, as he poured more cereal into a bowl and set it in front of his son.

Jay laughed, heading for the back door. "Thanks, I owe you one," he told his brother.

"More than one," he heard Mark say, as the door shut behind him.

CHAPTER TWO

"WHAT'S WRONG WITH A PARTY at Princess Pizza, I'd like to know?" Gail muttered while standing on the white Formica drainboard in her kitchen. Last year, nothing else would do for Mel but to have the party at the pizza place. This year she'd cried when Gail had mentioned it. She wanted the party at her house. Stretching, Gail taped another piece of bright pink crepe paper in place. Oh, well, what mattered was that her daughter was happy, not whether the kids turned the house into a shambles.

Still, it would have been nice to have the mess someplace besides her house. Gail glanced out the window and squinted. Rain. Definitely, rain. Which meant they'd have to hold the entire party inside. Her head pounded thinking about it.

Leaning back, she tried to judge what the decorations looked like. Of course, pink and purple, Mel's favorite colors, didn't look so hot next to Gail's bright red kitchen cabinets, but that couldn't be helped. Mel wouldn't notice the colors clashed. There was room for more balloons, but her jaws were aching.

Someone knocked on the kitchen door. "Come in," she called. *It's about time Cam showed up.* Her brother had promised to come by and help her decorate, and though he sometimes ran late, he was usually pretty dependable.

She heard the door open and before he could speak she said, "Where the heck have you been? Twenty giggling little girls are coming over in two hours." Steamed, she continued. "Never mind, just hand me that purple streamer there on the table."

"Here you go," an unexpected voice said as a hand reached up with the streamer.

Her head whipped round and she looked down into Jay Kincaid's dazzling green eyes. Straight, dark-blond hair fell over his forehead, a dimple winked in one lean cheek, and that lethal weapon smile of his was out in full, blinding force. He looked even better than he had the last time she'd seen him.

Damn, isn't this just my luck? She wore her oldest cut-offs, an ancient blue T-shirt with an unraveled hem, and she'd bet her next commission that she hadn't managed to brush her hair this morning. And unlike Meg Ryan, she didn't look good with messy hair.

It occurred to her she probably looked like a guppy staring at him with her mouth hanging open, so she snapped it shut. "Jay? What are you doing here?"

"I came bearing gifts," he said, nodding toward the kitchen table where a plastic cake holder sat. "Cat was afraid hurricane Max would demolish the birthday cake, so she and Mark drafted me into cake delivery."

"When did you get into town?"

"Last night." His gaze seemed to slide up her body.

Was he staring at her legs? It was hard to tell, from her angle above him, but since they were at his eye level, she thought he might be. At least she'd shaved her legs the night before.

Not that it mattered, she reminded herself. He's a man. Of course he's going to look at a woman's legs, especially when they're right in his face. Even if he wasn't particularly interested in said woman.

"So, what else can I do to help?"

Turning around, Gail taped the streamer, then walked down the counter to tape the other end. "Nothing." She leaned back again and surveyed the job. It needed something. "Unless you want to blow up a couple of balloons."

"My brother Brian always said I was full of hot air." He picked up a balloon and started blowing.

Over her shoulder, she watched him. "Don't you have anything better to do than help me decorate for an eight-year-old's birthday party?"

He handed her the balloon, lips twitching as he picked up another. "Nope."

"Thanks. And thanks for bringing the cake."

He gave her the last balloon and watched as she taped it in place. "Mel's eight? How is that possible? Jeez, talk about making me feel old."

"Try being her mother," she said as she turned around. "Roxy's ten."

"No way. Your kids can't possibly be that old."

Golden tongue, she thought. He sounded so sincere. "Too true. If you move, I'll get down."

He looked up at her and grinned. "Don't do that on my account. From this angle your legs look about a mile long."

"As lines go," she said, taking the hand he held up and hopping down, "that was pretty weak." He released her hand, but not before she felt an odd little tingle. *Get a grip,* she lectured herself.

He shrugged and tucked his hands in the pockets of his khaki shorts. "I'm out of practice."

No way could she pass that up. She tapped a finger to her cheek and looked up into his face. "Funny, I hear tell you're footloose and fancy-free again. I would have thought you'd be practicing up a storm."

"Hey, it takes a while to get back into circulation." He leaned closer and his voice dropped. "Could be I need some help."

Their eyes met and she saw the laughter in his. "Try the Internet," Gail said. "I hear you can find anything on the World Wide Web."

He gave a shout of laughter and she found herself chuckling in response. One of the things she'd always liked about Jay was that he didn't take himself too seriously.

"Actually," he said after a moment, "I do need some help. And I think you're just the woman for the job."

Tilting her head, she considered him. "Uh-huh. How's that?"

"I need a real estate agent."

"Jay, I'm a commercial Realtor in Corpus Christi. I don't know the market here." Not that there was a market to speak of in Aransas City, anyway. Which was one reason she worked in Corpus.

"Come on, Gail, have mercy. Did you know Max gets up at 6:00 a.m.?" He shoved a hand through his hair and shuddered. "And Mark says that's every day. You have to take pity on me. I'm a desperate man. I need a place of my own."

He attempted to look miserable, but failed. The man had too much charm to look woeful for long.

"Poor baby," she said. She could do it, of course. Why was she hesitating?

Because he's too damn tempting, that's why, she told herself. And she didn't intend to get into another situation that led to rejection. She'd had plenty of rejection in her life—just look at her marriage. Nevertheless, she said, "All right, but don't say I didn't warn you. When do you want to go?"

"Today's obviously out. What about tomorrow?"

"Fine. I'll get Mom to take the girls." She pulled a notepad and pen from a drawer and gave it to him. "Give me a price range and an idea of what you're looking for."

"Great." He flashed her another killer smile. "I really appreciate it. You're saving my life."

"That's what they all say." She sighed as she watched him, extremely conscious that he stood close to her, that he smelled good and looked even better. Jay still fascinated her every bit as much as he had the first time she'd met him. *Any sane, single woman would be attracted,* she consoled herself. *You'd have to be dead not to be.* A good thing she had too much sense to ever think anything could come of it.

He handed her the paper, keeping hold of her hand when he did. "It's good to see you again, Gail."

"It's good to see you, too," she said, and meant it. But she still wondered just exactly what she was getting into.

GAIL PULLED THE VAN TO A HALT by the curb. Jay looked out the window at the fifth house of the afternoon, and his mood nosedived to his toes. "Well, the outside sucks." He saw no reason to sugarcoat his reaction. Gail had eyes, too.

"It's listed as a fixer-upper," Gail said, her tone doubtful.

He followed her up the broken concrete walkway, admiring the fact that her white sleeveless summer suit with its short skirt showed off her legs. Very nice, shapely legs. She probably imagined she looked businesslike, and she did. But Jay found himself imagining what was under that suit.

Opening the lockbox hanging on the doorknob, she withdrew the key. It took her a minute to get the key to work, but she finally did.

She pushed open the door, and tried the lights as Jay walked in behind her. "No electricity," she said, as he looked around in the gloom. "I'll open the curtains."

Light—even the murky dimness provided by the natural light filtering through dirty windowpanes—

didn't improve the place any. The carpet was red shag, the entryway wallpaper gold with white flocked designs. He'd bet a thousand bucks it hadn't been updated since it was built. They went into the kitchen, which boasted ancient appliances and cabinet doors listing from the hinges. The house had a musty, nasty smell to it, as if the owners had cooked liver and onions too many times without ever airing it out. No, not food... It was more like...something dead?

"What is that smell?" Jay asked, sniffing the air.

"I have no idea." Gail cast a worried glance around. "It's been unoccupied for some time. I think the owner died and the bank took it over."

Depressed, he looked around as well. "Died, huh? What did they do, forget to bury the poor sucker?"

Gail stifled a giggle. "I'm sorry, Jay. You never can tell. Sometimes you get a real bargain with a fixer-upper." She opened a closet door and jumped back, swearing as a shelf came crashing down inches from her toes.

"I think we can cross this one off," Jay said. "I'd like something habitable, at least. I don't mind fixing a few things, but I'm not that skilled in construction."

"Are you sure you won't consider an apartment? There just aren't that many houses available in the price range you gave me."

"I can go up, if I have to." He didn't want to, since he had no idea what kind of money he'd be making, and wouldn't for some time. But he had to have a decent place to live, and he needed it ASAP.

"Let's get out of here, and we'll talk about it. This place is making me suicidal."

At Gail's van, Jay stuffed his hands into the pockets of his khaki shorts and squinted in the bright sunlight as Gail pulled out another flyer.

He looked back at the house and grimaced. Five houses so far, and he hadn't liked any of them. He didn't think he was being too picky. He wanted a decent sized house, in a decent neighborhood, for a decent price, and not a falling-apart ticket to disaster. So far, only one had come close, and while it hadn't been a mess, at best it was dull.

"I know you're against it, but I really think an apartment might be your best bet. At least until something you like better comes up," Gail said.

Frowning, he glanced at her. "I don't want to live in an apartment. I've spent the past twelve years in an apartment. I want a house. With a yard for my dogs."

Her eyebrow lifted in surprise. "I didn't know you had dogs. Where are they?"

He lifted a shoulder, aware he was being unreasonable, but he didn't care at that point. "I don't have any. Yet. But I'm getting them, as soon as I have a place to live."

Propping her hands on her hips, Gail tilted her head and considered him. "You're buying a house because of a dog—*dogs*—you don't even have?"

"No, I'm buying a house—or I would if I could find one—because I'm sick and tired of apartment living. I didn't move to Texas to live in another damn

sterile apartment complex. And I'm getting dogs—
puppies—because I don't want to live alone. I like
dogs, and I've wanted some for a long time now.''

Gail gazed at him a moment, then heaved a deep
sigh and muttered, ''Puppies. Oh, Lord.'' She jerked
her head at the car. ''Get in. There's one house we
haven't looked at yet.''

She handed him the last flyer to read on the way
over. A short time later, she pulled up in front of a
cream brick, one-story house. Huge oleander bushes
grew in the front, sporting flowers of brilliant pink.
A live oak tree, bent from the prevailing winds, occupied a large spot in the green St. Augustine grass.
A couple of bougainvillea, in shades of scarlet,
flanked the front door.

They got out of the van and stood looking at it.
''Nice. I like it already.'' He cocked his head at Gail.
''Why didn't you show me this one first?''

''Notice the location?''

He grinned, and nodded. ''Two doors down from
yours. Trying to keep the riffraff out of the neighborhood, Gail?''

''Very funny.'' She shot him a dark glance. ''You
know that's not it.'' A faint flush rose in her cheeks.
''What would you have thought if I'd showed you
this one first?''

''Oh, I don't know.'' He glanced at it again, then
back to her. ''That you'd found me a nice house?''

''Ha.'' She propped her hands on her hips. ''You'd
have thought I was making a move.''

''Are you?'' he couldn't help asking.

Instead of backing down, she lifted her chin and asked, "What would you do if I did?"

A little surprised, he stared at her. "What would I do if you made a move on me?" A smile tugged at his mouth. "Why don't we try it and see?"

She laughed. "Sorry, that was a rhetorical question. Come on, let's go see the inside."

"All right. I want to get this settled today, if I can."

"You know, most people want to think about it a while, once they see a house they like."

"They don't have my time constraints. I want to be moved in and settled as soon as possible. Tim wants to open the clinic next week, so the sooner I get this done, the better."

"You're talking as if you've decided, and you haven't even seen the interior yet."

"I'm waiting on my beautiful real estate agent to show me," he said, as straight-faced as he could be.

They entered and walked through the empty rooms slowly. By the time they reached the master bedroom, he knew he wanted it.

Pale blue walls rose above a lush, thick beige carpet. Glass-paned French doors opened into a fenced back yard. Another live oak shaded part of it, and a large palm tree graced one corner. Several beds were planted with a variety of flowering plants. Plenty big enough for a couple of dogs, he thought.

"Okay, let's do it. Can you write up the offer now?"

Gail stared at him for a minute. "Are you sure? Don't you even want to think about it overnight?"

"Nope. I'm used to making quick decisions. I like the house. It's going to suit me just fine."

Clearly baffled, she shook her head. "All right. I'll go get the papers."

He took her arm, detaining her before she could leave the room. "Are you all right with this? With me moving in here, I mean?"

"Of course. Why wouldn't I be?"

It dawned on him that this wasn't the woman he remembered from five years ago. Then she'd been a little tentative, a little unsure of herself. Still reeling from her divorce. But in the five years since, she'd changed. Which shouldn't surprise him. After all, he'd changed, too. A very strong, confident woman stood before him today. He had to admit she intrigued him as much as, or more than, the woman he remembered.

But he'd bet one thing hadn't changed. Those lips would taste every bit as sweet now as they had at his brother's wedding.

She must have seen the speculation in his gaze. Her smile turned saucy, and just a little bit wicked. Those slick, red lips pursed invitingly. Then she turned and sauntered from the room. He'd also make a bet she knew he watched her go. Man, when had she become so dangerous?

Her cell phone rang before she reached the door. After fishing it out of her purse, she glanced at it and then answered. "Cat?" She was silent a moment, then said, "Well, hello to you, too." She frowned as she listened, then handed the phone to Jay. "It's Mark."

He took it. "Mark, what's up?"

"Cat's in labor. Can you come over?"

"Are you sure? She's five weeks early. Could be Braxton—"

Mark interrupted. "Her water broke. It's for real. The contractions are coming real close together. She doesn't think we have time to drive her to the hospital. And the ambulance is at least forty minutes away. Maybe more."

"I'm on my way."

CHAPTER THREE

GAIL HAD NEVER SEEN Jay at work. He'd always been on vacation when he visited, and no emergencies had ever come up. She found the transformation from teasing companion to compassionate physician fascinating. She just wished the transition hadn't come about because her sister was in premature labor.

While she drove, she heard snatches of Jay's end of the conversation, spoken calmly and soothingly. After a few questions, he gave Mark some detailed instructions, then said, "Probably a good thing Max is with Cat's mother, but be sure to put up Buddy. You don't need a parrot in the mix." He chuckled and added, "Yeah, boil some water and we'll be there in a couple of minutes." He hung up and held up a hand before Gail could start firing questions.

"Cat is fine, but she's definitely in labor. She thinks it's coming too quickly for Mark to drive her to the hospital."

"Isn't this way too early?" Her fingers tightened on the steering wheel and she shot him a glance. "What if something goes wrong? What if..."

Jay placed a hand over one of hers and squeezed gently. "Dates aren't always correct. She might not be as early as she thinks. Besides, Cat and Mark are going to need you to stay calm.'' He smiled and added, ''Especially Mark. He sounded a little frantic.''

Gail drew in a deep breath, then let it out slowly. He was right, but she couldn't quite get a grip on herself. And she knew why. ''I don't usually panic, but I have a friend who delivered her son six weeks early.'' She glanced at Jay and tried to force a smile. ''I know it doesn't always happen, but her son has a lot of health problems they say are directly related to his prematurity.''

He hesitated a moment before he spoke. ''I wish I could tell you otherwise, but as you obviously know, sometimes premature birth is a problem. Most of the time, though, especially this late in the pregnancy, the baby is fine. But that's one reason we've called the ambulance. Just to be safe.''

''So you don't think I'm overreacting?''

''No, but I think it would be more productive if you focused on the positive.''

Gail nodded. ''You're right. I'll try.''

''Good. Can I use your cell phone to check on the ambulance?''

''Sure.''

They were a block away from Cat's when he hung up, frowning.

''Problems?'' Gail asked.

He gave her a reassuring smile. ''No, nothing to worry about.''

She pulled up in front and put the car in park. "The ambulance isn't coming, is it?"

He hesitated, then shook his head. "It's going to be a while. But don't worry. And I don't think we need to tell Mark and Cat yet. It could still get here in time."

Gail didn't think he believed it, but she let it pass. Mark had left the door unlocked and Jay entered with Gail right behind him. A blast of profanity hit her ears, so loud she winced. It took her a minute to realize it was her sister's parrot, Buddy, unhappy at being banished to his cage.

"Cover the cage, Gail," Jay said, on his way to the bedroom. "I think we can do without Buddy's input."

She found the cloth cover and dropped it over the large cage, muffling the bird's invectives. A moment later she found everyone in the bedroom. Clothes were scattered everywhere, and all of the bedclothes except the single sheet covering the bed were piled high in the middle of the floor. A suitcase stood open beside the closet, with all manner of things thrown in haphazardly and overflowing the top.

Her sister was standing in the middle of the room in a pretty, soft pink nightgown, with Mark and Jay beside her, doing their best to get her into the bed.

"I haven't finished packing," Cat said. "And besides, I need my Lamaze stuff. I have to have my focus object."

Mark's hair was standing straight up in dark, tortured spikes. His eyes were wild with fear and concern, and at the moment, Gail realized with a grin, frustration.

"For God's sake, Cat, who cares about a stupid focus object?" He patted her arm, tried to pull her toward the bed. "Just get into bed, sweetheart. Please?" he added desperately.

"I need something to focus on," Cat insisted.

Since Mark looked ready to strangle either himself or his wife, Gail stepped into the fray. "I'll get it, Cat. Let Mark and Jay help you into bed, okay? Where do you want me to put it?"

Cat started to speak, then doubled over in pain. "Bad...one," she said, panting.

"That's it," Mark said, scooping her up and taking the few steps to the big bed. "Come on, honey, breathe." He laid her down gently, then turned to his brother. "Do something! For God's sake, don't just stand there!"

"Calm down," Jay said mildly. "Have you been timing the contractions?"

Mark rolled his eyes, but looked at his watch. "Three minutes."

Jay frowned. "Looks like this is going to be a quick one. I'd better wash up. Did you find my bag, Mark?"

"Yeah. I put it in the bathroom," Mark said.

"Good. I'll be right back." Jay glanced at Gail and jerked his head toward the bathroom.

After placing Cat's focus object—a Play-Doh bird Max had made—on the dresser, and speaking a word of encouragement to Cat, Gail followed him.

He turned on the taps and began lathering the soap. "Unless the ambulance gets here soon—and the possibility of that is between slim and none—she's going to deliver here."

"Oh, man, she's having another one!" Mark said from the other room. "Two minutes this time. Hurry up!"

"Coming," Jay called. To Gail he said, "I need your help, because Mark is going to be busy with Cat. You okay with that?"

"I've had two babies and was with them when Max was born. I think I can handle it."

"Great. I knew you could." He flashed her a brilliant smile and reached for a towel, before pulling on a pair of thin latex gloves that lay on the counter beside his medical bag. "Let's go deliver a baby."

IT WASN'T QUITE THAT SMOOTH and easy, but almost. Gail brought the sterilized water, multiple towels, and the scissors into the room and settled down to do what she could to help. Mark got behind Cat and held her, soothing her, telling her to breathe, and laughing when she cursed him and said he wasn't coming near her ever again.

Watching them together, Gail's eyes stung. So different from her experience. Barry hadn't showed up at the hospital until long after she delivered both girls. What would it be like to have children with a man who actually loved you? Why had she ever imagined Barry cared about her?

She shook off her melancholy thoughts. This was

her sister's day. Sadness and regrets had no place here. She smiled as Cat alternately yelled at Mark and then apologized.

"The pains are coming awfully quickly," she murmured to Jay.

He nodded, his expression calm and unemotional. "You're dilated to ten centimeters. It won't be long now."

"Can I push?" she gasped out.

"Next contraction," he promised. "This baby's in a hurry to be born." He looked at his brother. "Did you tell me you don't know the sex?"

"Cat wouldn't let them tell us. She wanted it to be a surprise."

"I'm betting a boy, six pounds, two ounces." Jay glanced up at Gail. "What do you say?"

"I think it's a little girl."

"We're going to know real soon. The head is crowning. Mark, do you want to catch the baby? There's another set of gloves in the bathroom. Can you get them for him, Gail?"

Mark leaned down and murmured something to Cat. When Gail returned with the gloves, she switched places with Mark. She patted Cat's arm, then held her hand, wincing when Cat bore down. "Almost there."

"Can't—" she panted. "Hurts."

"I know." She squeezed her hand. "You'll have her soon. Just a little more time."

"The head's coming out," Mark said reverently.

"Look at all that hair. This is amazing. Unbelievable."

"Yeah, it is. You didn't catch Max?" Jay asked him.

"No, Cat had a death grip on me, so we figured the doctor should do it."

Gail had never thought Mark and Jay looked much alike, with Jay being so fair and Mark so dark. But just now, with identical expressions of happiness, the resemblance was remarkable.

"Come on, Cat, you can do it," she said, as Cat bore down again. Then she heard a cry, thin at first, but rapidly turning loud and indignant. Relief swept her.

"What is it?" Cat asked, trying to sit up.

Mark put the child in the waiting towel Jay held out. "It's a girl." Jay handed the baby back, and cuddling her, Mark smiled at his wife. "A beautiful little girl with her mother's eyes."

"She may even go six pounds," Jay said. "She looks great, Cat. You did great."

Mark laid the baby on Cat's stomach, then leaned over to kiss Cat long and lovingly. Gail swallowed, blinking back tears of happiness.

"What are you going to name her?" Jay asked after a moment.

They both looked at the baby, and then at Jay. "Miranda," Cat said softly. "After your sister."

SHE SHOULD BE HAPPY, Gail thought as hung up the phone after a final call to family. Her new niece was beautiful and healthy, her sister was fine, everything had worked out wonderfully. So why did she want nothing more than to have a good, hard cry?

Emotions. She pressed her hands to her eyes and willed herself not to cry. Fear, excitement, relief had all cascaded through her. Naturally, now the crisis had passed she felt a little let down. But hell, that wasn't the problem and she knew it.

She wanted what Cat had. A faithful, loving husband, her children, a career she loved. And while Gail did have two out of the three, she'd never had anything resembling a faithful loving husband. A man who wanted to share his life with her, a man she could depend on.

Jay walked into the bedroom. "Are you going to the hospital right away?"

Gail shook her head. "I want to clean house for them first. I'm meeting the rest of the family there later. You go on, I'll see you there."

"Let me help you. There's no reason for you to do it alone."

Her smile grew more strained. "I work faster by myself. You go on. Really."

"Is something wrong?" Concerned, he looked at her closely. "You look upset."

"Of course nothing's wrong. My sister just had a beautiful baby. Everything's p-p-perfect," she said, a sob choking on the last word. Horrified, she turned around. Unfortunately, now she stared into the mirror. She closed her eyes and prayed he'd go away.

No such luck. His hand dropped to her shoulder.

"Hey." He squeezed it reassuringly. "Cat's doing great. The baby's going to be all right. You don't have to worry anymore."

She gave a strangled laugh and opened her eyes. If he knew what she was really thinking he'd think she was terrible. Tears welled, threatening to spill as she shook her head. "I know," she managed to whisper.

"Come here." Ignoring her protests, he turned her around and held her firmly in his arms, his hand going to her head to place it against his shoulder. "Go ahead. I've been cried on before."

"I'm not crying," she said after a moment, the words muffled by his shoulder. In fact, the desire to cry had left her the minute he took her in his arms. A frisson of sexual tension crept up her spine, as she remembered the last time he'd held her in his arms. And that time, he hadn't been offering comfort.

Relax, she told herself. You're overreacting to a friendly hug. No big deal. "I'm okay." She raised her head to look at him.

He searched her eyes, then smiled. "Yeah, you sure are."

Tension hummed between them. Both of them knew he wasn't referring to her emotions. "You can let me go now." No, she hadn't imagined it. The glint in his eyes told her comfort wasn't all he offered.

"I could." But he didn't let her loose. He drew her closer.

Mesmerized, she watched his eyes darken to jade, his mouth come closer to hers. Could almost taste the kiss as his warm breath washed over her lips. Her legs wobbled, her breasts tingled. And then, thank God, she remembered. She slapped a hand on his chest. "Don't even think about it, buster."

He blinked and looked confused. "Don't think about kissing you? Why?"

She pulled away and crossed her arms over her chest. It infuriated her that a part of her desperately wanted to forget her pride and kiss him anyway. Her spine straightened. Pacing away a few steps, she turned back and nailed him with a hostile glare. "Gee, I don't know, Jay. Maybe because the last time you kissed me I ended the evening feeling like the biggest loser on the planet."

For a minute, he just looked at her.

Pleased, she saw that she had truly left him speechless. "What, no easy answer?"

He blew out a breath and shook his head. "Well, shit. I had a feeling you were ticked at me about that."

She gave a humorless laugh. "Brilliant deduction. Yes, Jay, you could say I'm still ticked." And humiliated.

"Gail, let me explain." Man, talk about having murder in her eyes. He'd screwed this up, big time. "Why don't we sit down."

"There's nowhere to sit in here," she said, indicating the messy bed and the chair piled high with clothes. "So go ahead. And while you're at it, explain how I managed to totally misread the situation. Did you or did you not come on to me from the first time I met you?"

There was no way to answer that except the truth. "Yes."

"Wasn't the entire weekend of Mark and Cat's wedding a prelude to getting me into bed?" When he tried to speak, she held up her hand. "Because if all that flirting and kissing and dancing and romancing wasn't intended to get me into bed, then I'm stupider than I thought."

"I did want to take you to bed." Still did, especially now as she vibrated with emotion. What would it be like if desire had caused that passion, rather than anger?

"Thanks for clearing that up. It makes perfect sense then, that you'd go home with me and then turn me down flat when I asked you to stay. I couldn't figure out what had happened. What I'd done wrong."

Her words made him wince. "You didn't do anything wrong." He hadn't been at his smoothest that night, obviously. "I didn't want you to...I didn't want to hurt you."

"Why would you have hurt me? Are you that clumsy?"

He smiled, amused as always by that smart mouth of hers. "Not physically. Emotionally. I didn't want to hurt you emotionally."

"Oh, please." She tossed her hair back in a gesture of irritation. "That is such a load of cow manure."

Frustrated, he jammed his hands through his hair. "It would have been a one-night stand." And she'd been vulnerable, still hurting from her divorce. The last thing he'd wanted was to add to those problems. Once they'd arrived on her doorstep he'd managed to think past the haze of lust and realize maybe taking her to bed wouldn't be the best thing for either of them.

One glance at her narrowed eyes and grim expression decided him. No way he'd tell her all this. She'd rip his face off.

"I'm not a moron, Jay. I knew you were going back to California the next day. So what?"

"I didn't want you to regret it. I thought the best thing would be to avoid it. Obviously, I hurt you. I'm sorry for that."

Her chin lifted. "As you can see, I lived through it. Hell, I lived through my divorce, don't think I can't handle something as insignificant as a failed—" she hesitated, then shrugged. "Whatever it was."

Insignificant? That pricked his ego. Still, if it had been so insignificant, she wouldn't be so pissed. But he wasn't going to point that out. Nope, no way. Instead, he said, "You haven't ever brought this up before."

"You hadn't made a move on me since then, either," she reminded him. "Besides, I didn't see you for a long time, and by then you were tied up with Carla. What would have been the point?"

"How long are you planning to stay mad at me?" Her lips twitched and he breathed a sigh of relief.

Regally, she inclined her head. "I haven't decided. Possibly forever."

"Then why are you biting your lip to keep from smiling?'' He wanted, badly, to nibble on those lush, enticing lips himself. But even though he'd handled the situation so poorly five years before, he wasn't a total fool. Giving her his most charming smile, he held out a hand. "Friends?"

She took it and smiled. "Friends," she echoed.

Jay had an idea that smile hid a plan. He just wasn't sure what that plan was. But he'd never backed off from a challenge.

CHAPTER FOUR

AFTER WORKING for two weeks—actually, after one—Jay knew he'd made the right decision in moving to Aransas City. He liked the clinic setup. His office, while conservative, suited him, holding a handsome mahogany desk, a comfortable deep blue leather desk chair and a couple of burgundy leather side chairs for his patients.

One of the things he especially appreciated was the slower pace of practicing in a small town. Most emergencies went directly to the Corpus Christi Emergency Room. No more weekend calls, no more trauma. And he was able to spend time with his patients, to get to know them instead of moving them in and out as fast as humanly possible.

He and his partner, Tim Kramer, worked together well. Tim had moved his practice from Corpus Christi, where many of his patients came from the outlying communities. He'd been wanting to open a clinic in Aransas City for some time, believing that given a choice, the locals would prefer a doctor nearby, rather than having to go to Corpus for all their medical needs. If the brisk business they'd been doing since opening was any indication, Tim had been absolutely right.

The first week Jay had been in town, Tim invited him over for a cookout to meet his family. Following the tradition found in small towns everywhere, Tim's wife immediately tried to set him up with a friend. Never one for blind dates, he'd wiggled out of it without offending her, but it gave him a taste of things to come.

It seemed as if everyone in Aransas City had a great idea of who to fix him up with. Too bad the one woman he wouldn't mind seeing hadn't shown any inclination to date him. While their talk had cleared the air, and Gail had been friendly enough when they'd closed on his house, she hadn't shown any signs of wanting to get together. And for reasons Jay didn't fully understand, he couldn't seem to drum up much interest in other women.

Closing the medical journal he'd been leafing through, he glanced out his window and smiled. The beige brick clinic surrounded a central courtyard with a small gazebo and a couple of benches. White clouds of seagulls circled overhead and hopped on the ground, hoping for a handout. He got up, deciding to break for an early lunch, then heard a commotion in the hallway. Just as he reached his office door, it burst open and his receptionist tumbled in.

"Dr. Kincaid!" Normally cool and collected, she wheezed his name breathlessly. "I tried to stop her but she wouldn't even let me buzz you."

"What is it, Bridget? Is it an emergency?"

Bridget shook her head and stepped aside. "I don't think so."

"It's only me, darling," a musical, feminine voice said as a woman stepped into view. "Surely you're not going to have me barred from your office."

He stared at her, hoping she was a bad dream and knowing she wasn't. "Carla? What are you doing here?"

"Can we do this...alone?" She turned to Bridget with a conciliatory smile. "You'll excuse us, won't you? I need to talk to my fiancé in private."

His jaw tightened at the comment. Damn Carla for following him here. He might as well deal with her now, though, because his ex-girlfriend was as tenacious as a pit bull. A good quality in a lawyer, but a pain in the ass otherwise.

"It's all right, Bridget. You can go now. And for the record—" he glanced at Carla, then back to his receptionist "—Miss Burkett isn't my fiancée."

He folded his arms and leaned back against his desk. "All right, Carla. Why are you here?"

A moment before she'd been frowning, but the smile she now turned on him was all sweetness and light. "Jay, I've missed you so much. I couldn't stay away any longer." She crossed the few steps between them, put her arms around him and laid a kiss on him that once upon a time would have had them horizontal in a matter of seconds. With difficulty, he extracted himself from her clutches and pushed her away from him.

Her eyes widened. He felt like a jerk until he remembered that Carla was very good at making a person believe what she wanted him to.

Her hands clutched his shirt. "I thought—I hoped you'd had enough time to realize what a terrible mistake you've made. You can't tell me it's truly over. Not after what we meant to each other. Why don't you come home, Jay?" She glanced around his office, obviously puzzled. "This place isn't for you. You can't be happy here. I've driven through the town and there's hardly a grocery store, much less any kind of entertainment. Come back to L.A. with me, Jay."

He shook his head. "You know I'm not going to do that."

Her composure breaking for the first time, her lips, full, lush and painted a deep red, tightened into a pout. "Are you trying to hurt me? Because you're succeeding."

Again, he felt a flash of guilt. "I never wanted to hurt you. But we've been through this often enough. I'm sorry, Carla, we're not getting back together."

He could still admire her beauty. It would be hard not to. Her blond hair fell in a riot of waves to her shoulders. Her eyes were a sharp, brilliant green, and she had one of the most luscious bodies he'd ever seen. Carla was bright, beautiful, and everything he'd once thought he wanted in a woman. Until he finally figured out that it didn't matter. He didn't love Carla, and he never would.

She placed a shaky hand on his arm and gave him a tremulous smile. "Haven't you missed me, Jay? Even a little?"

He didn't answer her question. Truthfully, he hadn't missed her at all. "It's been over between us for months. I don't want to say things we'll both regret. Don't do this. There's no point to it. You need to let it go."

Her eyes filled with tears, which she allowed to spill and track slowly down her cheeks. His more cynical side whispered that Carla knew she cried beautifully and didn't mind using the trick to ruthless advantage.

"I can't bear to see you throwing your life away. You don't belong here, Jay, any more than I do."

Frustration had him speaking more sharply than he'd intended. "I'm staying. And you'd better go. It's over, Carla. Accept it."

Her hand fisted over her heart. She looked stricken, every bit the tragic beauty. But Jay didn't quite buy it. He knew he'd hurt her, but he suspected her determination arose from the fact that he'd been the one to call it quits, rather than from any deep and abiding love she held for him.

One last, melting look, one last, husky plea. "Call me. I'll be waiting."

"Don't," was all he said.

He shoved his hands through his hair and sighed in relief. *Thank God that's over.*

GLAD TO HAVE taken care of her insurance physical, Gail left Dr. Kramer's office. She glanced down the hall and saw a woman step out of Jay's office, her posture defeated, despairing. Yet the moment the door closed, she straightened and took on a completely different attitude. Gail pegged her as furious.

"Carla? Is that you?" She walked toward her and held out a hand. "It's Gail Summers. We met last summer at my sister's house."

The woman looked at her hand as if she carried the plague.

Her gaze, frigid with disdain, swept over Gail from top to bottom. "Of course. You would be here, wouldn't you? I remember you. Don't think he'll fall for you, you pathetic little loser. You're nothing more than a hair follicle in this armpit of humanity." And with that, she stormed out in her three-hundred-dollar sky-high heels.

"Well, that'll tell me," Gail murmured as the door opened.

"Gail, what are you doing here? You're not ill, are you?" Jay asked.

Gail shook her head. "I had to have an insurance physical with Dr. Kramer. Wasn't that your ex-girlfriend?"

He glanced down the hall and grimaced. "Yeah."

"Or maybe not so ex?"

"What do you mean?"

With a wry smile, Gail tapped the corner of her mouth. "Lipstick. I guess she hasn't heard of the non-smudge variety."

He frowned and reached into his pocket for a handkerchief. "Forgot she kissed me." He scrubbed at the telltale stain, then stuffed the handkerchief back. "Definitely still ex."

"That would explain it, then." When he raised an eyebrow, she continued. "Why she called me a hair follicle in this armpit of humanity. I take it you told her no go."

"You take it right. Sorry. I guess she's angrier than I'd realized. She tends to lash out at whoever's handy when she's in a mood."

"Lucky me."

He smiled at her. "Let me make it up to you. Can I buy you lunch?"

He really was charming. And she'd spent the last two weeks since his house closing deliberately avoiding him. She figured she was the only single woman in town who hadn't yet pounced on him. "All right. What did you have in mind?"

"Your brother's place. I'm addicted to the fried shrimp plate."

THE SCARLET PARROT, Cameron Randolph's waterfront bar and grill, did a brisk lunchtime business. Jay usually ate there at least once a week, sometimes more. He liked the atmosphere, unpretentious and casually coastal. Fish—sailfish, marlin, redfish and tarpon—decorated the walls and huge fans hung from the ceiling, spinning lazily and helping clear out the inevitable odors of seafood, ocean and cigarette smoke. The bare planked floor and dark wood tables hadn't changed in the last five years, and Jay didn't imagine they would in the next five either. Not unless Cam Randolph married and his wife decided to redecorate. However, in the five years Jay had known Cam, he'd always seemed determinedly single.

Jay and Gail stopped by the bar to greet Cam on the way to their table. Of the four Randolph siblings, Cat and Gabe were dark, Cam and Gail fair. Cam resembled Gail the most. He was also, Jay thought, the most protective of her, but maybe that came from being the oldest in a family of four.

Content to let the Randolphs carry the conversation, Jay watched Gail. She must have come from work, he thought, because she wore another one of those suits she favored, this one a bright cherry red that hugged her slim hips. He wondered if her matching lipstick were the non-smudge variety. He wanted a chance to find out.

"I know what you want, Kincaid," Cam said.

"You do?" He sincerely hoped not. Because if Cam knew what Jay had been thinking about his sister, he'd slug him for sure.

"Sure, what you always get. The shrimp plate. But Gail is always changing her mind. What are you having, little sister?"

"We're going to take that table over there," she said, pointing to a corner. "Tell Sally to bring me a cheeseburger and French fries. And don't skimp on the fries this time."

He laughed and threw his towel over his shoulder. "Just trying to make sure you keep your girlish figure."

"I'm pretty sure I'm up for the job without your help," she said.

Not girlish, Jay thought, following her. Those curves were all woman.

"So, do you want to talk about it?" Gail asked, after they were seated and the waitress brought their drinks.

He blinked, still thinking about her figure. Then he realized what she referred to. "About Carla?" he asked, a little surprised. "No, why would I?"

"I forgot, you're a guy." She picked up her iced tea and sipped, her expression innocent. "Why would you want to talk about messy things like emotions?"

He leaned forward and caught her gaze. "Why would I want to talk about another woman when I'm a hell of a lot more interested in you?"

Her breathing hitched, then she smiled. "Oh, that was smooth. Very nice."

"But true. Carla and I are over. But you and I—" he picked up her hand and smiled at her "—have all sorts of possibilities."

"Do we?" she asked skeptically.

His fingers skimmed her pulse, which pounded appealingly.

The waitress interrupted just then, setting their food down. The subject changed naturally when she left, but Jay was well satisfied with the conversation. Gail wanted to play it cool, but he sensed the spark between them, and would've bet his last dollar she did too.

They ate quietly for a moment. "I saw Miranda yesterday," Gail said. "I swear, I can't believe how much that baby has grown in just a few weeks."

"Yeah, she's a charmer, isn't she?" He took a bite of shrimp and smiled, thinking about his brother's family. "I still can't get used to calling her Miranda," he said, after making some progress on his meal.

Gail touched his hand. "Does it bother you? That they named her after your sister?"

"No, and I think it means a lot to Mark. He was much closer to Miranda than either Brian or I were. We were only six and seven when she ran away. It's just," he hesitated, unsure how to put his feelings into words. "I never stopped hoping we'd find her. Naming the baby Miranda makes it seem more certain that she's gone for good."

"A lot of people name children after family members."

"I know. I didn't say it was rational."

"Are you afraid she's…" She broke off, apparently unwilling to complete the sentence.

"Dead?" he asked, his heart heavy. "Yeah. Mark tried to find her for years. Private investigators. So did our mother. I suppose it's possible she's alive, but she was only fifteen when she left home. The statistics on teenage runaways are pretty grim."

"I know." She put her hand over his and squeezed. "I'm sorry, Jay."

"Me too," he said simply, and turned his hand over to clasp hers. Their gazes met, held. Her eyes were blue, a deep blue like the ocean churning outside, and fringed with thick, dark lashes. The kind of eyes a man could drown in, and count himself lucky. In them he saw compassion, and something more, a sensual awareness that grew the longer he held her hand.

Her tongue touched her lips, exactly where he wanted to touch them himself. She cleared her throat and tried to pull her hand free, but he held on a few seconds longer before he released it.

"Are you going to eat those fries?" Gail asked after a moment.

"No, you go ahead." He watched her for a moment as she tucked into his fries. "Do you always eat like that?"

"Mostly." She gave him a cheeky grin.

Obviously, she didn't have a problem with her weight. She was slim, yet curved in all the right places. Subtle curves, but they were definitely there.

"You've got a funny look in your eyes."

"Do I?" He blinked, thinking she probably wouldn't appreciate knowing he'd been imagining those subtle curves without benefit of clothes.

She waved a fry at him. "I don't have an eating disorder, in case you're worried. I just have a fast metabolism. I always have."

He couldn't help grinning. "Believe me, Gail, an eating disorder was the last thing on my mind."

CHAPTER FIVE

A COUPLE OF DAYS LATER, Gail walked in from work just as her phone rang. *Probably Barry with an excuse for why he can't take the girls this weekend,* she thought, and dumped her bag of groceries on the counter. Ordinarily she didn't mind when Barry canceled out, but the girls did. However, her boss was throwing a big party Friday night. A party she'd yet to find a date for.

"Hello?" she said, a little breathlessly.

"Hey, can you come over?"

"Jay? Why, what is it?" He sounded pleased, which made her curious.

"Come over. You'll see when you get here."

"I just walked in the door. What's going on?"

"Where's your sense of adventure?"

She started putting away groceries. "I have children. They killed it."

"Speaking of kids, bring the girls, too. See you in a minute."

A dial tone. Baffled, she stared at the receiver. He'd hung up on her. She finished putting up the refrigerated items, then changed out of her work clothes into shorts and a T-shirt. Then she called the girls and explained they were going over to Jay's.

Mel, naturally, wanted to ride her pink Barbie bike that she'd gotten for her birthday. Roxy and Gail followed behind her. "Why are we going to Uncle Jay's?" Roxy asked.

"I'm not sure. He called and asked us to come. Maybe he wants us to see his new house."

Roxy skipped a step and glanced at her mother. "How come you didn't make him any cookies, like Aunt Cat said you should? She said you're supposed to give him a house hunting present, on account of his new house."

Gail laughed. "I think you mean housewarming." She tugged a blond curl, then slid her arm around her daughter's shoulders. "Cooking is your aunt's thing, not mine." She could have made him slice-and-bake cookies, but that was about the extent of her culinary capabilities. Unless he liked macaroni and cheese, the girls' current favorite.

Jay opened the door before she could ring the bell. He wore khaki shorts, a green knit shirt the color of his eyes, and his feet were bare. Gail thought he looked too damned appealing for her own good.

"Must be my lucky day. Three beautiful blue-eyed blondes are on my doorstep."

Both girls giggled. "Do you have any cookies?" Mel asked. "I haven't had my snack yet."

"Mel, it isn't polite to go to someone's house and ask for food," Gail said.

She turned a puzzled face to her mother. "But it's

Uncle Jay. And I'm hungry. I do it all the time at Aunt Cat's,'' she said, with unassailable logic.

He held the door open and motioned them inside. "I do have cookies, if it's okay with your mom. Chocolate chip.'' Smiling at Gail, he added, "Several people dropped by with food. I can't tell if they're just being nice or if Cat told them to because she's afraid I'll starve to death.''

"Don't you know how to cook?'' Roxy asked as they followed him into the kitchen, concern creasing her round face.

"Not according to your Aunt Cat,'' Jay said, and grinned.

"Mommy does. She's a good cook. You can eat with us tonight. Mommy's making macaroni and cheese.''

Gail laughed. "Thanks, honey, but, not everyone likes macaroni and cheese.''

"It's one of my favorites,'' Jay said solemnly, handing a plate of cookies to the girls. He caught Gail's eye, his own gleaming with humor. "Unless you don't have enough.''

"I'll make two boxes,'' she said, thinking it served him right. "So, why are we here?''

"Let's wait until the girls finish their cookies and I'll show you.''

A few minutes later, he opened the back door and whistled. Nothing happened. Looking around, he whistled again. Still nothing happened. "Just got them this afternoon,'' he said. "They don't mind very well yet.''

From around the corner, two brown-and-white balls of fur appeared, tumbling over their feet and yapping excitedly. One carried a plant in its mouth, the roots dangling.

"Puppies!" Roxy and Mel said in unison, falling over themselves to get to them. Laughing delightedly, they sat in the grass and instantly the puppies climbed all over them.

"Oh, man," Jay said, leaning down to take the plant from one brown and white fuzzball and scold it gently. "That's the third plant that's bitten the dust since I brought them home. They've only been here a couple of hours."

Gail laughed, sinking into the grass beside the girls and reaching over to rub soft puppy fur. "I'm afraid your yard is toast. Or the flowers are, at least." Scratching one of their tummies, she said, "They're so cute and pudgy. What breed are they?"

"Mostly Springer Spaniel, with a little Labrador Retriever mixed in. Or at least, that's what the Humane Society thinks." He squatted down beside Roxy and picked up a puppy's paw. "I have a feeling they're going to be bigger than I'd planned, but I couldn't resist them."

Gail thought he looked pretty irresistible himself, with a round bundle of fur on either side of him. Smiling, she met his eyes. "So, how's the proud father?"

"Stumped. He can't think of what to name them, so he thought he'd ask the experts for advice." He turned to her daughters. "How about it, girls? Can you help me name them? They're both girls."

He got to his feet, his mouth twitching while a vigorous discussion took place between Roxy and Mel. "What about you, Gail? You have any ideas?"

"I don't— Ouch!" One of the puppies had sunk its little teeth into her palm. Gently, she pried it off. "That smarts. I'd forgotten puppy teeth were so sharp."

"Are you bleeding? Here, let me see," Jay said, kneeling beside her and turning her palm over. "Yeah, she broke the skin all right. Sorry. Let's go inside and see about it."

"It's no big deal, Jay," she said, even as he got to his feet, tugging her up along with him. "Just a tiny bite."

"I can see that, but it needs to be taken care of." He spoke to the girls, still arguing over names. "Your mom and I are going in for a minute. Be careful, one of them just bit your mother. Give them one of these rawhide sticks to chew on." He pulled a couple from his pocket and handed them to the girls before dragging Gail inside.

"I can't believe you're making such a big deal out of a puppy bite," Gail protested.

"I'm not. Wash," he commanded, pointing at the kitchen sink. "I'll find a bandage."

He returned a few minutes later just as she turned off the water. Apparently considering her incapable of doing it herself, he dried her hands with a clean towel, then placed the bandage over the wound. Turning her hand over, he touched his lips to her knuckles. "All better," he said, his eyes sparkling as he released her hand.

Such a simple, silly thing, and it had her heart beating like a drum. "Do you do that for all your patients?"

He shook his head, smiling. "No. You're not my patient." His finger pushed up her chin. "And your hand isn't really what I want to kiss."

"Oh." Keep it light, she told herself. Her heart fluttered. *Yeah, right.* When in doubt, change the subject.

"You must do this sort of thing at work. Minor injuries, I mean. Don't you find it boring after working in the emergency room?"

The look he gave her very clearly said, "Chicken" but he answered her. "You sound like Mark. The emergency room is full of minor injuries, colds, flu. A lot of boring, tedious things go on. It's not like the TV shows, where something exciting is always happening."

"Still, the emergency room must be more exciting than the clinic."

He shrugged, put his hands in his pockets. "Depends on your definition of excitement. After a few years of the Saturday night knife and gun club, that kind of action gets old."

"The Saturday night—"

"Knife and gun club," he finished for her. His eyes closed and he rubbed the back of his neck. "Yeah." When he looked at her, his smile was weary. "Saturdays were especially fun. Gang members, teenagers looking for trouble, husbands and wives drinking and fighting—and every damn one of them has access to a knife or a gun. I worked in one of the biggest trauma centers in L.A. We saw more gunshot wounds, more knife wounds, more vehicular trauma, more domestic violence in a year, than you could see in a lifetime in a place like Aransas City. After a while, the futility of it wears on you."

He paced a few steps, stood with his back to her. "Some of the gang members were repeats. They'd come through, we'd patch them up, then they'd be back again. Next week, next month," he turned around, spread his hands. "Maybe even two or three months. But it didn't matter. We knew that sooner or later, they'd have a wound we couldn't fix. Or they'd come in DOA." He glanced at Gail, his gaze solemn. "Do I miss that? No, I can't say I do."

"I'm sorry. I had no idea."

"You wouldn't unless you worked in an emergency room. Some people really thrive on it. Some of us burn out."

She wanted to comfort, but didn't know how. Tentatively, she touched his arm. "You're not burned out on medicine. If you were, you wouldn't have come here."

"True." His lips curved. "No, I like medicine, and I like working at the clinic."

"What do you do when something happens you can't handle at the clinic?" she asked curiously, relieved that his melancholy mood seemed to have passed. "Like a test you need to run or something?"

"Tim and I have hospital privileges at Varner Memorial," he said, naming the hospital nearest Aransas City.

"That's a nice hospital. My OB works out of there, so that's where my kids were born." She glanced out the window. "Speaking of kids, I should take the girls home, but I'm not sure they'll go for it."

"Let them play with the puppies a while longer. It's not late."

She didn't have much choice, unless she wanted to drag them away kicking and screaming. "Don't feel like you have to eat with us. I mean, macaroni and cheese from the box doesn't exactly compare," she said, waving a hand at the massive amounts of food on his counter. If she knew the single women in town, and she should after all these years, there was an equal amount in his refrigerator and freezer.

He tucked a strand of hair behind her ear. "Would you rather I didn't eat with you?"

"No, that's not what I meant. I just—"

His fingers stroked her cheek lightly and his lips twitched. "Are you trying to avoid me, Gail?"

Her pulse kicked up. She swallowed, hard. "Not…exactly."

"What are you afraid of? That we'll enjoy being with each other?"

She met his eyes. "Yes."

He smiled. "Do you know what I think about every time I see you?"

The intensity in his eyes was making her feel faint. She put her hands behind her and gripped the counter. "What?"

He moved even closer, but he didn't touch her. "Your mouth," he said, his voice deep and quiet. "And how much I want to kiss you."

The back door burst open. Roxy and Mel trooped in, each holding a ball of fur in their arms. "We did it!" Roxy said.

"We named them, Uncle Jay," Mel confirmed. "This is Fudge, and Roxy's holding Fluffy."

"Fluffy and Fudge. Perfect," he said, still gazing at Gail.

Just in time, she thought, unsure whether to be frustrated or relieved. "Okay, now put the puppies back outside. We need to start dinner. It's a school night, remember," Gail said. "Give us half an hour, Jay, and then come over."

She let the girls go ahead of her. "Jay." She waited until his eyes met hers. "I think about it, too."

JAY AND GAIL WASHED the dishes together after dinner, while her daughters got ready for bed. He enjoyed the meal and the conversation, which hadn't subsided for a moment. In what was obviously a nightly custom, each of the girls, then Gail, had talked about their day. If something bad had happened, Gail encouraged them to think of something good to offset it.

To his surprise, after they finished, they ganged up on him and made him talk about his day. So he told them the story about the elderly lady, the wife of a farmer, who came in for the third time, insisting on being given a flu shot. No amount of talking could convince her that the vaccine wasn't available yet. Worse, she brought her pig with her every time, planning on using him as payment. They couldn't convince her they didn't take farm animals as barter, either.

Gail served strawberries with powdered sugar for dessert. Thinking about it now nearly made him groan as he remembered what her pretty red mouth had looked like closing around the succulent fruit.

"What are you smiling about?" Gail asked him.

"You eating strawberries."

She handed him the clean, wet pan to dry. "Why, do I eat them weird or something?"

"Not weird." He raised an eyebrow at her and grinned. "Sexy."

She laughed. "Oh, right."

"No, really." He glanced at her to find her staring at him. "With you, it's an art form. You can tell you're really enjoying them. Every bite."

"You're very strange," she said, and gave him the lid.

He dried it, placed it on top of the pot. "Nah, I'm just a guy."

"So you're saying all guys have a strawberry fetish? Or is it only you?" Finished with the dishes, she turned around with her back against the counter.

Her baby-fine blond hair feathered around her face in a simple, casual style that looked at the moment as if she'd just crawled out of bed. Some women might have called it messy. Jay thought it looked sexy and tousled. He already knew how silky her hair felt, and he wanted to run his fingers through it—preferably while he kissed her.

"You're staring at me," she said, her voice a bit husky.

Nodding, he traced a finger over her lips. Her lips parted, her tongue touched her lips nervously. "I'm thinking about doing a lot more than just staring." He slipped his hands in her hair, on either side of her face.

Her eyes widened. "The girls," she said, hitching in a breath. "I have to tuck them in."

He bent his head until their lips were close, but not touching. "I'll wait for you."

A few minutes later, she returned, closing the swinging door behind her. For an instant, they stared silently at each other. Then they met in the middle of the room, her arms in a stranglehold around his neck, his wrapped around her, pressing her to him. He couldn't do subtle, and she didn't seem to want it either. He kissed her, plunged into the ripe taste of her, his tongue meeting hers as she demanded as good as she gave.

Warm. Potent, like a straight shot of whiskey on a cold winter night. He left her mouth to taste the pulse raging at her throat. "Thank God," he managed to say. "I wasn't sure you were ever going to let me kiss you again. I've been going crazy."

She tugged his head back to hers and kissed him again. "Don't talk. Just kiss me."

She vibrated in his arms, tasting like strawberries and sweet sin. He backed her against the door, used his teeth on her throat, felt her pulse leap and quiver before he returned to her lips. Those lush, inviting lips that tasted even better than he remembered.

"We shouldn't be doing this." Even as she said it, she pulled him closer, rocked her lower body against his. "I know there's a reason."

With one hand on her rear, pressing her near, he slipped his other beneath her T-shirt, thumbing her nipple. She sucked in a jerky breath, then moaned.

"I think my brain is fried."

"Mine, too." He couldn't remember getting this hot, this fast since high school. He pushed her shirt up, and keeping his eyes on hers, cupped both her breasts. Rubbed them. They both groaned.

The door swung forward, hitting Gail in the head. She yelped and swore.

"Mommy," a childish voice said as their eyes met and they froze. "I need a drink of water."

"Go back to your room. I'll bring it to you."

He didn't move his hands. Smiling, he took her nipples in his fingers and tugged gently.

Gail's eyes half-closed and her head fell back against the door.

"But Mommy, I'm thirsty," she whined.

"Mel, honey, go back to bed." She sounded a little desperate. "I promise I'll be right there."

"O-kay," she said, dragging each syllable out as she obviously shuffled away.

Jay's smile widened as he gave her breasts one last, lingering caress, then dropped his hands. "You'd better take care of her."

"You're wicked," Gail said.

"And you're irresistible."

She smoothed her shirt down, ran her fingers through her hair, then left the kitchen with the requested water. When she returned, she held up a hand and said, "Stay away from me."

"Now you've hurt my feelings."

"Ha, ha. I mean it. I'm not sneaking you into my bedroom with my daughters here."

"Does that mean if they weren't here, you would?"

"It means we have to be sensible."

Jay smiled and closed the distance between them. "There was nothing sensible about what just happened. But I can respect your wanting to protect your daughters."

"Good. As long as we're clear."

He took her face in his hands and touched his lips lightly to hers. "We're clear. Can I see you tomorrow?"

"I have a PTA meeting. I'm not sure how late I'll be."

He put his arms around her and tugged her against him. "I'll wait. Call me when you get home."

She sighed, then pulled back to look at him. "Last time we got to this point, nothing happened."

"My stupidity," Jay murmured. "But that was five years ago. And I'm rarely that stupid twice."

"Are we sure about this? What if something goes wrong? What if we wind up hating each other? Think how awkward that would be. We've got mutual family. We'd never be able to avoid each other."

"Gail." He cradled her cheek in his palm. "I want, very much, to make love with you. What do you want?"

Her mouth curved. "The same thing you want."

"Then relax. What could go wrong?"

"You're right. I do that sometimes. Dissect and analyze until I drive myself crazy."

"Analyze this," he said, and kissed her again, making sure she knew exactly how much he wanted her.

"We have to stop," she said, eventually, but she didn't move away.

"I know." He forced himself away from her mouth, leaned his forehead against hers. "When?"

"This weekend. The girls are going to be with their father."

"I think I can live that long."

She laughed. "My boss is having a party Friday at the Omni Hotel in Corpus Christi. Command performance. Will you go with me?"

"I can't think of anything I'd like better." When she smiled, he added, "With one exception. And I think you know what that is."

"I can guess," she murmured, as he kissed her one last time.

CHAPTER SIX

As soon as Jay left, Gail called Cat. "I have to cancel lunch tomorrow," she told her sister when she answered.

"You're just saying that because it's my turn to choose. No, Max, don't throw grapes at Buddy."

"I'm going shopping."

"You're standing me up to shop? For what? What's so important?"

"I have to find the perfect dress to begin a passionate affair." Something she'd imagined, but never really believed would happen to her.

Cat choked, then swore. "Damn it! No, I mean, darn it! I just spilled my tea everywhere. Hold on a minute."

Muffled background noises indicated her sister had handed the baby to her husband, informed Max he wasn't to repeat bad words, and then took the phone into another room.

"Okay, repeat that. I thought I heard you say you're going to have an affair."

"I did." A thrill of anticipation ran up her spine. "And I need a dress that will bring him to his knees. Something that will make him crazy." Gail wasn't certain why that was so important. Maybe because she needed to feel strong and in control, unlike she had five years ago.

"Do I get to guess the identity of this mystery man or are you going to tell me?"

Getting comfortable on the couch, Gail tucked her feet beneath her. "If you don't know who it is, then motherhood has drained all your brain cells."

There was a long pause. When Cat finally spoke, her voice sounded troubled. "I was afraid of that. It's Jay, isn't it?"

Gail held the phone away from her ear and stared at it before bringing it back. "What do you mean, you were afraid of that? Isn't this exactly what you've been pushing for?"

"Well, yeah, but—" She hesitated before adding, "I hadn't thought it through before. Maybe it's not such a hot idea. Mark said—"

Infuriated, Gail interrupted. "How nice of you and Mark to decide what I should do with *my* personal life. It might have escaped your notice, but I'm a grown woman. Older than you, as a matter of fact."

"Don't get all huffy with me," Cat fired back. "Mark and I love you both, so of course we're concerned. You and Jay are connected. We're family. What happens if something goes wrong and you wind up hating each other?"

Exactly what she'd asked Jay, but she wouldn't tell Cat that. "We can handle it. I have an ex-husband I have to deal with, remember? Awkward situations are my specialty."

"So you're just going to plunge into this affair with no thought for the future?"

Her fingers tightened on the receiver. "I have thought about the future." And the past and how dull her life had been the last few years...until Jay showed up. "Besides, I'm not planning on marrying him. We're just having fun. There's no need for you and Mark to get your panties in a wad."

"So what are you saying? That this thing between you and Jay is just about sex?"

She sounded disapproving, which considering what Gail knew about Cat and Mark's romance struck her as a tad hypocritical. Gail blew out an exasperated breath. "Since when have you gotten so stuffy? No, it's not just about sex." A lot of it, maybe, but not all of it. "I like him. We have fun together. What's wrong with that?"

"Nothing, as long as it doesn't get messy. But these things have a way of getting messy. Especially when you're talking about family. You'll be thrown together all the time, like it or not. Right now that's fine. But what about when you break up?"

"You're just going to have to trust us. And Cat? Butt out."

Cat laughed at that. "Okay, I can take a hint."

"Good. I thought I was going to have to slap you upside the head."

After a moment, Cat said, "One last question, and I promise, I'm done." Gail didn't speak, figuring it was better to go ahead and let her sister have her say.

This time. "Does Jay know this is just fun? Is that what he wants, too?"

They hadn't discussed it, but Gail thought she knew his sentiments. "He's just come out of a long-term relationship that didn't work. I can't imagine he's looking for serious any more than I am."

GAIL SMOOTHED DOWN the skirt of her sleeveless midnight-blue cocktail dress and eyed herself critically in the mirror. The glittery material caught the light and shimmered, picking up a hundred different hues. It hadn't looked like much on the hanger, but the saleslady had talked her into trying it on. And she'd been absolutely right.

Her skin glowed creamily above the low-cut bodice, where the material molded to her figure, then flared at the hem to swing above her knees. Perfect, Gail thought, even if it had cost a small fortune.

But she didn't feel guilty. Not much. She deserved to have some fun. In the years since her divorce, she'd dated, of course. She'd even had sex. Not very often, but she'd had it. After a couple short relationships, she'd decided she just wasn't cut out for that part of the singles scene and she hadn't been even tempted for a very long time now.

Until Jay moved to town.

Since her meeting had run late and she'd been exhausted, she hadn't seen him the evening before. But she'd talked to him on the phone, and she knew that if they had been together, they wouldn't have managed to keep their hands off each other for long.

The doorbell rang as she sprayed on a mist of cologne and twisted the back of the small gold and pearl earring dangling from her ear. Luckily, Barry hadn't canceled, but as usual, he was late.

She heard shrieks of "Daddy, Daddy, Daddy" and the pounding of little feet as the girls ran to answer the door. They adored Barry, particularly Roxy. Gail admitted, albeit grudgingly, that Barry seemed to love his daughters. Since he'd come back to town and begun sharing custody, he swore he was a different man, but Gail didn't believe a person could change that much. Not deep down.

Roxy and Mel had been so young when he left the first time. If he did it again, how much worse would it be for the girls now that they had grown to know him and love him?

Barry was smiling, trying to listen to both girls at once when Gail entered the room. Seeing him like that reminded her of why she'd fallen for him in the first place. With his light brown hair, hazel eyes, and lean, fit body, he was a very good-looking man. And Barry could be very charming when he wanted to be.

He looked up just then and saw her. His eyes widened and he smiled. "Looking good tonight, Gail. Hot date?"

"As a matter of fact, yes," she said, pleased when the smile turned to a frown.

"Mommy." Roxy tugged insistently on her skirt. "Daddy said you could come with us tonight. We're going to eat pizza and then Daddy said he'd take us to a movie."

Gail ruffled Roxy's hair. "Thanks sweetie, but I have a date." She'd told the girls about it, seeing no reason to keep them in the dark. Especially not if she intended to keep seeing Jay for a while.

"You can come on a date with us. Can't she, Daddy?" she persisted. "You don't need to go out with Jay. *Daddy* can be your date."

Mel picked that moment to interrupt with a chant of "Mommy's got a da-ate," repeating it until Roxy pulled her hair. Mel started to cry, but her tears dried magically when Barry promised her ice cream on the way home from the movie.

"Sounds like your mom's busy, Rox," Barry said, with a smile for Gail. "Maybe next time. Why don't you two go get your bags. We need to get moving if we're going to catch the movie."

Still looking mutinous, Roxy left the room with her younger sister in tow. Disturbed, Gail stared after them. She didn't date often but it wasn't as if she never went out. What had gotten into Roxy?

"Who's the lucky guy?" Barry asked, taking a seat on the sofa. "Anyone I know?"

Knowing her girls and how long they took to gather their things, she sat in a chair to wait for them. "I doubt it. Jay Kincaid."

"Kincaid? Any relation to your brother-in-law?"

She nodded. "His brother. Not that it's any of your business."

"Whoa, a little defensive, aren't you?"

He was right. Roxy's reaction must have bothered her more than she realized. But she wouldn't let on to Barry. "I don't happen to like my ex-husband grilling me."

Barry lifted his hands, palms up, then leaned closer to her. "Roxy's right, you know," he said, his voice dropping to an intimate tone. "It wouldn't be a bad idea."

Confused, Gail stared at him. "What wouldn't be a bad idea?"

"You and me. Dating." He smiled at her, leaned even closer and skimmed his hand down her bare arm. "In fact, I think it's a great idea."

Dumbfounded, Gail couldn't speak for a moment. She jumped up, away from that caressing hand. "Well, think again. It's not going to happen. Not ever."

"Why not?"

He was smiling indulgently, as if he knew she'd fall into his hands like the proverbial ripe plum. And the pitiful thing was, she'd done it once. She'd taken one look at that handsome face and fallen for him head over heels. But she'd been young then, and stupid. *And what about those years of marriage you endured when you suspected he didn't love you anymore? You weren't so young then, were you?*

No, she hadn't been young, but she'd felt trapped all the same. She'd wanted the marriage to work, for the children's sake. It still galled her that Barry had been the one to leave, and not her. She brushed aside those thoughts, as she brushed aside their past.

"We're divorced, remember?"

"So? Lots of people who are divorced date."

She parked her hands on her hips and gave him a good, long stare. "You're crazy. I wouldn't date you if you were the last man on earth."

His assurance finally cracked and he frowned. "How long are you going to punish me for one lousy mistake?"

"It wasn't one mistake. It was a series of them, and the last was the *mother* of all mistakes," she said.

Thank God, the doorbell rang. "This conversation is over. And in case you decide to bring it up again, don't." She turned her back and stalked to the door, yanking it open more forcefully than she'd intended.

"Hi. Sorry I'm late, I got held up at the office. You look great," Jay said appreciatively. He wore a light-weight summer suit that stretched elegantly across his broad shoulders, and tailored slacks covering long legs. She'd seen him in dress clothes before, at Cat's wedding. If possible, he looked even better now than he had then. Perhaps it was the added maturity that five years had given him. There was nothing boyish about Jay now. No, nothing boyish at all.

Realizing she'd been all but drooling, Gail stepped aside, motioning him to come in. "Thanks. And you're not late. The girls haven't left yet. Let me introduce you to their father."

She made the introductions. Roxy and Mel came in as the two men shook hands. Jay turned to them and smiled. "Hi, Roxy. Hi, Mel. How's it going?"

Mel ran to him, bombarding him with questions about the puppies. He laughed. "Yes, they're still digging holes," he said in answer to one of her questions. "I'm not sure when I'll be able to break them of that."

Roxy, standing beside her father, broke into the conversation. "Mommy, are you sure you can't come with us? Please?"

Gail's gaze met her ex-husband's. He shrugged, apparently as perplexed as Gail. "Your mom already said no, Rox. Come on, let's go."

Roxy looked at Jay, a clear challenge in her eye. "Daddy's taking us for pizza. And a movie," she added, her manner implying that whatever Jay's plans were, they ran a clear second to her father's.

Jay's lips twitched but he spoke to her solemnly. "That sounds like fun. Have a good time."

"We will. We *always* have fun with Daddy." She glanced at her father, then back to Jay. "Mommy would have lots more fun with us than with you. Except she already told you she'd go with you."

"Roxy, that's enough," Gail said, wanting to sink into the floor with embarrassment. Thank God, Jay looked more amused than offended.

"Roxy's being a poop-head," Mel confided in Jay.

"Am not!" Roxy said, starting toward her sister.

"Are too!"

Gail broke in before they could erupt into full battle. "Stop it, girls. Give me a kiss and go get in the car."

She opened the door for them and kissed each in turn. Barry said goodbye to Jay, then paused on his way out, putting his hand on her arm. "A little young for you, isn't he?" he murmured. "Have fun."

"Don't worry, I plan to," she said, giving him her brightest smile instead of shoving him out the door as she wanted to do.

After Barry left, she breathed a sigh of relief. That had been a lot more uncomfortable than she'd imagined it would be. She wasn't sure whether to apologize for Roxy or ignore the whole thing.

"That was interesting," Jay said. "I seem to have graduated to the top of Roxy's shit list. Any idea why?"

Gail started to deny it, then shrugged. "No, but I don't intend to worry about it. Whatever it is, it will blow over."

But she knew exactly why. Roxy wanted her parents to get back together. She couldn't have made it clearer if she'd held up a neon sign, and Gail didn't doubt Jay knew it as well. Obviously, Gail was going to have to have a talk with her eldest daughter. Tonight, though, it was out of her hands.

"Let me get my purse and we can go."

"Did I mention you look fantastic?"

Her lips curved upward. "Thanks. I think you said great earlier."

"Yeah. That too." His gaze caressed her like a warm breeze. He looked at her as if he wanted to start at the top and lick his way down her body.

Heat climbed into her cheeks at the image that brought to mind. But she had a plan, and she intended to follow it.

"Are you sure you want to go to this party?" Jay asked. "I can think of a lot of—" his gaze lingered on her mouth, dropped to her decolletage, then slid back up to her eyes "—intriguing things we could do."

Gail laughed. "I'll bet. But my boss will kill me if I don't show up. Come on, let's go."

Once inside his car, Jay leaned over her to pull her seat belt out, snapping it into place. His hand brushed her breast as he did so, and they both drew in a breath. Their eyes met.

His gaze dropped to her mouth. "If I kiss you now, we won't make it to the party."

She moved closer. "Then I guess you'd better not kiss me. Besides, you know what they say." She sat back, folded her hands together, and waited.

He was staring at her with a slightly glazed expression in his eyes. "No, what do they say?"

Deliberately, she touched her tongue lightly to her lips. "Anticipation is half the fun."

His pupils dilated and he sucked in a breath. "You're a wicked woman, Gail. I like that about you."

Fun, definitely fun, Gail thought as they drove away.

Still, it would be even more fun if she could shake that niggling worry that Roxy hadn't finished trying to get her parents back together.

"NICE," JAY SAID, as they walked into the gorgeous ballroom. Chandeliers sparkled, elaborately decorated tables stood laden with trays of seafood, crepes, and canapés, arranged artfully around ice sculptures of leaping dolphins. "What's the occasion?"

"Technically, it's a party for my boss's daughter and her new husband. Her third, I think," Gail added with a mischievous grin. "But believe me, he's schmoozing, too. I'm sure half the Corpus Christi business community is here. There's my boss," she said, pointing toward a group of people. "I'll introduce you. Charlie's a nice guy, you'll like him, but watch out for his daughter."

"I thought you said she just got married."

"She did." She glanced up at him and smiled. "There's a reason she's on husband number three."

Gail introduced him to several people, including Charlie Wade and his daughter, Muriel. Gail had pegged the sexy brunette perfectly, he thought, withdrawing a piece of paper from his pocket. He ditched her phone number on his way to the bar.

"White wine spritzer and a Sam Adams," Jay told the bartender. There was only one problem with bringing a beautiful woman to a party like this one, he thought, watching Gail from across the room. Every other man in the room wanted to know her, and about half of them hit on her. And he didn't want to share.

Tonight she looked outrageously good. Part of it, he suspected, was the dress. Sexy as sin, it clung to her in a way that had him counting down the minutes until they could leave. Hell, he'd spent the last two days doing very little else beyond thinking about making love to her. If he didn't have her soon, he just might die of frustration.

As he made his way back to Gail with the drinks, a distinguished gray-haired man slid his arm around her waist. Apparently, Jay wasn't the only one who thought Gail looked good enough to eat. The man's hand fell to pat her butt, with a hell of a lot more familiarity than Jay thought reasonable.

Gail said something to him and eased away. Jay reached them just as the man, apparently too stupid to understand no, tried again.

"Hey, buddy, you can take your hand off my date now," he told the older man as he handed Gail her drink and, putting his arm around her waist, pulled her next to him. "I can handle it from here."

Gail choked as he led her away. "Do you know who that is?" she asked, laughter lighting her blue eyes.

"No, but I know he's a jerk."

"Yes, he is. He's also one of the biggest condo developers around here. My boss has been courting him for the last three months. He's finally got him interested in a really big project."

"Sorry," he said, though he wasn't. "I guess it would have really queered the deal if I'd broken his fingers, like I wanted to."

Eyes dancing, she laughed. "Probably. His expression was priceless. I don't think a lot of people turn him down, or call him on his obnoxious behavior."

He didn't want to talk about jerks, or think about

another man's hands on Gail. Not when he wanted, very much, to put his own hands on her.

"Dance with me," he said. He found a darkened area of the dance floor and took her in his arms. Holding her close against him, he didn't speak at first, but let the music wash over them, a woman singing a bluesy, sexy ballad. Bending down, he spoke quietly in her ear. "Did you wear this dress to torture me? Because it's doing the job. All I can think about is getting you out of it."

Soft laughter was his answer. A few minutes later she said, "Jay?"

He looked down at her, saw those lush lips smiling and wanted to dive in right there. "What?"

"Matching lingerie."

By the time they left the party he was damn near whimpering.

For the first time in his life, Jay wished he didn't drive a sports car with bucket seats, a stick shift, and an extremely small back seat. So he wouldn't even touch her. With a thirty-minute drive ahead of them, he couldn't afford to. But he wanted to. The night was dark, the parking lot was deserted...maybe just one kiss. He drew in a breath and shook his head. *Start the car,* he told himself. *While you still can.*

He hadn't considered Gail kissing him, but he should have. She wrapped herself around him, locked those lovely lips on his, and he thought he'd died and gone to heaven. His hand slipped inside her bodice, inside her bra and he felt the bare, silky skin of her breast. His fingers touched her nipple, felt it pearl, and they both moaned.

He wanted to see her, had to see her. He tugged the clingy fabric down, pushed down her bra and gently lifted out one perfect breast. "Beautiful," he murmured, as the moonlight shone through the window. His lips closed around a deep, dusky rose nipple. He licked it and then sucked it, as it grew to a hard point to tease his tongue. The gearshift stabbed him in the side, and he released her breast, cursing.

They stared at each other, both of them gasping for breath. "There's a hotel right here," he said. "With a big, comfortable bed in the room. Why are we leaving?"

"The puppies. Don't you need to—" Her eyes fluttered closed when he cupped her bare breast. "See to them?" she finished, a breathless moment later.

He started to say to hell with the animals, they'd be fine, but he knew if he left them shut up in the laundry room all night, the place would be a shambles. And if he went into that hotel with Gail, he knew he wouldn't come out until morning. At least.

"You're right. Damn it." Regretfully, he pulled her bra and dress up to cover her breast, cranked the engine and started the long drive home.

As if he needed anything more to turn him on, she kept her hand on his thigh the whole way. And he discovered, once they got on the highway and he didn't need to shift, that she wore thigh-high hose and very little else under that sexy blue dress.

THEY MADE IT INSIDE, barely, before they started ripping off each other's clothes. Jay backed her up against the wall. His lips crushed hers, his tongue plunged inside her mouth with hot, rapid thrusts. She met him stroke for stroke, her hands grappling with his shirt buttons, even as she felt the zipper at the back of her dress slide down.

"This dress is really pretty," he said, and sucked on her earlobe. "I want you out of it."

She laughed as he pushed it down over her arms, past her hips, until it pooled at her feet. Stepping back, his hot gaze slid over her, and she felt as if she'd been blasted by a furnace. Then his mouth was on hers, his hands on her breasts, popping the front closure of her bra and peeling back the cups.

He cupped her bare breasts, caressed them, then his head dropped and he sucked her nipple, tonguing the tip of it until she put her hands in his hair and pressed him harder against her. He tormented one breast, moved to the other, gave it the same, sweet treatment. She nearly exploded right there.

He raised his head, his hands sliding down to grasp her hips, rocked his own against her. "The bedroom." His voice was deep, seductive, sliding over her like the tide.

Shaking her head, she put her hands on his belt buckle. Unbuckled it, opened the button, slid his pants zipper down, slowly, with difficulty, over a blatant erection. "Here. Now," she said, and closed her hand around him.

"I won't argue with you," he said, and pulled her

to the floor with him. His hand slipped inside her panties, palmed her, rubbed her until her hips bucked against him, and then he slid one long finger inside her.

"Jay!" His name burst from her with a shocked gasp as she crested, trembled on the edge.

"Yeah. Oh, yeah," he groaned, and kissed her mouth. He left her for a moment, to pull out a condom from his pants pocket.

"Hurry," she said, holding out her arms. He covered himself, then lay down, pulling her on top of him. He helped her straddle him as he thrust inside her in one smooth, long plunge, his hands on her hips, guiding, stroking.

His hands came up to caress her breasts as she rode him, at first slowly, then faster and faster. She looked down, into his eyes, fell into their depths with each deep thrust. He slipped his hand down to where their bodies joined and sent her tumbling, flying. She gasped, stifled a scream as her orgasm speared through her on a burst of light.

His hands grasped her hips again, and she looked into his face as with one last, welcome push, she saw his eyes cloud, close and felt his climax rip through him.

"I had no idea," she murmured, aeons later, still collapsed on top of him.

"That it would be so good between us?" he asked, his hand stroking her back.

"Hmm." She rubbed her cheek against his chest.

She didn't think she had a backbone left. She was certain she couldn't move without assistance.

"I did."

She raised her head and smiled at him. "You're a smart guy, aren't you?"

He smiled. "If I was so smart, we would have done this five years ago."

"True," she said, and laughed. "Is that the puppies I hear?" Sharp yaps came from the direction of his kitchen. "Shouldn't we see about them?"

Jay groaned. "Yeah. I'm sure they've demolished the laundry room. But it was worth it," he said, and kissed her. His hands slipped over her rear. "I meant to take you to the bedroom. To my bed."

"I liked it here, just fine," she told him.

He rolled them over, settled between her legs. Her eyes widened as she felt him harden against her. "Me too."

"Jay," she said breathlessly. "The puppies."

"Okay, I'm going." He kissed her mouth, tenderly. "Because next time, we're going very, very slow."

She looped her arms around his neck. "So, there's going to be a next time?"

"Definitely." He kissed her again, and again. "More than one, if I have anything to say about it."

CHAPTER SEVEN

THEY SPENT THE WEEKEND together. Talking, watching movies, playing with the puppies. And making love. Everywhere. A lot. By Saturday afternoon Gail could attest to the fact that Jay Kincaid had a number of moves, every blessed one of them smooth.

They sat on the couch, the puppies at their feet gnawing on chew toys, sharing a bowl of popcorn and a diet soda. Gail wore one of Jay's dress shirts and nothing else. He wore a pair of cutoffs, and, she was almost certain, nothing else.

At the moment, Jay's eyes were closed and he appeared to be asleep. Her fingers itched to trace their way down that muscled chest. If she thought about it very hard, her extreme preoccupation with his body might worry her. Then again, she acknowledged, it was some body.

"I've never done this before, you know." She dug into the popcorn bowl, munched a bit. "I had no idea my education was so lacking."

"Never done what?" he asked, eyes still closed.

Thick blond hair fell over his forehead, mussed from her fingers running through it. She wanted to do it again. His beard, like his hair, was light, though he'd shaved that morning, saying he didn't want to give her whisker burns. Progressing to his mouth, she sucked in a breath. Perfection. His lips were just full enough to be beautiful, yet they were unmistakably masculine. Unable to resist, she traced a finger over his mouth, remembering what it felt like on her own, and on her skin.

"Had marathon sex," she said, fingers still on his lips. "I like it."

He cracked open an eye. "You were married. You mean to tell me you never spent a weekend in bed? Was your husband a eunuch?"

Knowing Barry thought himself the ultimate sex machine, she gave a peal of laughter. "No," she gasped when she stopped laughing. She couldn't wait to tell Cat that one. "Maybe he just didn't have your stamina. Or maybe he wasn't interested." Not in her, anyway. She frowned at that, thinking it the most likely explanation.

"Then he's an idiot," Jay said succinctly. "He had you and your daughters and he let you go. How much more stupid can you get?"

She laid her hand on his cheek and smiled. "Have I told you I really like you?"

He grinned, turned his head to kiss her palm. "Not lately. Have I told you I really like you?" He set the popcorn aside, lay back on the couch, pulling her on top of him. "And that I find you extremely—" he kissed her mouth, trailed his lips to her neck "—extremely sexy?"

"Not lately," she said, and sighed as he unbuttoned her shirt.

ONE DAY the following week, Jay went to his partner's office. "Hey, Tim, you got a minute?"

Tim's office was somewhat less spartan than Jay's, for in addition to a desk, chairs and bookshelves, it held a kid's-size table in one corner, for when his children visited their father at work. His desk and bookshelves boasted a number of pictures, as well, most of his family at various stages. The office was like Tim, Jay thought. A little messy and very comfortable.

"Sure." Tim set aside the chart he'd been studying and sighed. "I don't know why I can't convince Mrs. Finch she can't expect her blood pressure to improve if she won't take her medicine."

"Maybe it makes her feel bad. Try a different one."

"I think I will." He leaned back in his desk chair as Jay took a seat across from him. "Now, what can I do for you?"

"I've got a patient with a lump in her breast. Almost certainly a fibroadenoma," he said, speaking of a tumor that while common in women in their twenties, was also benign. "Problem is, she won't let me excise it."

"Just you, or anyone?"

"Anyone. I explained that it was almost certainly benign, but that it still needed to be biopsied, and that the operation's a minor one. She said she didn't care, and has been adamantly refusing the surgery. I finally got her to admit she's just gotten married and she's afraid her husband will flip.''

He tapped his fingers on the desk and thought about the woman he'd seen that morning. It hadn't taken him long to realize she was scared to death. More of losing her husband than of the consequences of ignoring her medical problems. ''Seems she thinks he married her for her looks.''

Tim looked at him over his glasses. ''I take it these looks include a great set of....''

''Spectacular,'' Jay admitted. ''But you know as well as I do it shouldn't make a difference. It's a minor operation, you should hardly be able to see a scar. I even offered to set her up with a plastic surgeon, if she doesn't want me to do it, but she still said no go.''

''Do you mind if I ask who the patient is?''

Jay told him.

Tim laughed. ''Have you thought about having them in together and explaining it to the husband?''

''Yes, but I don't know if I can talk her into it.''

''Keep trying. I know the guy. He's crazy about her.''

''You're sure? I don't want to make it worse.''

''Positive. I don't know why she's so worried. The guy's sappy in love with her, and it's not just her looks. I wish all my problems were that easy.''

''Thanks, Tim. I'll see if I can convince her to bring him in.'' He got up to leave.

''Hey, hold on a minute. The wife's having another

barbecue this weekend. Saturday afternoon. How about dropping by?'' He stacked some papers and added, ''She's asked a friend of hers. Single, brunette, built.'' He waggled his eyebrows. ''What do you say?''

''Sorry, have to pass. I'm seeing someone.''

''Damn, Jay, you work fast,'' Tim said admiringly. ''You've only been in town a few weeks.''

He grinned. ''We go back a ways.''

''Mind telling me who she is? Tamara will make my life a living hell until she knows. Anyone I know?''

''Yeah, she's a patient of yours. Gail Summers.''

''Gail?'' He rubbed his chin and smiled. ''That's good. Tamara likes her. Why don't you both come, then? And tell Gail to bring the kids. There'll be a wad of them there. Not to mention, Roxy and my daughter Carol are friends.'' He paused, then added, ''Unless it's all too domestic for you.''

''I'm dating a woman with two kids. I think I can handle domestic. Thanks, I'll ask her.''

LATER THAT EVENING, when he saw Gail at Mark's house, Jay thought about his earlier conversation with Tim. Four kids and four adults made for a lot of domesticity. He liked the kids—all the kids. They were good kids, sweet kids. But he hadn't made love to Gail since her daughters had come home on Sunday. His frustration level was beginning to get seriously out of hand.

So when Cat complained all the popcorn had disappeared and she couldn't watch the movie without food, he spoke up. "Gail and I will fix more."

They managed to put a bag in the microwave and set the timer before they were in each other's arms.

"Oh, God, put your hands on me," Gail said, wrapping her arms around his neck and kissing him frantically.

Not about to argue, he put his hands on her sweet rear and pressed her tightly against him, plunging his tongue into her mouth. "I want to be with you," he said, sliding one hand up to cup her breast. "Inside you."

"I know, I know. I want you, too." She groaned and pushed her breast into his palm. "So much," she whispered. Their lips met, clung, parted. "Tomorrow night. I'll get a baby-sitter and come to your house."

"Good. Come here." He let go of her long enough to pull her into the room off the kitchen that Cat used to isolate the birds she rehabilitated. Currently it was empty. He leaned back against the door and wrapped his arms around Gail. Her breasts rested against his chest, the vee of her thighs against his hardening flesh.

"We should go back," she said, but she kissed him as she said it.

"We will. First I need to touch you." He slipped his hand beneath her skirt. They both groaned when he slid his hand over her panties, stroked her heat. Her hips thrust toward him, seeking more. He thought about easing that scrap of fabric off and sliding inside of her.

"Let me have you," he said against her mouth.

"Now?" she whispered hoarsely.

"Now."

Their gazes locked. Slowly, eyes still on his, she nodded. He tugged on her panties, slipped them over her hips, down her pretty legs.

Someone knocked on the door. "Gail, are you in there?" Mark asked.

Jay closed his eyes and swore. "Go away, Mark."

"Sorry. Mel needs Gail."

"Um, okay," she said, her voice a bit unsteady. "I'll be right there."

Jay kissed her, hard, then slowly, regretfully let her go. Her cheeks were flushed, her lips swollen. She looked tousled, a little dazed, and so damn sexy it hurt him to watch her. She pulled up her panties, adjusted the rest of her clothes, ran her fingers through her hair, then opened the door.

"Sorry," Mark said again.

"That's all right. Is something wrong?" she asked him.

"Yeah, Mel says she has a stomachache. She wants to go home."

"Too much popcorn, I'll bet," Gail said. "Thanks, Mark." She looked at Jay, her gaze regretful.

Jay leaned down and kissed her lightly on the lips. "I'll call you later. Go see about Mel."

She nodded and left the room.

He stood staring after her, wishing Mark had been five minutes later. But it couldn't be helped. Her child needed her. He'd live. A man didn't die of sexual frustration. Probably.

"Are you sure you know what you're doing?" Mark asked.

He turned around to look at his brother. "What?"

Mark gestured at the door. "You and Gail. Maybe you should cool it. Before you get too involved."

"Why would I want to do that?" And where the hell was Mark coming from? As far as Jay knew, Mark had never had a problem with Gail. Why would he have one now?

Mark took the popcorn out of the microwave, opened it and poured it into a bowl. "Gail had a lousy divorce. The bastard really did a number on her." He glanced up at Jay. "You and Carla haven't been broken up that long. If this is just a rebound relationship you're going to hurt Gail. And she's been hurt enough for a lifetime."

Annoyed, he stuffed his hands in his pockets and paced a step. Mark didn't have a problem with Gail, he had one with Jay. "I'm not on the rebound. And this is none of your business."

Mark crossed his arms. "It damn sure is. You're both my family."

"And we're both grown and capable of taking care of ourselves."

"Look, I didn't mean to piss you off, but have you thought about what will happen when it ends? What about the kids? What about all the family crap?"

He'd thought about it. Not a lot, but he'd thought about it. He'd just thought about getting Gail into his bed a lot more. His temper spiked, maybe because Mark's questions were reasonable. "Butt out, Mark."

Mark picked up the bowl and started toward the door. "Fine, but just think about it, will you?"

It irritated the hell out of him but the conversation did make him think. Gail and he weren't the only ones involved. She had children. They had mutual family. None of that made him want her any less, though, and no way could he step back now. No, they'd just have to be careful. He was damn near addicted to her. How could he think about ending it?

SATURDAY AFTERNOON, as Gail was getting ready for the Kramers' barbecue, Roxy came into her room.

"Daddy's coming to get me."

Gail paused while putting on mascara and looked at her daughter. "What do you mean, your father's coming? We're going to the Kramers' barbecue. You were at your father's last weekend."

Roxy shrugged and plucked at some of the doodads littering Gail's dresser. "Daddy said *we'd* barbecue. 'Sides—" she looked at her mother, accusation in the blue eyes so like Gail's own "—you don't care if me and Mel go. You just want to be with Uncle Jay."

Gail reached out for her daughter, but she jerked away.

Hurt, Gail dropped her hand. "Honey, that's not true. I want you and Mel both to be there, and so does Jay. What's wrong, Roxy?"

She dug her toe into the carpet and dragged it. "Last time, when we went to Daddy's house, he said you sure looked pretty. He said you looked *beautiful*," she quoted, emphasizing the word. "So why can't you go out with Daddy, and not Uncle Jay?"

Understanding dawned. "Your father and I are divorced, Roxy. We don't go out with each other."

Roxy muttered something Gail couldn't hear. "Roxy, honey, I'm sorry, but your daddy and I aren't going to get back together." Gail barely restrained a shudder.

"But you could." She pinned her mother with a hopeful gaze. "If you wanted to, you and Daddy could get married again. My friend Shauna's parents did that."

"I'm sorry, sweetie. It's not going to happen. But even though we're not married, both your daddy and I love you and Mel very much. That's not going to change."

Might as well give Barry the benefit of the doubt, because Roxy needed to believe in his love, even if Gail wasn't sure he was capable of it. She was very careful never to mention to the girls the two years their father had gone without seeing them. That or the fact he'd taken their savings with him when he walked out. Thankfully, the girls had been too small to remember it well.

But Gail remembered.

Her daughter's lip stuck out. "I'm still going to Daddy's. You can't stop me," she added defiantly.

"If you want to, then of course you can. But we would love to have you come with us, Roxy. Your friend Carol will be there," she reminded her.

For the first time, Roxy looked undecided. Then the doorbell rang. "There's Daddy!" Roxy ran out of the room. Gail finished putting on mascara and then followed.

"Daddy," Gail heard Mel say as she walked in. "Can I still come see you next weekend? Mommy wants me to go with her tonight."

"Sure, honey." He ruffled her hair, smiling when she ran out.

"Barry, can I see you a minute? In the kitchen?" To Roxy, who was hanging on her father's arm, she said, "Go make sure you have everything. Your father and I will be finished in a few minutes."

She let him precede her into the room. He held up a hand. "Before you start ragging on me, Roxy called me."

"I know that. But you should have at least warned me you were taking her on an unscheduled day."

"Why? I figured you'd be glad I was taking her off your hands. From what the kid says, you're too busy with your new boyfriend to give her the time of day."

Irritated, Gail propped her hands on her hips. "That's ridiculous. I've been with the girls every night this week."

"Yeah, and so has he."

"Not every night," she said, aware she'd been put on the defensive and hating it. "But even if he had, so what? I'm entitled to date whoever I want to."

"Sure, if you don't care what your daughters think. Roxy doesn't like him."

"Mel does." Gail strove for patience. "Roxy is understandably jealous. I haven't dated anyone more than once or twice before now. She likes Jay, she's just not accustomed to my dating. She'll get used to it, and things will be fine." Hoping what she'd said was true, she turned her back on Barry and attempted to cool off.

"There's an answer to this you haven't considered," Barry said from behind her. "Something I wish you would think about."

Suspicious, she turned around. "What's that?"

He smiled at her. The same smile that had once dazzled her into believing almost anything he wanted her to believe. But now it left her cold.

"You could give me another chance," he said.

Oh, he did sincerity so well. But it wouldn't work, not anymore. "No." She shook her head emphatically. "No way in hell. I have to say, I think it's a little absurd that you showed absolutely no interest in me until another man did."

He looked hurt. "That's not how it is. I've been thinking about the two of us for a long time now."

"News flash, Barry. There is no 'two of us.' And there won't be in the future. The only interest I have in you is as Mel and Roxy's father."

Roxy entered just then, preventing further argument. She barely allowed Gail to kiss her cheek before she was out the door.

Barry paused in the doorway. "We'll talk more later."

"No, we won't," Gail said automatically. Barry

simply smiled and waved. Gail's stomach sank even further. What would it take to convince her ex-husband she had no intention of taking him back? Worse, what would it take to convince Roxy to give Jay a chance?

CHAPTER EIGHT

JAY COULDN'T QUITE figure out what was wrong with Gail, but he knew something was up. At the Kramers', she'd seemed preoccupied, a little moody, but they hadn't really had a chance to talk. Now, on the way home, she'd hardly spoken, even though Mel had fallen asleep the instant she crawled into the car. Jay had a gut feeling Gail's mood had something to do with Roxy and the fact that she had gone with her father, rather than them.

"So," he said after Gail returned from putting Mel to bed. He patted the couch beside him. "Sit down and talk to me. What's going on?"

She sat beside him, clasped her hands together and looked straight ahead. "Oh, nothing. Besides the fact that Roxy's trying to get me back together with her father."

He didn't care for the sting of jealousy that gave him. "Is that what you want?" he asked carefully.

She shot him a glance that had the tightness in his chest easing. "I wouldn't go back to Barry if he were the last man on the planet."

He thought he'd known her answer, but hearing it still relieved him. "Then what's the problem?"

"I told you. Roxy. She's not very happy about you and I dating." She worried her lip. "I haven't, you know. I mean, not to speak of. Until you." She glanced at him. "What are you smiling about?"

"I don't know. I like knowing that."

"Do you?" She smiled, too.

"Yeah. Come here," he said, and put his arm around her shoulders.

Gail snuggled against him, tucking her feet up beside her. "I'm sure she'll get over it. After all, she liked you before. And she doesn't hate you, she just—"

"Wishes you'd get back with her dad. That's understandable. Don't you think this will blow over?"

"Ordinarily, I'd say yes. And I'm sure it will, eventually. But it would help if Barry didn't seem to have the same agenda in mind."

His stomach sank. He didn't like the sound of that. "Your ex-husband wants to get back together with you?"

Gail shrugged. "He's made some comments to that effect. I don't know how serious he is about it."

Jay didn't know why that surprised him. After all, he'd thought Barry was an idiot to leave Gail in the first place. "How long has he been hitting on you?"

"He hasn't been hitting on me. Exactly. He's just said things a couple of times. Don't worry, I set him straight."

Jay frowned. She looked a bit doubtful about her success in that area.

"What's wrong?"

He didn't answer.

"You're jealous," she said, watching him, a mischievous smile tilting her mouth.

Maybe. Okay, yes. Damn straight, he was jealous. "Do I have reason to be?"

"No." She put her arms around his neck, leaned in and kissed him. "No reason at all." She kissed him again, lay back on the couch, pulling him with her.

He settled between her thighs, gazing down at her. He believed her, yet he wondered if he'd have believed anything she told him with her so close and so damn tempting. *But she isn't with Barry,* he thought. *She's with me.*

"Do you know how much I want you right now?"

Her legs tightened around him, her hips rocked up against his. "I think I'm getting the picture."

He leaned down, murmured in her ear, so softly, so quietly, the air hardly stirred. "Do you think—" his tongue traced the rim of her ear "—if we're very, very quiet—" he set his teeth gently on her lobe "—we could go to your bedroom and make love?" His lips trailed to her neck, to taste the pulse beating at the hollow of her throat.

"Jay." She tugged on his hair until he looked at her. "Do you think if I sneak a man into my bedroom that makes me a bad mother?"

He smiled and kissed her mouth. "Not as long as I'm the man you sneak in."

"I'm serious."

"So am I."

Her lips curved. "What are we waiting for?"

They walked hand in hand to her bedroom

ONE EVENING a couple of weeks later, Gail took the girls to Cameron's restaurant to meet Jay. Very much at home, Mel and Roxy went off to the kitchen with Cam's head waitress. "You know the cook won't forgive you if you don't let the girls visit," Sally said as she followed the two.

Gail took a seat at the bar, daydreaming a little as she waited. At first, she had wondered if something so intense might not burn itself out, but that wasn't the case with her affair with Jay. They had spent every spare minute of the past few weeks together, and neither showed any sign of being tired of the other one.

The previous weekend they'd taken the girls to the beach and built huge sandcastles. Roxy had relaxed enough to remember she really liked Jay, and it had done Gail's heart good to see her girls laughing and dumping sand on each other, then ganging up on Jay.

And the nights. Gail closed her eyes and sighed. Once she'd weakened and let Jay stay with her, she hadn't been able to say no again. The enforced silence only made their lovemaking more intense, more intimate, somehow.

"Yo, Gail, what is with you?"

She opened her eyes to see her brother Gabe sitting on the stool beside hers, staring at her. "Nothing." She cleared her throat, thankful he couldn't read her mind. "What do you mean?"

Since he ran a charter fishing service, Gabe's face was sunburned and his dark eyes bloodshot from hours in the bright, coastal sun. That didn't make them any less sharp, though. He hadn't taken time to shave after coming in from a fishing trip and dark stubble lined his jaw. He looked tired, a little grumpy, and too damn curious for Gail's comfort.

"So, I guess the word's true." He picked up an unshelled peanut from the dish on the bar, cracked it, and tossed it in his mouth.

"What word?"

"That you're up to your ears in a red-hot affair. I got to wondering why I hadn't seen you or the girls in weeks, then Cam gave me the scoop."

She made a mental note to twist Cam's ear off when she got the chance. "Cameron, as usual, is exaggerating. I've been dating someone. So what?"

"Yeah, I know." He nodded. "Jay Kincaid. And I'd say it's a little more than dating." He grinned and touched a finger to her neck. "Love bite. Even if I haven't had a date in months, I can still recognize one when I see it."

Her face flamed. She remembered exactly when Jay had put that mark there. And remembered biting the back of her hand to keep from screaming, too. "You're my brother. You're not supposed to notice things like that."

"Believe me, honey," he said, shaking his head. "I'd a hell of a lot rather not. But I'm not blind."

"What you are is nosy. Mind your own business, Gabe."

"Hey, as your older brother, I'm duty bound to razz you." He took another peanut and smirked at her.

Gail considered dumping her soft drink on his head, but she never could stay mad at Gabe for long. "Don't you have something else to do?"

"Nope." He took a sip of beer. "Just catching up with you. So tell me, is he treating you right?"

Her brow furrowed. With only a year between them, she'd always been close to Gabe. "Gabe, are you worried about me? You don't need to be."

Gabe shrugged. "Goes with the territory. You haven't really dated anyone—not seriously—since the slime bastard."

She couldn't help smiling. That had been Gabe's name for Barry ever since she'd introduced the two of them.

"You're more naive than you think you are," Gabe continued.

"I'm thirty-five years old, and naive is the last thing I am. Barry took care of that, a long time ago." His indifference, his total self-absorption, his affairs. Yes, he'd destroyed her illusions about him. And perhaps herself, as well.

"I should never have let you marry that bastard. I knew what he was like. Even if I didn't have proof on your wedding day, I knew—"

"Don't, Gabe." She put her hand on his arm, to stop him before he became truly worked up. "It wouldn't have mattered. I was determined to marry him."

"I should have pasted him on your wedding day," Gabe mused. "On general principles."

Gail laughed. "For the record, Jay is nothing like Barry. So you can quit worrying, okay?"

Gabe circled a finger on the rim of his glass before looking at her. "You sure about that?"

"Positive." She leaned over and kissed his cheek. "But thanks for caring."

He smiled at her, then his expression changed. "Damn, if that's not enough to put you totally off your food. Speaking of the slime bastard..."

Gail turned around to see Barry walking toward them. "Behave," she muttered. "Don't forget the girls are here."

"Hello, Gail. Gabe," he said, nodding to him, though his eyes were on Gail. "I'm glad I ran into you. I wanted to talk to you about the girls." He glanced around. "Are they here?"

"In the kitchen. What do you want, Barry?"

"Privately, if you don't mind." He spared Gabe a false smile. "I'm sure Gabriel will excuse you."

Gail weighed her options. She could have refused to talk to him alone, but that seemed petty. Besides, he might actually have something of importance to say.

"All right." She glanced at her watch. "But make it fast, I'm meeting Jay and he should be here any minute."

"Of course." He led her to a table and pulled out her chair. He hadn't been that polite to her since before they married, she thought.

"Okay, what about the girls?"

Barry looked a little sheepish. "It's not actually about the girls. I just said that to get you away from your brother. I know he hates me."

"You could hardly help but know it. Gabe isn't particularly subtle."

Barry signaled the waitress, then ordered a scotch on the rocks after Gail declined a drink.

Exasperated, she glanced at her watch again, then over at the bar, wondering what was keeping Jay. She turned her attention back to her ex-husband. "What's going on, Barry? Get to the point."

His fingers tapped the table. He seemed different, more nervous than usual.

"Do you believe people can change, Gail?"

"I suppose. If they want to."

"Even people who have done some...not very admirable things?"

Not this again. Deliberately obtuse, she said, "Like what? Lie, cheat, steal? Or are we talking murder?"

He frowned, accepted his drink and took a healthy sip. "You're not making this easy on me."

Why should I? she thought. *I don't want to hear it anyway.* She remained silent.

He set his glass down and looked at her solemnly. "I'm trying to say I'm sorry. For the way I treated you. For the things I did."

Stupefied, she stared at him. "You've never in your life apologized to me."

"I—it's not an easy thing for me." He took her hand and she was so surprised, she let him. "I want you to know that I'm truly, sincerely sorry. I know it's a lot to ask you to forgive me but..." His voice trailed away.

On that, they were in total agreement. "Yes, it is. Why are you doing this, Barry? Groveling isn't your style."

Eyes soulful, he gazed at her. "I want you back, Gail. Give us another chance."

"You've got to be kidding." She tried to pull her hand away, but he held on.

"I've never been more serious."

"Let go of my hand." He released it, slowly, reluctantly. "You can't possibly believe I'd take you back after what you did." She glanced up and saw Jay, sitting at the bar beside Gabe. She couldn't really read his expression, other than to note he didn't look happy.

"I made a mistake," Barry said. "A terrible mistake. I've been trying to rectify it since I came back."

"It was a bit more than a simple mistake, Barry. Even if I could forgive the affairs, I couldn't forget the rest of it. You deserted us for two years. Not once, in those two years, did you see the girls or talk to them, or offer a penny for their support. For two years I had to borrow money from my family and work day and night, so I could get a decent job and support my daughters. My daughters, whose father decided he had better things to do than be responsible for a family. Maybe someone else could forgive you that, but I'm sure as hell not that woman."

"I'm sorry," he repeated. "I explained what happened. My God, Gail, I was married with two kids almost before I could turn around. And the offer, it seemed like a once-in-a-lifetime opportunity. I couldn't turn it down.''

"Even if it meant taking all our money and losing it.''

"It wasn't supposed to happen that way. Besides, you're the one who pushed for the divorce.''

"Gee, imagine that,'' she said, dripping sarcasm. "I divorced the man who deserted me and left me destitute with two kids. Not to mention, a man who was unfaithful, probably from the day we married.''

"Gail, that isn't true.'' At her look of patent disbelief, he added, "I stumbled. I admitted that. I thought we'd gotten past it.''

"You thought wrong.'' Stumbled, had he? That's how he described an affair that had broken her heart, and her faith. For her daughters' sake she'd tried to forgive him. But it had happened again. Several times, she suspected. By the time Barry left, she'd been on the verge of divorcing him anyway. Only the thought of her children had made her hesitate. Then Barry took the decision out of her hands by walking out on them.

Which didn't say a heck of a lot about her judgment.

"Can't you consider forgiving me? Trying again? For the girls' sake, if nothing else.''

"To tell you the truth, Barry, it's been all I could do to let you back into their lives, period. I have no guarantee you won't turn around and do the same thing to them all over again.''

"I wouldn't do that. I love my daughters.''

"That didn't stop you the first time. You said you loved them then, too.''

"So that's it.'' He sighed heavily. "You're never going to forgive me. No matter how many times I tell you I've changed, you're just not going to believe me.''

"I'd say that sums it up real well. I don't trust you, Barry, and I never will.'' She'd made that mistake once, she would never make it again. She looked for Jay but didn't see him. "I've got to go. Don't bring this up again. I won't change my mind.''

She stopped by the bar to talk to Gabe. "What happened to Jay? I was supposed to meet him.''

Gabe took a long pull of his beer before setting it down and looking at her. "He left. Maybe he got sick of watching you and lover boy there cozy up to each other. I know I did.''

Astonished, she stared at him. "We were not cozying up to each other. The reverse, if anything. Jay couldn't have thought that.''

"I don't know what he thought, but I can tell you it's been giving me some bad moments.'' His mouth thinned into a grim line. "You're not thinking about taking that slime bastard back, are you?''

"Don't be an idiot,'' she said crossly. "Why would Jay leave like that?''

"You spent the last twenty minutes oblivious to anyone but your ex-husband. What's the poor sucker supposed to think?" He took another sip, closed his eyes and rolled his head. "Well, at least I don't have to go break Barry's face. Again."

Gabe was exaggerating. Surely Jay didn't think she and Barry... Yet obviously something was bothering him, or he wouldn't have left without even waiting to speak to her.

"I need you to do something for me, Gabe. Will you take the girls home and put them to bed? I'm going to find Jay and clear this up."

"Yeah, I'll take care of Roxy and Mel." He paused, then added, "Good luck. You're gonna need it."

JAY LEFT the Scarlet Parrot for a very good reason. If he'd had to watch Gail and her ex-husband gazing into each others' eyes for one more damn minute, he'd have thrown up. So he left.

He picked up his glass and took another sip of whiskey, feeling the burn as it went down. He rarely drank hard liquor, but tonight seemed like an appropriate night for it. Cradling the glass in his palm, he slumped down and leaned back against the couch cushions.

Fluffy laid her head on his thigh and gave a heartfelt sigh when he scratched behind her ears. Fudge, with her head on Fluffy's rump, wagged her tail, but was apparently too comfortable to demand equal treatment. The dogs weren't supposed to lie on the furniture, but right then he didn't give a shit about dog hair on the fabric. Besides, he liked having the company.

No, he was a lot more concerned about the fact that he'd fallen for a woman who, apparently, hadn't quite finished with her ex-husband.

Gail had sworn she didn't want to get back together with Summers. Maybe he *was* overreacting. All she and her ex had done was hold hands. And gaze at each other. And totally ignore everyone else in the place.

Hoping to block that image, he poured more whiskey into the glass and took another drink. It didn't help. Much. The doorbell rang. Fudge opened one eye, but Fluffy didn't budge. "Some watchdogs you are," he told them, and went to answer it.

He opened the door to Gail. Figuring it was her move, he didn't speak.

"Can I come in?" she asked.

He shrugged and stepped aside.

She walked into the family room. Pausing by the couch, which the dogs still sprawled on, she looked down at the table. "Rough night?" she asked, gesturing at the partially empty whiskey bottle.

"It didn't start out that way," he said, and took a seat on the couch. "Want a drink?"

"No, I want to know why you left the Scarlet Parrot. I was supposed to meet you there, remember?"

"I remember." He took a drink. If he didn't watch it, he'd be drunk. He took another sip. At this point getting drunk seemed preferable to the current conversation. "You're the one who appeared to have forgotten that."

She sat down beside him. "Is that what this is all about? You're upset because I was talking to Barry and didn't rush right over when you came in?"

"No, Gail. All this—" he waved his glass and some of the liquid sloshed out, dripping onto his pants "—isn't because you were talking to your ex-husband. It's because you were totally wrapped up in your ex-husband. Hell, there could have been a fire and the two of you wouldn't have noticed."

"I—we— He's Roxy and Mel's father. I have to talk to him. You're being ridiculous."

"Yeah? Then why are you twisting your hands together like you do when you're nervous?" Her hands stilled and he smiled grimly. He got up and with some difficulty, managed to convince Fudge and Fluffy to go out in the back yard.

A moment later, he came back in. She was sitting just where he'd left her, hands clasped together on her knees and eyes brooding.

He sat down again, careful to keep some distance between them. "Let's get this over with. Then you can go home and I'll finish off this whiskey and feel really bad in the morning."

She gripped his arm. "Do you honestly think I came over here to tell you I'm getting back with Barry?"

"The thought crossed my mind." He started to take another drink but she snatched the glass out of his hand and set it on the table with a bang.

"Stop that. You're only making matters worse."

That was a matter of opinion. He found the numbing effect of the liquor quite pleasant. A lot more so than thinking about Gail and her ex together again. "So what was that deep conversation about? Your kids?"

Her gaze faltered and fell. "No. Barry apologized for what he did during our marriage. For walking out, among other things. He wants us to try again." Her eyes lifted to Jay's. "I told him no."

He searched her face, looking for answers. She wouldn't out and out lie to him. But Jay wondered if there wasn't more to it than that. "And now you're regretting you turned him down."

"Of course I'm not!"

"You're still tied up with him. Because of your daughters, you always will be." Gail and Barry shared a bond that would never break. Because Barry was her children's father. "A part of you is bound to be thinking how much easier your life would be if you just went back to him." He closed his eyes and added, "Roxy would be happy. I'm sure Mel would be too."

Gail took his hand and squeezed it. "Jay, look at me."

He opened his eyes. Her eyes were blue, and troubled. Earnest. Honest. He touched her hair, so blond, fair and pretty, skimmed his fingers over her cheek before his hand dropped away. "Why is it I can't look at you without wanting you?"

She smiled ruefully. "I don't know, but I've wondered the same thing about you."

"Barry wants you back."

"I know he *says* he does. But I don't want him back, Jay. I don't trust him, and I don't love him. I made sure he believed me. Do you?"

"I don't know." He wasn't thinking clearly, and with Gail so close, smelling so good, looking so...sweet, damn it, he didn't know what to do. "I want to."

"Then believe me." She kissed him, slid her tongue inside his mouth, put her arms around him. Pulled him to the floor with her.

"I want you," she said, her voice low and husky, tempting. "Only you. Make love to me, Jay."

So he did. And he buried his reservations, just as he buried himself in that soft, yielding body.

CHAPTER NINE

GAIL STARED AT THE WAND in her hand, the plus sign glowing like a neon sign. Positive. She was pregnant. Which, since she'd been throwing up every morning for the past four days, shouldn't have come as such a shock to her. Yet it had.

How could she be pregnant? They'd used birth control faithfully. The condom hadn't broken. No possible way should she be pregnant.

She looked at the wand again.

Still positive.

What was this, some kind of cosmic joke? Surely once in a lifetime had been enough.

Thank God she'd taken a sick day. She couldn't possibly have concentrated on work. Not when her world was busy falling apart. She told herself not to be overly dramatic, but the lecture didn't help much.

Barry had the girls this weekend. Gail had a date with Jay tonight. He'd told her he had a surprise for her and to come to his house. She'd bet her surprise topped his.

She crawled back into bed and pulled the covers over her head. Maybe if she went back to sleep, some brilliant answer to her problem would occur to her.

Yeah, right, she thought as she dozed off. *If I was that lucky, I wouldn't be pregnant.*

LATER THAT EVENING, Gail stood on Jay's doorstep for a solid ten minutes, trying to get up the nerve to ring it. She'd considered telling him she was sick and canceling, but first off, he'd have come over to see her regardless, and secondly, there was no point putting off telling him the news. Waiting wouldn't make her any less pregnant.

He's a decent man, she reminded herself. *He's not going to murder you.* Sucking in a deep breath, she jabbed her finger on the bell.

Jay opened the door, pulled her inside and kissed her before she could say a word. Just like every time he kissed her, her knees wobbled, her blood heated, and her mind turned to mush. Before she could weaken, she put her hand on his chest and turned her head. "Jay, we have to talk."

His arms encircling her waist loosely, he kissed her cheek. "Okay, but can't I kiss you first?"

"No, because then we'll wind up in bed, and we have to talk."

He let her go, then put his fingers under her chin and tipped it up, studying her. "You look a little pale. Is something wrong?"

"Nothing. I'm fine." *Just pregnant, that's all.*

"Are you hungry?" He took her hand, pulled her with him into the kitchen. "I thought I'd cook for us. I've got chili simmering. It should be ready in a little while. Do you want a beer or a glass of wine first?"

Touched that he'd gone to so much trouble, she started to say so. Then the spicy smell hit her nostrils, strong and overwhelming. Her stomach rolled, twisted on a wave of nausea. She clapped her hand over her mouth and made a dash for the bathroom.

She made it, barely. After heaving up the crackers she'd eaten earlier, she felt a little better. During pregnancy, she remembered, certain smells had always gotten to her, no matter the time of day. One more sign, as if she needed any more.

She splashed cold water on her face, rinsed her mouth out and used some of Jay's mouthwash. Peering into the mirror, she combed her fingers through her hair. She looked, she thought, like one of the walking dead in the horror stories Roxy loved. *Great, just terrific.*

Jay was waiting by the door when she emerged, arms crossed, one shoulder leaning against the wall. "I take it you don't like chili." Though he smiled when he said it, he looked concerned. "I turned it off. If I'd known, I'd have made something else."

"No, I love chili. Ordinarily. It was very sweet of you." Still a bit unsteady, she asked, "Can we sit down? In the den?" No way would she risk the kitchen again.

"Sure." He put his arm around her and led her to the couch, as if afraid she'd keel over without support. Then he sat beside her, took her hands in his and kissed them. His gaze met hers, concerned, questioning. "Tell me what's wrong. Are you sick?"

She shook her head. Took a deep breath and just told him, straight out. "I'm pregnant."

His expression turned blank as he stared at her. "You're—you're pregnant?"

"Pregnant." She nodded. "Yes."

He dropped her hands and got up, pacing away a moment before returning to stand in front of her. She braced herself, wondering if he'd yell at her, blame her, like Barry had done when she told him about Roxy, all those years ago.

"We've been using birth control. Every time."

Though he didn't raise his voice, didn't sound accusatory, she felt a twinge of defensiveness all the same. "I know." She lifted a shoulder. "One of them must have leaked. Or something."

"I don't remember—" he began, then shook his head, stuffing his hands in his pockets. "No, how it happened doesn't matter at this point. Have you taken a test? How sure are you?"

"I took a home pregnancy test this morning. It was positive. If you want, I'll take another test, but I've got all the symptoms. I'm late, my breasts are tender, and the kicker, of course, is the morning sickness." She made a frustrated gesture, waving a hand. "I've been throwing up for the past four days, every morning, regular as clockwork. I'm sorry, Jay, but I'm sure."

He blew out a breath and sat down again. Resting his forearms on his thighs, he shook his head and muttered, "Pregnant. Wow."

Her throat tightened so she could hardly breathe.

"I'm not trying to screw up your life, but I thought you should know. So we can talk about it and de-cide...what we're going to do."

He turned his head to look at her, lifted an eye-brow. "Do? That's obvious, isn't it?"

If possible, her heart sank another level. "I can't have an abortion. I won't."

He straightened and glared at her, for the first time showing some expression. Mostly irritation. "I wouldn't expect you to. Is that what you thought?"

She tossed a hand in the air. "How was I to know how you'd react? We don't even know each other all that well. We've only been dating a few weeks."

"We've known each other for five years."

"Casually. We never talked about anything like this."

He sighed and leaned against the back of the couch, his legs stretched before him. "Come here." He put his arm around her shoulders and tugged her next to him, tucking her head onto his shoulder. "Don't worry. We'll work it out."

He held her silently, offering comfort. It worried her that he could make her feel better by doing noth-ing more than holding her in his arms. Tears stung her eyes. Blinking rapidly, she willed them away. Tears wouldn't help now. Nothing would. "What are we going to do?"

"The obvious solution." His hand skimmed up her arm, soothingly. "We get married."

Gail jerked herself out of Jay's arms and stared at

him. "Get married? Are you crazy? You can't be serious."

"Damn right I'm serious. I don't joke about things like marriage." He'd never asked a woman to marry him. Not Carla, not anyone. Of course, he hadn't exactly asked Gail. Maybe that's why she was so bent out of shape.

"I want you to marry me, Gail." And if part of him wasn't so sure about that, then he'd just have to deal with it later. Marrying Gail was obviously the right thing to do, and he would do it.

"Jay." Her expression changed from shocked and surprised to touched. "It's really sweet of you, and I appreciate you asking me very much, but you don't want to marry me. You're not in love with me."

"Are you sure about that?" Because he wasn't.

She frowned. "Well, if you are, you sure haven't mentioned it before now."

He touched the back of his fingers to her cheek, smiled. She had some color back now, as if arguing with him had steadied her. Now that the first shock had passed, he was beginning to get used to the idea. Besides, he was a practical man, and in this situation, marriage was the only logical course of action. But he owed it to both of them to be as truthful as he could be.

"I don't know about love. I've had a couple of serious relationships in the past, thought I was in love, but they never worked out." He'd thought, after Carla, that he simply wasn't cut out to be married. To have a wife, kids. Looked like he'd been wrong.

He picked up Gail's hand, rubbed her wrist with his thumb. "I care about you, Gail. I want to be with you." He smiled and added, "I'm damn well addicted to you."

She patted his knee with her free hand. "That's sex, not love."

"Great sex."

"Good sex isn't enough to base a marriage on."

"It's fantastic sex, and it sure doesn't hurt."

She gave him a dirty look, but didn't speak.

"I care about you," he repeated. "You care about me. And the baby is mine. My responsibility."

"You don't have to marry me to take responsibility," she insisted. "There are plenty of ways to be responsible without getting married."

"So what's your solution? If you don't want to marry me, what do you suggest we do?"

"I'm not going to keep you from your child, if that's what you're afraid of. I'll have the baby and we'll figure something out. Later, when we need to. I won't show for a few months, at least."

Her chin had that determined tilt to it. She'd taken a stand and would stubbornly adhere to it. He'd seen it before, when she felt strongly about something. Time to hit her with the big guns. "And what do you plan to tell Roxy and Mel? *Oh, gee, girls, I'm having my lover's illegitimate child, and no, we're not getting married.*"

A flood of color rushed to her cheeks, but she answered steadily enough. "I'll think of a way to tell them. Women have babies alone every day."

Not my baby, he thought. "This isn't New York or L.A., Gail. You're not a celebrity in a town where your sex life is a continuous scandal, and no one cares if the father of your child is a sperm bank or a movie star." She shook her head, started to speak, but he held up a hand and continued, "You're living in a small town on the Texas coast. They don't have the same attitude toward illegitimate kids...and their mothers."

"News flash, Jay, this isn't the fifties. No one's going to think a thing about it."

"How sure are you about that? Sure enough to risk hurting your daughters?"

"I—of course I don't want to hurt the girls." She jammed her fingers in her hair as if she wanted to pull it out. Repeated desperately, "We can't get married."

"Think, Gail. Do you really want Roxy and Mel to have to face the gossip? About their mother? You've lived here all your life. You know what it's like. And you know what label they'll slap on our child. Bastard," he said deliberately. "Is that what you want?"

She closed her eyes, put her head in her hands. Long moments later, she looked at him. "I've never told you about my marriage."

"Not much," he said, wondering where she was heading. Her hands were clenched in fists, resting on her knees. "I know your ex is a jerk, and I know he wants you back. What else do I need to know?"

"I was pregnant with Roxy when Barry and I married." She shot him a wry smile. "Barry wasn't thrilled about it. At first, he went ballistic, but he did marry me, eventually. I was young, stupid, in love. I thought it would work. It didn't.'' She gave a humorless laugh. "He made a pass at Cat just two weeks after the wedding. I let him convince me he hadn't meant anything by it, that Cat had overreacted.'' Her hand passed over her eyes. "God, I can't believe I was so dumb.''

"You loved him, you wanted it to work. That's not dumb.'' He hated that the bastard had hurt her so badly. No wonder she was gun-shy.

"Doesn't matter,'' she said, shrugging the would-be comfort away. "I have my daughters, and Barry can't hurt me anymore. But after my marriage ended, I swore I'd never again marry anyone for the wrong reasons.'' Her gaze lifted to his. "So you see why I can't marry you, Jay. It wouldn't work. I have first-hand experience with a shotgun wedding.''

"No one is holding a gun to my head, Gail. I want to marry you.''

She patted his hand. "No, you don't. You feel obligated to marry me, which is a whole different subject. I'm trying to save us both a lot of heartache.''

"You're being stubborn and unrealistic.'' He didn't just feel obligated, he was obligated. "Would it be so bad, to marry me?''

She stared at him a long moment and then her mouth lifted in a half smile. "No,'' she said softly. "I think if we did get married I'd be a very lucky woman.'' Her gaze dropped and she shook her head. "Everyone will say I…trapped you.''

"Both of us know that's not true. What else is going on?"

She was silent for a long moment, biting her lip. Jay put his arm around her and pulled her close, against his side. He kissed her cheek, then the corner of her mouth. "Come on," he said softly in her ear. "Talk to me. Tell me what's bothering you."

"The girls." She smiled sadly. "Well, Roxy. She hasn't been pleased about us dating. Can you imagine what she'll do if I tell her I'm going to marry you? And then eight months later, we have a new baby."

He couldn't deny Roxy was a problem. But was it as bad as Gail thought, or was Gail using Roxy's resistance as an excuse? "You said you thought she'd come around. You were willing to keep dating me until she did. She doesn't hate me, does she?"

"No, but this will crush her hopes about her father and me."

"She has to accept sometime that you aren't getting back with her father. And you have another child to think of besides Roxy and Mel." He laid his hand on her stomach. "Our child."

"I'm thinking about all of them. That doesn't mean I know what I should do."

"I think we could be happy together. You, me, the girls. The baby."

"Do you? Really?" She gazed into his eyes solemnly. "Or are you just saying that because you want to do the right thing, and you're convinced that's marrying me."

"Do you believe I'd lie to you about something so important?"

"Barry did," she said, as if the words were forced from her.

"I'm not Barry. And I'm not lying. I think we could all be happy. Together. If you're willing to try."

"I hope you're right." She wrapped her arms around his neck and kissed him. Their tongues met, tangled. She moaned, leaning toward him as the kiss grew hotter, more urgent. She moved closer, or maybe he pulled her so her breasts lay against his chest.

He wanted her, had to have her. He swung her up in his arms and carried her into his bedroom. She didn't argue, but kissed his neck and started undoing his shirt buttons. He placed her on his bed, pulled his shirt off over his head.

"Are you trying to seduce me into saying yes?" she asked, her lips curving into a smile.

Unbuckling his belt, he paused. Grinned. "It's a thought. Not one I'd considered, but I'm willing."

"It's a mistake," she said, suddenly sober.

"No, it's not." He finished undressing, then helped her out of her clothes. She was warm, fragrant. Soft. That lithe, tempting little body lay stretched out before him, begging for attention. Her breasts, a little heavier now, called to him. He traced the fine blue veins, smiling when her back arched and her breasts thrust upward. Slowly, carefully, he touched the pale flesh, caressed her, sucked her nipples until she cried out, quivering on the brink of climax.

He slid his hand down to her slick heat, stroked her, teased her, his fingers gliding into her, his mouth tasting, touching, testing their limits.

Parting her legs, he entered her slowly, rode her gently until her hips pushed against him impatiently, demandingly, and her arms clung to him, her breath sobbing out of her lungs. He thrust deep, long, groaned out her name as she shattered around him and he emptied himself into her sweet warmth.

When he could breathe again, he rolled onto his back, adjusting her until she lay bonelessly on top of him. He tugged her head back and looked deep into her eyes, as serious as he'd ever been. "Marry me, Gail. Say yes."

She stared at him, her eyes as blue and turbulent as a storm tossed ocean. "Yes," she whispered, and kissed him.

IN A REPLAY of the last several days, Gail found herself hugging the toilet bowl the following morning. But this time, she got to do it in front of Jay. She didn't realize he was in the bathroom shaving until it was far too late.

Miserably embarrassed, she tried to wave him off, but he ignored her and helped her anyway.

"Go away," she managed to croak when she'd finished heaving.

He ignored that, too, dampened a washcloth, and wiped her forehead and neck with it. "Gail, I'm a doctor. Believe me, I've seen worse things."

Feeling a little better, she glanced up at him. He

looked amazingly good, she thought, wearing only a white towel wrapped around his lean waist and shaving cream on that handsome face. "You haven't seen *me* doing them. It's not the same."

"No, it's not." He squatted down beside her and wiped her mouth with a fresh towel, then laid his palm against her cheek and smiled. "Those other people weren't having my baby."

It shouldn't have, but hearing him say *my baby* in that deep, sexy voice gave her an undeniable thrill. "What are we doing?" she whispered.

"Having a baby," he said, and helped her up.

She rinsed out her mouth, then stumbled back to bed.

"I'll bring you some crackers," Jay said. "Would that help?"

"Yes, and Sprite, if you have it."

A little while later, she felt almost human. Jay sat beside her on the bed, still wearing the towel. Drops of water clung to his chest. She followed one as it snaked its way down to his washboard stomach and disappeared beyond, into the towel. Okay, so she wouldn't mind seeing that gorgeous specimen of manly chest in the mornings. Or any other time of day.

"I thought you were sick?" he asked, grinning.

She lifted her nose in the air and sniffed. "I'm feeling better."

"Good." He leaned over and kissed her. "So, how does next weekend sound?"

"Next weekend? For what?"

"The wedding. I don't think there's any way Brian can get here, but I'm sure my mother and her husband will be able to make it." He broke off as she gaped at him. "You know, my brother, Brian. He's in London on a job. At least, I think he is."

"You want to get married next weekend?" she asked, trying to focus. "But—but—that's so soon."

"That's the point, isn't it? The sooner the better."

"Jay, maybe we should wait. I'm not very far along. What if something happens?" But the thought of losing her child had her curving a protective hand over her stomach.

"Gail." He put his hand over hers, where it rested on her flat stomach. "I know we didn't plan this, and neither of us expected it to happen, but tell me something. Do you want this baby?"

"Yes," she said, surprised at how fiercely she already loved it.

"So do I."

She searched his eyes. "You mean that, don't you?"

He smiled, that slow, sweet smile that made her heart beat faster. "Yes. Let's get married. Next weekend."

She put her arms around his neck and kissed him. "Next weekend," she agreed. "Do you ever lose an argument?"

"Not very often. And not when it's important. Now get dressed. We've got a wedding to plan and I know just the two people to help us plan it."

CHAPTER TEN

"SAY THAT AGAIN," Mark said, staring at Jay and Gail as if they had sprouted alien wings.

"Gail and I are getting married." He squeezed Gail's hand reassuringly. "Next weekend."

Mark opened his mouth, then closed it without saying anything. Then he looked at his wife and demanded, "Did you hear that?"

"Of course I heard him," Cat said, looking up from nursing the baby. "I'm not deaf, am I?" She didn't seem nearly as shocked as Mark had. "When and where is this wedding taking place?"

"We thought Friday night would be good. Jay can take Friday and Monday off, but he has to be back at work Tuesday. We haven't really discussed much beyond that. Like where to have the ceremony, or anything. We thought you two could help us plan things."

"Help you plan things," Mark repeated hollowly.

"We're keeping it small," Jay added. "Just family and a few friends."

"Jay, can I see you in the kitchen a minute?" Mark asked. "Alone?"

"Sure." He leaned down and murmured in Gail's ear, "Older brother lecture."

"I know." She smiled, but he thought she looked a little anxious. "I have a feeling I'll be getting the younger sister one at the same time."

He kissed her, then followed Mark to the kitchen. "How about a cup of coffee?" he said, tucking his hands in his pockets and leaning back against the counter. "I could use another dose of caffeine."

Ignoring him, Mark planted both hands on the counter across the room, his back to Jay. "Getting married. Next weekend. Good God."

"Last I heard, congratulations was the appropriate response."

Mark spun around and stared at him incredulously. "It would be if I didn't believe you'd lost your ever-loving mind." He began to pace, waving his hands in the air for emphasis. "I realize you're thirty years old and don't need my advice. Hell, you wouldn't listen when you were a kid, why should I expect you to listen to me now?"

He halted in front of Jay and glared at him. "Are you completely nuts? For God's sake, you just came out of a relationship. You lived with Carla for two years, and you never decided you had to get married. You're obviously on the rebound here. Have you thought about what this will do to Gail?" He sucked in a breath and continued. "Hell, no, you haven't thought about anything at all. At least have a long engagement. Why next weekend? Why are you in such a damn hurry?"

"Gail's pregnant."

That stopped him cold. Jay had known it would.

"Oh, shit."

"I think my word was wow." Jay took his hands out of his pockets and crossed his arms over his chest. "She's pregnant, Mark, and it's my child. What else can I do, but marry her?"

"I don't know. Oh, man," Mark said, and scrubbed a hand over his face. "Are you sure this is what you want?"

He thought about that a moment. At first, he'd been so wrapped up in doing the right thing, he hadn't taken time to consider what living with Gail would be like. He smiled. "Yeah, I'm sure. I want to marry her."

Mark pinned Jay with a sharp glance. "Is this— this marriage what Gail wants?"

He shrugged, walked away a few steps. "Not initially. I talked her into it."

"Jay, if Gail isn't sure…"

Jay interrupted him impatiently. "She has an eight-and a ten-year-old daughter. How are they going to deal with it, if I don't marry her? The gossip, the snide comments. They'll hear them, and so will Gail." He took a few steps, closer to Mark. "You know this town. I'm a professional here. Can you imagine the talk it will cause if Gail has my baby and I don't marry her? And believe me, there won't be any doubts about whose baby she's having. We haven't tried to hide our relationship."

Mark winced. "It wouldn't be pretty."

"No, it wouldn't. We may be living in the twenty-first century, but as far as the people around here are concerned, it might as well be 1950. Gail isn't having this baby alone. It's decided, we're getting married."

Mark gazed at him for a long moment, then nodded. "It's your decision. I can't say I wouldn't do the same in your place."

"You would," Jay said, knowing how seriously Mark took his own responsibilities.

"Are you in love with her?"

"I don't know." He passed a hand over his forehead. "I care about her. A lot. But I don't know about love." He shot Mark a sideways glance. "The sex is incredible."

For the first time since Jay had dropped the news, his brother smiled. "That helps." Mark sighed, then put a hand on Jay's shoulder and squeezed. "I don't know what to say to you."

"Say you'll be my best man."

He looked surprised again. "What about Brian?"

"He won't be able to make it. Hell, for all we know, he may not even be in London, he could be in China. But even if he does come—" he met his older brother's eyes and smiled "—I still want you to do it. So, will you stand up for me?"

Mark cleared his throat and rubbed his jaw. "Yeah, I will. I'd be...happy to."

Jay didn't often talk about his feelings. But now seemed like the time to take care of some things he'd neglected to say over the years. "Mark, I'm pretty sure I've never told you what it meant to me when you took Brian and me in after Mom left. We would have ended up in the system if you hadn't.''

Mark glared at him. ''Don't get mushy on me here. I'm having a hard enough time without that.''

Jay laughed. ''Okay. I just wanted you to know how I felt. Thanks.''

''Forget it.'' Mark cleared his throat again. ''Well, hell.'' He glanced at his watch and frowned. ''Forget the coffee. You're getting married, I vote we have a beer.''

''Damn straight,'' Jay said, and pulled out a chair. ''And Mark, while I'm asking for favors, will you take care of the dogs while we're gone?''

Mark laughed and set a beer down in front of him. ''Sure. Anything else?''

Jay smiled and popped the top. ''I'll let you know.''

UNLIKE MARK, Cat didn't lecture. She sent Gail a speculative look, but she didn't speak. After she finished feeding Miranda she said, ''I'm going to put her down for a nap. Unless you want to.''

''I would love to.'' Gail took Miranda from her sister and cuddled her. ''I haven't seen nearly enough of my niece. Or my nephew. Where is Max, by the way?''

''Next door, playing.'' Cat followed her into the baby's room, watched as Gail changed her diaper, then laid her in her crib and kissed her cheek.

''She's so sweet,'' Gail said, rubbing her back. ''So unbelievably tiny.''

"Not for long. She's gaining weight like crazy." She paused and said, "So, Gail, when are you due?"

Gail's hand froze in midmotion. She gave the baby a final pat and turned to her sister. "How did you know?"

"It's the only reason I can think of that you'd be in such a hurry to get married."

"I'm not. Jay is." She sat on the bed and put her face in her hands. "Oh, God, Cat, am I making a terrible mistake? Again?" Despairing, she raised her head and gazed at her sister.

"I can't answer that. But don't compare Jay to Barry. He's an infinitely better man than Barry ever thought of being."

"I know." But that didn't make their marriage right. "I haven't even seen the doctor yet. I'm going to see her next week. Maybe it was a false positive."

"Come on, Gail. If you believed that the two of you wouldn't be here talking marriage."

"No, you're right. We wouldn't." She plucked at the bedspread, thinking about that, and about Jay's reaction. "Do you know what Jay said when I told him? He said it didn't matter how it had happened. He said it was his baby, his responsibility."

"It is," Cat said reasonably.

Gail gave a half smile. "Yes, but I can tell you from experience that not all men respond that way."

"But Jay did, and that's what matters."

Her throat tightened and she nodded. "He says he wants the baby. I almost cried when he told me that. I think he really means it."

Cat patted her shoulder. "He's a good guy, Gail."

"I know," she said again. That was the problem. Jay *was* a good guy and she was afraid she was ruining his life. Forcing him into a marriage he didn't want, but felt duty bound to provide. Trapping him.

"Are you in love with him?"

"I don't know. I care about him," she said, remembering Jay's words. "And I'm—" She paused, considering how to describe her feelings. Obsessed, maybe. "I want to be with him. All the time."

Cat cocked her head. "Define be with him."

Gail squirmed a little uncomfortably. "Sex," she finally admitted. Her eyes closed, she felt the heat rise in her cheeks. "I've never had sex like this in my life." Concerned, she opened her eyes and stared at her sister. "I can't help but think it's clouding my judgement."

"Spectacular sex will do that." Cat grinned. "So, he's a stud, huh?"

Gail laughed. "Oh, honey. The word doesn't begin to do him justice."

"So." Cat took her hands and pulled her to her feet. "Let me get this straight. You're marrying a man you like and respect, and who likes and respects you."

Gail nodded.

"In addition to that he is one extremely fine piece of eye candy."

Smiling, Gail nodded again.

"And last but certainly not least, the two of you have dynamite sex. Have I covered everything?"

She hadn't exactly thought it out in quite those terms. "Pretty much." Provided she ignored the problems.

"Then what are we waiting for? Let's go plan a wedding."

Gail laughed, then hugged her sister. "You're so logical sometimes. Must be the accountant in you. Thanks for listening."

"What are sisters for?"

Ready tears sprang to Gail's eyes, but she blinked them away. "I love you, Cat."

"I love you, too." Cat led the way into the den, shooting Gail a mischievous glance over her shoulder. "I think we should have it at Mom's and put her in charge of whatever we don't want to deal with." Cat rubbed her hands together, gleefully. "She's going to totally flip. One of her girls is marrying a doctor."

"Oh, Lord." Gail stopped and stared at her sister in dawning horror. "I hadn't thought of that. She'll drive him insane."

Cat laughed. "We won't tell him until after the ceremony. Can't have him backing out."

GAIL DECIDED TO TELL Roxy and Mel the news by herself. Mostly because she feared Roxy's reaction, and thought she could smooth things over more easily if they were alone.

But how to tell them? She didn't want to lie, yet she couldn't tell them the truth, either. She planned to put off telling them about the baby for as long as possible.

So she called them in, sat with one on either side of her on the couch and with only a little beating around the bush, she told them she and Jay had fallen in love and decided to get married.

Both girls stared at her without speaking for a moment, but then Mel found her voice. "You and Uncle Jay love each other?"

It wasn't precisely a lie. Anyway, it was a necessary one. She wasn't sure how to explain complex adult relationships to an eight- and a ten-year-old. Still, she felt tempted to cross her fingers behind her back when she answered. "Yes."

"And you and him are gonna get married? On Friday?"

"That's right."

"He's gonna live with us? In our house?" Mel persisted, obviously wanting everything spelled out.

"Actually, we're going to live with him, in his house." Besides being newer and nicer, Jay's house had more bedrooms, so it was the obvious choice. "But you'll each have your own rooms, just like you do now."

"Can my room be pink and purple?" Mel asked suspiciously. "My room now is pink and purple and I like it. You said I could have pink and purple 'long as I want."

Gail smiled and ruffled her hair. "We'll paint it first thing."

Mel put her hands on Gail's knees and leaned on her. "Mommy? What about Daddy? Is Uncle Jay gonna be our new daddy?"

"No, honey. You have a father. Jay's going to be your stepfather." She glanced at Roxy's expressionless face. "I think you should both call him Jay from now on."

"Mommy?" Mel asked again. She glanced at her older sister, then back to Gail. "I like Jay."

"I know, sweetie. He likes you, too. We'll have fun. You'll see."

Roxy didn't say a word. Gail watched the storm clouds gather in her older daughter's eyes and wished she didn't have to hurt her. "Mel, honey, why don't you go to your room and let me talk to Roxy."

"I love you, Mommy." Mel hugged her fiercely. "Can I have a new dress to wear to the wedding?"

"Yes. Both of you can." She smiled. "Really pretty dresses," Gail said, accepting the hug gratefully.

Once Mel left, the real problems started. She sighed and began, "Roxy, I know this is sudden, but—"

The storm broke. "No! You can't marry him! I won't let you! You're supposed to marry Daddy." She started to weep, huge gulping sobs. "I want you to marry Daddy," she wailed.

Gail gathered her close and let her cry it out. Eventually, the sobs turned to soft hiccups, and Gail judged it time to talk.

"Roxy, your daddy and I don't want to be married. But Jay and I do." She grasped her upper arms gently and looked into her eyes. "Now I know it's hard, and I know it hurts, but you're going to have to be a big girl and accept this. Do you understand?"

"Don't have to." Roxy thrust out her lower lip. "I'm going to live with Daddy."

Pain sliced through her heart. Even though Gail knew Barry would never go for it, hearing Roxy say she wanted to live with her father hurt. "We'll talk about it, once Jay and I have been married awhile. For now, you're still living with me. You can still spend some of the weekends with your father, just like you do now."

Roxy hunched a shoulder. "Can I go now?"

"Not yet. I'm still talking. You used to like Jay," she said. "You didn't decide you didn't like him until we started going out together. If you give him a chance, I bet you'll like him again." She put her fingers under Roxy's chin. "Will you do that for me, Roxy? Will you give Jay a chance?"

Roxy lifted her shoulders in the age-old "I'm not promising anything" gesture. Gail didn't think she'd make any more headway tonight. "All right, you can go." Gail hugged her. "I love you, Roxy."

Roxy didn't say anything, didn't return the hug, she just got up and ran out of the room.

Gee, that was fun, Gail thought, and sank her head in her hands. If she'd needed something more to stir up her doubts, Roxy's reaction had done it. Could she and Jay really be happy? In a marriage made from practicality, from obligation, not from love? What if Roxy never adjusted to Gail's remarriage? What would Gail do then, married, with another child? Oh, God, what a mess.

A little while later her phone rang. Checking caller

ID, she cursed silently. Just who she didn't want to talk to.

"What do you want, Barry?"

"What the hell is going on over there? I just got off the phone with Roxy. The poor kid is totally hysterical, but from the little I understood, I gather you're getting married."

"Yes, I am. To Jay."

"Yeah, I got that, too. Did you ever plan to tell me?"

"Of course I intended to tell you." She tapped her fingers on the table, irritated to be on the defensive. "You need to know, because it affects the girls, but I saw no reason to rush out and call you. You were way down on the list," she couldn't help adding.

"When's the big event?" Barry asked sarcastically.

"Friday. I know you had the girls last weekend. If you don't want to take them, I'm sure Mom will. She'll be keeping them Friday night, anyway. But I know Roxy would like to be with you."

"This Friday? You're getting married this Friday?"

"Yes." She braced herself for what she knew was coming.

Barry started laughing. A nasty, snide sound. "You're pregnant, aren't you? Does Kincaid know that's how you trapped me? My God, Gail, can't you convince a man to marry you any other way?"

"Go to hell, Barry," she said, and slammed the receiver down in his ear. So much for the new, improved Barry. That had been vintage Barry, calculated to hurt.

Trapped, she thought as she got ready for bed. Barry wasn't the only person who would believe Gail had trapped Jay. Face it, she thought glumly, the whole town would think so if they knew.

But she didn't care about what the town thought. She cared about whether Jay felt trapped. Because if he did, their marriage was doomed before it even began.

Gail didn't fall asleep for a long time that night. The thought had come to her, persistent and unwelcome, that maybe part of her resistance, and her doubts, came from feeling trapped herself. But there was a big difference this time. She was older, experienced, self-sufficient. She could take care of herself and her daughters now. Support them emotionally and financially. No matter what happened in her new marriage, she'd never again be that clinging dependent woman who'd been afraid to be without her husband.

CHAPTER ELEVEN

JAY'S WEDDING DAY dawned bright, clear and beautiful, a prime late October day. A great day for a wedding, so why couldn't he shake the uneasiness that crept up his spine? He didn't think Gail would stand him up at the altar. Still, he knew she harbored doubts that their getting married was the right thing to do. To be honest, so did he. He pulled on a pair of shorts and let the dogs out, then went to the kitchen in search of caffeine. He still believed marriage was the best solution to their situation, but he admitted to being worried about the practicalities. First of all, he wouldn't be living with Gail alone, but with her daughters, as well.

Gail had told him a small part of her conversation with the girls. Not the entire conversation, but enough to let him know Roxy wasn't a bit happy. No surprise there, but it didn't help matters. And it sure as hell didn't make him feel perky about things. Still, Roxy was young. She was bound to come around, and no good purpose would be served by thinking negatively.

He poured water in the coffeemaker, then grabbed the can of coffee from the cabinet above. The empty can, he realized when he opened it. After scrounging around, he came up with instant, which he hated. But at least it was caffeine.

He put a mug of water in the microwave and turned it on. Nothing happened. Flipping the light switch, he realized the electricity was off. "Damn it!" He scrubbed his hands over his face and wondered if the lights were out all over the neighborhood. If not, he could go to Gail's.

A loud, sort of grinding noise came from outside, from the front of the house. He trudged to the front door, opened it and saw an electric company truck parked by the transformer down the street. Probably got the whole neighborhood, he thought. After a brief stop in his bedroom for a T-shirt, he went outside to investigate.

A few minutes later he came back in and called Gail on his cell phone. Fortunately, he knew she kept a phone in the bedroom, for just such emergencies.

"'Lo," she answered, her voice thick with sleep.

"Did you know the electricity is going to be out all day?"

"Hmm. That's nice."

"Gail, are you still asleep? It's seven-thirty. Aren't the girls supposed to be getting ready for school?"

"Huh? What? I'm awake."

He heard rustling, then she dropped the phone. While he waited, he looked out the window into the back yard. Damn puppies had dug a hole the size of China back there. How had he missed that yesterday? It was just too damn bad, because he wasn't spending his wedding day digging in the mud. He'd fix it when they came back.

"The electricity's out," Gail said when she came back on the line several minutes later. "The alarm didn't go off."

"Yeah, I know. It's going to be out all day. Do you want me to take the girls to school for you?"

"No, I'd nearly decided to keep them home anyway. Their mother doesn't get married every day. Even though the wedding isn't until this evening, I think they'd like to spend the day with me."

"I'm sure they'd rather be with you than at school." And he had a feeling Gail needed to be with them, too. "So, what are you going to do about getting ready?"

She yawned. "I'll just go to Mom's early. It will be easier, anyway. And it will make Mom happy. She can fuss over all of us that way. Are you going to Mark's?"

"Yes. His electricity better not be out. Do you need anything? I'm going out for coffee."

"No, nothing." She paused, then said, "Jay? We're doing the right thing, aren't we?"

His bride-to-be needed reassurance. Unfortunately, so did he. But he was a man, and if he'd learned one thing from Mark, it was that a man took care of those who needed him. "Gail, would you have said yes if you didn't think we were doing the right thing?"

"No, I guess I wouldn't have." She was silent a moment, then added, "Although, you are very persuasive when you want to be."

"Do I need to come over and persuade you some more?"

She laughed. "No, it's bad luck to see each other on our wedding day."

Glad to hear the lighter note in her voice, he played along with her. "Only if I see you in your dress. I'd be perfectly willing to see you not wearing a thing. More than willing, I'd be happy to."

"Dream on," she told him, and laughed again. "We're not supposed to see each other at all the day of the wedding."

"You're not superstitious, are you?"

"Yes," she said, and had him laughing as well. "I'm fine. Just a little nervous. Go get your coffee."

LATE THAT AFTERNOON, everyone gathered at Meredith Randolph's opulent house in Key Allegro, just north of Aransas City. More like a mansion, Jay thought, seeing the beautiful showplace for the second time. The first time he'd seen it had been after Mark and Cat's wedding, he remembered, when he'd spent the entire evening with Gail. Appropriate they'd have the wedding here, he thought, where it had all begun.

Though they had scheduled the ceremony for six, Jay didn't hold much hope that it would begin on time. Cat had told him Gail wasn't feeling too great.

Mark and Jay's mother and her husband had come down from Dallas. His brother Brian, still living in London, hadn't been able to make it, though he'd called and talked to Jay that morning to give him his best wishes. Unfortunately, since Brian could imagine nothing worse than being married, his best wishes had sounded more like condolences. It ticked Jay off, even though he realized Brian didn't mean any harm.

Jay's partner, Tim, and his wife had come, as well as a couple of Gail's friends from work, and a sprinkling of her old friends who still lived in the area, or could make the wedding on such short notice.

They'd invited Gail's boss, as well, since he'd offered them the use of his luxury condo on Padre Island for their honeymoon. That meant they wouldn't be traveling far, but since Jay had to be back at work by Tuesday, and Gail planned to spend the following week moving, they'd been just as happy to stay close to home.

Both Gail's brothers and Cat were there, of course, as well as Meredith Randolph and a few of her friends. Mark was currently occupied dealing with the baby. He'd enlisted Roxy and Mel to help him with Max, while Cat and her mother helped Gail do whatever it was brides did at times like this. Jay wasn't too sure what that entailed.

While Mel had talked to Jay and even hugged him, Roxy had yet to speak a word to him. Not a very good sign, but maybe he should have expected it. He didn't remember much about being ten, but he did remember that every change was a big deal. Hell, he was thirty and this wedding was knocking him off-balance.

After being cornered by a couple of Meredith's cronies, both of whom made veiled references to the speed of the wedding, he escaped with his tea to the terrace overlooking the canal.

"Lovely old bats, aren't they?" Cam said, coming up behind him. He nodded his head at the two women, who'd now surrounded Gabe and appeared to be talking a mile a minute.

"Scary," Jay said, repressing a shudder. "Very scary."

Cam smiled. "They're really pussycats when you get to know them."

"I'll have to take your word for it." He took another sip of tea and turned back to the canal, leaning his forearms on the railing. Gulls circled overhead, giving an occasional lazy caw. The water was calm, protected as it was by the concrete-lined cays.

"I heard your car got stolen today from Buster's convenience store," Cam said, joining him at the railing. "Some wedding present."

He shook his head. "Not stolen." At least he'd been spared that. "Buster had it towed."

"Man, that's low, even for that old buzzard."

He shot Cam a sideways glance. "Yeah, it hasn't been the greatest day so far." It couldn't help but get better.

Cameron laughed. "You know, if I were the type to believe in omens, I'd say it was a sign."

"I'm not superstitious," Jay said, though he was beginning to wonder, considering the kind of day he'd had. "But Gail is. I don't think I'm going to tell her what happened today."

"What else happened?"

"Oh, not much. Max finger-painted my suit with chocolate, and when I went back to my house to get another one, the puppies were gone. It took me an hour to find them and fix the fence." And those were only the major things that had gone wrong.

"You're a stronger man than I," Cam said, tapping Jay's tea glass. "I'd have hit the bottle by now."

"Nah." He shrugged. "I figure the day can only get better." They fell silent a moment, then Jay glanced at him. "You ever think about getting married?"

"Once." Cam's mouth turned grim. "A long time ago."

"Why didn't you marry her?"

"Found her doing the horizontal tango with another guy." He shrugged. "That pretty much took care of that."

Jay winced. "Yeah. That would do it for me, too."

"After that I decided women were better in quantity."

They both laughed, then Cam asked, "So, you ever think about it? Before Gail, I mean."

"Not really."

"What about the blonde you were living with?" He made an obvious gesture with his hands. "The one with the body that wouldn't quit."

"Carla." He set his glass down on a nearby table and rubbed his jaw. "I don't know, I never could convince myself to ask her. Pissed her off royally."

Cam laughed, then sobered. "You're going to tell me this is none of my business but I don't see it that way. I see it as being Gail's oldest brother and looking out for her."

Jay sighed and rubbed a hand over the back of his neck. "It's a little late to ask me my intentions. Besides, I think they're obvious. We're sitting here waiting for the wedding to start."

"Yeah, that part's obvious. But I want to know if the baby is the only reason you're marrying Gail."

Jay stared at him a minute. "Is this where you slug me if you don't like my answer?"

Cam grinned, but shook his head. "I promised Cat, no hitting."

Maybe. But Jay had a feeling Cam would ignore that promise if he thought it necessary. "There wouldn't be a baby if Gail and I didn't have feelings for each other. But I don't think either of us would have chosen to get married so quickly without a damn good reason."

"And you think a baby is a good reason."

"Yeah, I do. I'm not going to leave Gail to raise my kid alone. If you don't like that, you might as well slug me now and get it over with. But whether you do or not, I'm still marrying your sister."

"I'll pass." Cam held out a hand. "Sounds like a straight answer to me."

They shook hands. Jay cocked his head. "Do I get to go through this with Gabe, too?"

"I'll tell him you passed." Cam slapped him on the back. "Welcome to the family, Jay."

"Thanks." Jay looked toward the doors opening

onto the terrace. ''Mark's waving at us. Gail must be ready.''

''Hey, Jay?'' Cam said as they walked inside. ''You look a little green around the gills. You wouldn't be nervous, would you?''

''Not nervous.'' He took a deep breath and tugged on his tie. ''Petrified.''

JAY'S NERVES DISAPPEARED when he saw Gail. She wore an ice-blue silk suit that set off her fair prettiness to perfection. In her hands she carried a bouquet of white roses. Her skin was milky white, with just a touch of color on her cheekbones and on her mouth. Her blue eyes stood out, deep and intense, in the paleness of her face. She looked calm, untouchable, and very, very beautiful.

The desire hit him suddenly, urgently and completely by surprise as his bride took her place beside him. He wished she were marrying him because she wanted to. Because she loved him, and not because she was pregnant.

Then their eyes met, and in hers—wide, distraught, moist with the sheen of tears—he saw all the nerves and doubts she'd hidden so well until now. He smiled at her, held out his hand, and waited as she slowly, hesitantly put her own hand in his. He brought it to his lips, kissed it. ''It's a wedding,'' he murmured, low enough that only Gail could hear. ''Not an execution.''

Her smile broke, those lovely lips curved upward, and he could see her struggling not to laugh. ''I know what it is. I'm ready,'' she said, and they turned hand-in-hand to the minister.

"Dearly Beloved," the minister said, and the traditional ceremony began.

As Jay listened, he watched Gail closely, and not solely because she looked so beautiful. Was it his imagination, or was she becoming paler and more unsteady before his eyes? He wished the minister would hurry, and wondered if there was a way to tactfully tell the man to speed things up. Instead, he droned on. And on. And on. Jay had nearly decided to stop him when suddenly, he began reciting the vows.

"Wilt thou, Gail, take this man, Jason, to be thy wedded husband? Wilt thou love him, comfort him, honor, and keep him in sickness and in health; and, forsaking all others, keep thee only unto him, so long as ye both shall live?"

Instead of speaking, Gail looked at Jay, her eyes wide, her complexion as pale and fragile as he'd ever seen it. Then she clapped a hand over her mouth and bolted from the room.

There was a stunned silence. "Oh, dear," the minister said, breaking it. "Is she all right?"

Everyone began talking at once. Cat squeezed Jay's arm and said, "I'm going after her. You know she's sick, don't you? She's not running out on you."

He didn't bother to answer. He knew he should say something, anything to break the heavy, awkward silence that had settled once again in the room following Cat's departure. But he couldn't for the life of him think of a word to say.

Thankfully, Mark stepped into the breach. "I think the bride's a little under the weather. I'm sure she'll be back shortly."

Gail's mother left the room a short time later.

Jay felt someone tugging on his jacket sleeve and looked down into Roxy's face. She looked very like her mother, with her light blond hair, blue eyes, and ice-blue dress. Except Roxy was steady as a rock and not a bit pale.

"Mommy doesn't want to marry you," his almost-stepdaughter said, calmly and clearly enough for everyone in the place to hear. "She ran away so she wouldn't have to marry you." Her maturity deserting her, she stuck out her tongue and added, "So there."

A collective gasp went up, along with a few groans. Cameron took his niece by the shoulders and spoke to her, more sternly than Jay had ever heard anyone address the child. "That's enough, Rox. Tell Jay you're sorry."

"Won't," she said, her lip thrust out mutinously.

Jay saw behind the stubbornness, to the pain and uncertainty in her eyes. "Don't worry about it, Cam," Jay said, and watched as Cameron marched her off.

Great. Terrific. His soon-to-be stepdaughter hated his guts. Not only that, she'd just informed everyone at the wedding of her feelings. It looked like changing Roxy's attitude was going to be a lot harder than he and Gail had believed.

Hard? Or impossible?

CHAPTER TWELVE

GAIL LAY on her mother's bed, a cool, damp washcloth on her forehead, a half-eaten cracker in her hand and total misery in her soul.

Seated beside her, Cat asked, "Are you any better?"

"Oh, peachy. Just dig the hole and let me crawl in it." She stuck the remainder of the cracker in her mouth, chewed and swallowed.

Cat gave a gurgle of laughter.

Gail flung the washcloth aside and glared at her. "It's easy for you to laugh. You're not the one who just abjectly humiliated herself in front of all those people. Not to mention, humiliating my poor husband-to-be. Or maybe not to be. Jay probably doesn't even want to marry me now. For all we know, he's hightailed it out of here. God knows, most men would have, long before this."

Her eyes filled with tears and she turned her head away. Was she cursed? At least at her other wedding she hadn't almost barfed in front of the guests. Of course, that marriage had failed. So maybe in a bizarre sort of way, this was a good sign. A sign their marriage would last.

"You know better than that. Jay is still here. And he's waiting for you to come out." Cat patted Gail's arm. "Gail, you know I'm sympathetic. Really I am."

Gail turned her head and looked at her. "I hear a but in there."

Cat nodded. "You're being ridiculous."

Gail's mother entered the room just then. "Are you feeling better, dear?"

"If you mean am I going to barf again, no, Mom, I believe I'm past that. For now."

Meredith's perfectly arched eyebrows drew together in puzzlement. "Then what in the world is keeping you?"

"Try embarrassment. No, try humiliation. In case you didn't notice, Mom, I sort of ran out on my bride-groom at a crucial moment."

"Oh, that." Her mother waved away her words, and her misery, with a flip of her hand. "Jay knows why you ran out, doesn't he?"

"Of course he does!" She looked from her sister to her mother, both of whom held identical expressions of disapproval. "Oh, go away, you two. You don't understand. Just leave me alone." She turned her head away again.

"Gail, look at me," Meredith said, in the commanding voice Gail remembered as a child. When she'd done something bad and her mother was about to let her have it.

Unwillingly compelled, she turned her head to look at her mother.

"I'm ashamed of you. Positively ashamed. Lying

on that bed whining—'' she held up an imperative hand when Gail would have spoken ''—yes, whining, while your bridegroom, not to mention, your guests, are patiently waiting for you. A better man I doubt you'll find. Are you thinking of him at all, while you're lying on that bed feeling sorry for yourself?''

Gail stared at her mother, unable to believe her ears.

''Sorry, Gail, but I agree with Mom,'' Cat said, adding the clincher. ''I hate to say it, but you're being a wimp.''

''Wimp, am I?'' Incensed, Gail sat up and glared at her sister. ''Whining, am I?'' she demanded of her mother. Pointedly ignoring the two of them, she got off the bed and stalked into the bathroom, slamming the door behind her.

She looked in the mirror and moaned. Grabbed a brush and went to work on her hair. Rinsed her mouth out and reapplied her lipstick. Added a little blush and mascara.

Now, that's more like it, she thought, eyeing her reflection critically. She was strong. In control. Invincible. She nearly giggled as the words to ''I Am Woman'' began to run through her mind.

Cat and her mother were right. Oh, she'd had reason to be upset. But enough was enough. Shame tugged at her, because her mother had been right about something else, as well. She hadn't been thinking of Jay, left standing at the altar. She'd been too concerned with her own feelings to consider his. It can't have been very comfortable to have his bride run out on him. Even if he knew the reason, not everyone did. But she would make it up to him.

She intended to go out there with her head held high and enjoy her wedding. And later, when they got to the condo, she'd make Jay forget everything but his name. He certainly wouldn't be thinking of the fact that his bride-to-be had run out of the wedding smack in the middle of the vows.

Not if she had anything to say about it.

"I'm ready," she said, and swept past her mother and sister.

She could have sworn she heard them give each other a high five as she passed through the door.

SOME WEDDING NIGHT, Jay thought, hours later. But after the day he'd had, what else had he expected? His bride lay sleeping in the bedroom. The cable reception for the condos was out, and the only thing he could pick up on the TV was an incredibly grainy, pitifully bad horror flick.

He didn't even have a book to read, since he hadn't imagined he'd do much reading on his honeymoon. All he'd found in the condo was a dog-eared copy of a paperback thriller he'd read several years before, and for some bizarre reason, a Farmer's Almanac from the same time period.

The heroine of the horror flick screamed and dripped more blood. Jay picked up the paperback. It was looking better all the time.

At least he had champagne, even if he did have to drink it alone. He chose a fluted glass and toasted his invisible bride. Gail hadn't even managed a glass of sparkling grape juice before she'd fallen asleep. Fallen asleep, hell. She'd crashed, dead to the world the instant she'd changed into her nightgown.

Did wanting to make love to his bride on their wedding night make him a terrible person? An insensitive bastard?

He'd dealt with the interrupted ceremony without much problem. Ignored Roxy's behavior, which went from bad to worse, until finally, her mother had sent her to bed before the reception ended. He'd endured the speculation by those who didn't know, as to exactly why Gail had run out on the wedding.

My God, he remembered, shuddering, he'd even listened with an appearance of interest to his mother-in-law and her friends go into exhaustive detail of all their physical ailments, most of which sounded like pure hypochondria to him.

He'd dealt with it all because he knew he'd be alone with Gail soon, and he'd assumed they would do what most people did on their wedding night. Make love.

Stupid assumption, obviously.

He picked up a cheese stick and bit into it, glad that Cat had sent along some of the food from the reception. He thought about getting out the chilled shrimp, but decided he'd save that for later. It looked like it was going to be a long night. A long, lonely night.

Brooding, he sipped champagne. He wasn't a total jerk. He didn't blame Gail. She was pregnant and exhausted and had fallen asleep. She hadn't done it to frustrate him, he knew. Nevertheless, he *was* frustrated. Extremely.

He walked to the bedroom door and looked at her, curled up asleep on top of the covers. Her sheer white nightgown was very pretty, and very sexy. Unfortunately. Afraid he'd wake her if he put her under the covers, he picked up a light blanket and covered her with it. Better, though he could still see her face, and those luscious lips just made for kissing.

He thought about getting in bed with her and holding her while she slept, but the truth was, he wasn't too sure of his control. They hadn't made love since the previous weekend, and he had an idea if he held her next to him, all his good intentions would go out the window. And she obviously needed to sleep.

His wife. Funny, but the words didn't seem as strange to him as he'd thought they would. He touched his fingers to her cheek and smiled as she snuggled down under the blanket. Until a week ago, he'd never envisioned himself married at all. Much less married with a baby on the way. And two stepdaughters.

But he wouldn't think about his stepdaughters tonight, especially the one who hated him. Time enough later to worry about how to handle Roxy, and eventually win her over.

So, he didn't want to think about problems, and if he stood staring at Gail for much longer, he'd say to hell with it and wake her up and make love to her.

The thriller it is, he told himself and left his wife sleeping.

He woke hours later, hard as stone, with Gail's mouth on his and her hands sliding over his body, mercilessly arousing. Reaching for her, he found nothing but bare, silky flesh. He groaned. "Is this a dream?" he asked hoarsely.

"Take off your pants," she whispered, spreading her hands over his bare chest. "I want you naked."

"If I'm dreaming I'm going to be extremely—" he sucked in a breath as her warm mouth traveled over his chest, kissing, nipping "—disappointed."

She unbuckled, unzipped his pants. "Now," she said. "Right now."

In seconds he'd shed his clothes and Gail knelt beside the couch, her hands and mouth working magic. She leaned over, kissed his mouth deeply, her tongue dancing a long, slow tune with his, her bare breasts teasing his chest, tormenting him with their softness.

"Did you think I'd sleep through our entire wedding night?" she murmured, her hand closing around his aching flesh, sliding up and down, slowly, torturously. "Without ever making love?"

He could barely breathe, sure as hell couldn't think. "Yes," he managed to say.

"You were wrong. I want you too much." Her mouth traced its way down his body, while her hands drove him toward oblivion. "I want this to be a night you'll remember. Always." And her mouth replaced her hands.

He put his hands in her hair and groaned. "Believe me, I'll remember."

THE FOLLOWING DAY they walked the beach, half empty because of the season, looking for driftwood and shells. They played in the surf and built an elaborate sandcastle, and talked about their families, and how different their childhoods had been.

Gail knew something about Jay's childhood from Cat, via Mark. But she'd never heard about it from Jay's perspective.

She was very touched to discover that Jay quite simply adored his older brother. Of course, he didn't phrase it quite like that. Still, it was clear he admired Mark tremendously and loved him very much.

"So Mark worked in construction before joining the Fish and Wildlife Service?" Stretched out on the sand leaning on one arm, she watched as Jay very carefully shaped a tower on his side of the castle. Gail had long since stopped, content to watch him. "He must have taught you some of those skills. Your part of the castle is much more elaborate than mine. Mine's just kind of a square blob."

Jay grinned. "Well, he tried. Both Brian and I had part-time jobs, and we did a little construction, but our hearts were never in it. Of course—" he frowned a little as he dripped some wet sand over the structure "—Mark's never was, either. But he had to support Brian and me."

"Where was your mother during those years? I mean, you see her now, obviously." Gail had enjoyed a nice visit with her and her husband after the wedding. It was hard to reconcile the woman she knew with the one who'd left her children to be raised by her oldest son.

Jay nodded, still concentrating on his building. "Yes, but Brian and I didn't see her at all until about six years ago. Mark and she reconciled about a year after that, around the time he met Cat. None of us realized it at the time, but our mother left because she was sick. She spent a couple of years in a hospital, being treated for depression." He glanced at Gail. "Didn't Cat ever tell you any of this?"

"Not really. Oh, I knew you'd been estranged from your mother, and that Mark had raised you and Brian, but I didn't know any details. It must have been hard, putting that behind you."

"A lot easier for Brian and me than for Mark. But then, we didn't have to put our lives on hold at twenty-one to support a family." He stopped building for a moment and looked out at the ocean. "Mark's the most responsible person I've ever known. And he never once made Brian or me feel like we were a burden." His mood shifted and he smiled. "A pain in the ass, yes, but not a burden."

Gail laughed. "Yes, I can hear Mark saying that."

Idly, she tossed sand at the castle. "When did you become interested in medicine? Did you always want to be a doctor?"

"No, I had all sorts of ideas." He shot her a quick grin. "Wanted to be a rock star for a while, but I couldn't sing, and couldn't play a musical instrument, so I gave that up.''

"That would make it difficult,'' she agreed, hiding her smile. "What else?''

"Thought about baseball.'' Carefully, he added more sand, leaned back and considered his creation. "I played first base. Had a minor league team scout interested my senior year. Then I tore my ACL—the anterior cruciate ligament—in a slide into home and that idea bit the dust big-time. Nowadays they can fix that, but back then, it was a career-ending injury.''

"I'm sorry. Did you mind terribly not being able to play?''

"I wasn't set on it. So, no, it was no great loss. And it did lead me into medicine.''

"How?''

He stretched out on the sand as well, the castle between them. "They took me to the emergency room. I'd been in before, but for some reason, that time I paid more attention. The doc who treated me was a great guy. He helped me get an orderly job there, took some interest in me. I left for college that fall as pre-med.''

"Were they hard? College and medical school?''

"Yes, but I had a lot of fun. California,'' he said, and waved a hand at the ocean. "Beaches, pretty girls, surfing. What more could a guy ask for? Mark used to razz me about the surfing. I think he was afraid I'd chuck medicine and end up a beach bum.'' He winked at Gail. "Sometimes I was tempted.''

She remembered thinking when she first met him

that he looked like a surfer. "Was Mark strict? After seeing him with Max, I have to wonder. That child has him wrapped around his finger. And I'm sure he'll be even worse with Miranda."

"They've got his number, all right. He wasn't all that strict, but he remembered perfectly what goes on in a male teenager's mind, so we couldn't get around him very easily. He knew what we were going to pull before we did."

"I thought all that goes on in a male teenager's mind is sex?" Gail teased.

"Pretty much." He shot her a calculating look and reached across the castle to trace a finger down her chest to her cleavage. "And for the record, the male doesn't have to be a teenager for that to happen."

She smiled. "Is that a hint?"

Jay rolled across the sand until he was next to her, then kissed her. "How did you guess?"

"You mean, you being so subtle and all?" she asked with a gurgle of laughter.

He kissed her again, and before long they went back to the room and made love.

For dinner that night they went to an off-the-beaten-track dive, one rumored to have the best seafood in the area. The place—called Piggy's, of all things—was dark, noisy and oddly enough, intimate. They chose a table in a corner at the back. Most of the action took place up front, near the pool tables. Their waitress, once she brought their food and drinks, mostly ignored them.

Gail took a bite of melt-in-your-mouth flounder and

sighed. "Will you think I'm terrible if I ask you why you and Carla broke up?"

"No." He took a bite of his own flounder and cocked his head. "But if I have to talk about Carla, then you have to tell me about the slime bastard."

"You've been talking to Gabe," she said, recognizing her brother's name for Barry.

"A little." Jay picked up a French fry, browned to perfection. "Neither of your brothers are too fond of your ex-husband."

"No, they're not." She chose to tell him about the beginning of the marriage, bad as it had been, rather than the humiliating end of it. "I told you Barry made a pass at Cat two weeks after we were married."

Jay nodded. "Knowing Cat, I'm surprised she let him live."

Gail laughed. "Gabe walked in, just as Cat slapped him. If Cat hadn't stopped him, I think Gabe would have killed Barry. As it was, Barry had a broken nose and a very clear hand print on his cheek."

Jay reached for her hand, gave it a light squeeze. "How did he explain that to you?"

"He said he'd given Cat a friendly hug and both she and Gabe overreacted."

"Did you buy it?"

She sighed, shrugged. "I tried to. It's amazing what you can convince yourself of when you're young, naive and in love. Besides, I was pregnant, married and I didn't know how else to handle it. And I really was amazingly naive. I wouldn't tell them, but some of that was because of Cam and Gabe."

"What do you mean?" He let go of her hand and picked up his water.

Gail pushed her food around the plate and tried to organize her thoughts. "I went through high school with two older brothers who threatened to kill any guy who made a wrong move toward me. Then, I went to a small college in Corpus Christi, and every time I brought a guy around home, Gabe and Cam put the fear of God in him. I'd just finished college when I met Barry. I didn't let him near my family for a long time. Didn't want to scare him away."

Jay grinned. "Yeah, your brothers can be pretty intimidating."

A sudden hideous thought struck her. "Tell me they didn't harass you." She grasped Jay's hand. "I swore I'd kill them if they did."

His lips quirked. "They didn't harass me. Cam talked to me, the day of the wedding." He held up a hand when Gail began to sputter. "They love you and are concerned about you. I don't have a problem with it, and neither should you."

She relaxed a little. Besides, there was nothing she could do about it now. "I take it you passed."

Jay's mouth curved upward. He took another bite of fish. "Well, he didn't slug me."

They both laughed. "I'm glad." She patted his cheek. "It would be a shame to mess up such a pretty face."

Jay flashed her a grin. "Men aren't pretty."

She leaned over and kissed him. "You are. And you're a man."

He looked embarrassed, she thought, finding it endearing.

"I'm not sure how to answer that. Are you trying to distract me?"

"Probably." She smiled. "I bet you're wondering why I ever fell in love with Barry."

"He must have had something good in him, or you wouldn't have."

Gail shook her head. "No, but I thought he did. Barry was very charming. I thought he loved me. He put up a good front. I didn't figure out it was all a fake until after Mel was born." Unwilling to talk about how she'd felt when faced with proof of Barry's infidelity, she changed the subject.

"So." Gail laid her fork down and laced her hands together beneath her chin. "Tell me why you fell in love with Carla. And why you broke up."

Jay used his napkin, then pushed his plate away. "I didn't fall in love with her. Which, come to think of it, is pretty much why we broke up."

"You lived with her for two years. I just assumed you were in love with her."

"I thought I was. At first. She's beautiful, smart. Ambitious. Successful."

Gail's stomach sank as he talked. Carla, who was everything Gail wasn't, hadn't been able to hold him. How did she expect to keep his interest?

"I wanted to love her, but I just didn't. Eventually, she became unhappy with the way things were going. She gave me an ultimatum." He looked at Gail and those warm green eyes had gone cold. "I don't respond well to ultimatums."

"What did she say?"

"Marry me or move out." He shrugged. "I moved out."

Wonderful. He'd broken up with Carla over the issue of marriage, and here Gail was, married to him because of a child neither one of them had planned on. "Obviously, she regretted her ultimatum."

"I didn't. I felt like I'd been let out of prison." He was silent a moment, his finger circling the rim of his water glass. "You know the first time you and I had dinner at your house, when you made macaroni and cheese?"

Gail nodded, wondering what was going on in his head.

"We talked to the kids, and everyone told something about their day?"

A little embarrassed, Gail blushed. "It's a way to get the kids talking. To find out what's going on with them."

"Don't apologize. It was great. And you asked me about my day, and the three of you were really interested. You listened, and asked more questions. You cared how my day had been." He took Gail's hand and held it. "Mark used to do that. Not exactly, but he'd get us to talking about the day, if something bad or good happened."

"I guess a lot of people do something like that."

"Not Carla." He shook his head decisively. "We never had a conversation that didn't revolve around her. Her career, her caseload, her problems, whatever. If we did talk about my career, it was only because it affected her. And the pitiful thing is, I never realized it until that night in your kitchen.''

''Maybe you realized it on a subconscious level. You did leave her.''

''Maybe.'' He brought Gail's hand to his lips and kissed her wrist. ''But I'm glad I did. Because if I hadn't moved out, I'd never have come to Texas. And then I wouldn't have gotten together with you.''

''You wouldn't be married with a baby on the way, either.'' It hurt, when she thought of it, to know he'd married her because of duty. Obligation.

''I don't regret any of it. Do you?''

How could she, with him looking at her so openly? So sweetly. Even lovingly. But he didn't love her, she thought, any more than he'd loved Carla. ''No, I don't regret it. But I wish I didn't feel as if I'd given you the same ultimatum Carla did.''

''As I recall, I'm the one who talked you into marriage. I was hardly coerced.'' He tugged her forward until his lips met hers. Then he drew back, and his eyes were troubled. ''But maybe you feel coerced.''

''Not by you.'' Perhaps by circumstances, but never by him. She laid her palm against his cheek. ''You make me happy.''

He smiled, kissed her again. ''You make me happy, too. So why don't we go back, and make each other even happier?''

She let him kiss her, take her home, make love to her. And her doubts slid away with each stroke of his hand, each lingering caress, each tempting kiss.

CHAPTER THIRTEEN

"OKAY, THE CAR'S LOADED," Jay said late Monday afternoon. "Are you ready to hit the road?"

Gail sighed and glanced longingly toward the bedroom. "Do you think if we hurried we could have one more bath in the Jacuzzi?"

He smiled, wishing they could. The whirlpool tub was big enough for both of them, and they had put it to good use, on several occasions. Jay came up behind Gail, put his arms around her and kissed her neck. "No. Because if we get in that tub I won't be able to resist making love to you and then we won't get home until very, very late. But I'm game if you are."

"Sex fiend," she accused.

"Hey, it's our honeymoon. I'm allowed to be a sex fiend."

"It was nice, wasn't it?" she asked, snuggling back against him. "I had a wonderful time."

"Yeah, me too." He kissed her again. "I hate to say it, but we'd better get going."

She sighed and followed him out.

"I've been meaning to bring something up," Gail said, once they were on their way. "I promised Mel something I realize now I should have discussed with you first.''

Curious about her apprehensive tone, Jay glanced at her, then back to the road. "What's that?"

"I said we could paint her room first thing."

"Is that all?" he asked, relieved to find it was something so simple. "Of course you can have her room painted, and Roxy's too, if she wants. She can paint it purple if that's all it takes to make her happy."

Gail didn't say anything. He glanced over to see her biting her lip, struggling not to smile.

His stomach sank. "Mel wants a purple room?"

Fighting laughter, Gail nodded. "I know it's sort of strange, but her room at home is purple and pink and she wants the same thing. I can't help it, I promised her she could have whatever colors she wanted, and she didn't have to change it until she grew tired of it. Do you mind terribly?"

Not as long as his bedroom didn't have to be purple. "No. Could be worse," Jay said philosophically. "What color does Roxy want?"

"I don't know. She won't discuss it."

He was silent a moment. "Until the wedding I didn't realize quite how strong her feelings were. The fact that she hates my guts, I mean." He could still hear her saying, "Mommy doesn't want to marry you."

"Jay, she doesn't hate you. But she isn't used to sharing me. It's just going to take her a while to become accustomed to it. But she will, I promise you, she will.''

"I hope you're right.'' Because if she didn't get used to him, they were facing major problems. Problems he didn't know how to solve.

Gail continued, ''I guess I'll paint her room blue, like it is now.''

Jay drove onto the ferry and put the car in park. ''Do you know a painter?''

She glanced at him, obviously surprised. ''Why would I need a painter? I can do it this week. After we move in.''

''No, you can't.''

''Of course I can.''

He shot her an irritated glance. ''You're pregnant, remember? You don't have any business climbing around on ladders, painting walls.''

Her eyebrows drew together and she frowned. ''Don't be ridiculous. I'm perfectly fine.''

''Right now you're perfectly fine. But what if you have one of those dizzy spells while you're up on a ladder?'' Which, he thought, clinched his argument.

She waved his concerns aside. ''I'll be careful. I won't do it unless I'm sure I feel all right. Besides, I can't afford a painter.''

''I can.''

''I'm not going to ask you to pay for a painter to paint my daughters' rooms.''

''You're not asking, I'm offering.''

''Absolutely not. It wouldn't be right.''

"Why not?" he asked, but he suspected he knew her reasoning. And he didn't like it a damn bit.

Gail didn't answer, remaining silent for a moment as the ferry docked. "I guess we should have talked about finances before we got married," she said after a moment.

"Looks like." Still irritated, and growing more so by the minute, he drove off the ramp.

Gail folded her hands together in her lap. "Well, it's not too late. I think we should figure out our estimated common expenses, and then we can split them up. You know, mortgage payments, groceries, that sort of thing."

He shot her an incredulous glance. "You do, do you? Well, think again."

"What do you mean? It's the only fair thing to do. My daughters shouldn't be a drain on you financially."

"And what about you, Gail? Are you not going to be a drain on me either?"

"Why should I be?" she fired back. "I have a perfectly good job, Jay. There's no reason for you to pay for my expenses."

"Is that so?" he said pleasantly. "I happen to have a perfectly good job, too, and I can damn well support my own damn family."

"But the girls—"

He interrupted, more hurt than angry, but he led with the anger. "Your daughters aren't my family. Thanks, you've made that clear."

"Jay, that isn't what I meant. But I don't think you should have to pay for Mel and Roxy. They're my responsibility. And Barry's."

And none of his. He heard the words, even though she hadn't said them. He didn't speak. Didn't trust himself not to say something he'd regret.

They rode the rest of the way with a strained silence between them, reaching her ex-husband's house a short time later. Again, he didn't speak, but put the car in park and waited for her to go get the girls.

Tentatively, Gail touched his arm. "Jay, I didn't mean to hurt you."

"Forget it. You'd better go get your daughters."

He waited, and brooded. How was he supposed to bond with Roxy when Roxy's own mother—his wife—didn't think of the four of them as a family?

GAIL DIDN'T HAVE A CHANCE to talk to Jay again until late that night. He'd gone to his house to tend to the puppies while she put the girls to bed. She knew he'd been angry, and hurt, but she had no idea how to fix it. Especially when he'd been wrong.

She decided the open approach would be best. "Are you still mad at me?" she asked him when he came in.

He sat on the bed to pull off his shoes and socks, before angling his head to look at her. "I wasn't mad at you. Exactly."

"Could have fooled me."

He shrugged. "You were right. We should have talked about finances before."

"So you agree we should split our expenses?"

He pulled his shirt off over his head, then tossed it on a chair. All that lovely golden skin distracted her, but she tried to focus on the discussion.

"No," he said, pulling his wallet out of his back pocket and tossing it on the dresser. "I still think it's a dumb idea, but if that's the way you want it, that's the way we'll do it."

Incensed, she glared at him. "It's not dumb, it's practical."

"Practical, huh?" He stroked a hand over his chin and looked at her. "We're going to have two mortgages to pay until you can sell your house. Don't you figure you'll be strapped enough making the payments on your house, not to mention what you spend on the girls, without additional expenses?"

Damn it, he was right. She crossed her arms and tapped her fingers on her arm. "I'll figure something out. Maybe you can cover these expenses, until the house sells, and then I'll pay you back."

He tilted his head, considering her. A slow smile curved his mouth. "You don't know me very well, do you? Do you really think I'd take money from my own wife? That I'd allow *my wife* to pay me back?"

Barry would have, she thought. But Jay wasn't Barry, thank God. She huffed out a breath. "No. Damn it."

He grinned, dimples flirting, then reached for her. "Come here."

She allowed him to tug her down next to him on the bed. "Jay, we haven't solved anything."

"Yes, we have. Or we will. Let me take care of our living expenses here. It's important to me, Gail. Will you let me do that?"

His green eyes were fringed with surprisingly dark lashes. Beautiful eyes, especially when he looked at her so intensely. She wondered if he knew how distracting he could be, and suspected he did. "You make it sound as if I'm doing you a favor."

"You would be. Because then we could stop talking about finances." His hands slid slowly up her arms and drew her nearer. "And do something more interesting." His lips cruised her jawline. "Much more interesting."

"What about—" She paused, struggling to think clearly, but he made it impossible with that talented mouth driving her wild with slow, heated kisses sprinkled over her skin. "My house. The girls."

"You pay for your house. Until it sells." His mouth was busy on her neck, at her fluttering pulse.

Now those clever hands were cupping her breasts, at the same time his mouth savored her as if she were a fine wine. "And when it does?" Unable to stop herself, she gave a small moan and raised her hands to his chest.

He drew back and smiled at her, his eyes heavy-lidded with desire. "We'll renegotiate."

His mouth covered hers and his tongue slipped inside, sipping, savoring. Seducing. She couldn't think when her skin was on fire and her mind grew numb with pleasure. She wrapped her arms around his neck and lay back on the bed, pulling him with her. "Make love to me," she whispered.

"I will. I am," he said, and kissed her again.

"Do ME A FAVOR," Jay said the next morning as he got ready for work.

"Anything," she said. "Since you're taking the girls to school and I get to be wonderfully lazy and lie in bed." Of course, she'd have to get up and make sure the girls had everything, but the point was, she could go back to bed. Even better, she'd only had one small bout of morning sickness this morning.

He sat on the edge of the bed and smiled at her, flicking a finger beneath her chin. "I had no idea you were so easily bribed."

"Depends on the bribe, and the briber."

He ran a hand over her hair. "Don't paint the girls' rooms today. I swear I've been having nightmares thinking about you getting dizzy on the ladder and crashing."

"Oh, Jay. I promised Mel. And I don't feel right letting you pay—"

He interrupted. "Mark's going to help me do it after work. It'll take a couple of nights, but we should be finished before you move everything in. Can you get the paint today?"

"Yes, but you don't have to do this, Jay. It's sweet, and I appreciate it, but I never intended you to go to so much trouble."

"It's a done deal. Mark's coming over right after work. I need to get going," he said, and kissed her.

"How did you get Mark to agree?" she asked him as he started out the door.

"Bribed him." The grin flashed. "Said we'd baby-sit once we get settled. Poor guy's so desperate to get Cat alone, he'd have re-roofed the house if I'd asked.''

"Mommy," Roxy said, nearly running into Jay in the doorway. He stepped aside to let her in and she swept past without looking at him. "I can't find my hair clip. I can't go to school without my clip.''

"Can I help you find it?'' Jay asked.

Roxy shook her head. "I want Mommy to. How come you're not dressed?'' she asked Gail. "Don't we have to leave for school?''

"Jay's going to take you two today. Is Mel ready?''

Her lip thrust out in a mutinous pout. "Don't want to go with him.''

"I thought you liked my car, Roxy?''

She hunched a shoulder. Gail wanted to shake her, but reminded herself that her daughter was making a huge adjustment. Roxy needed understanding, even if it killed her mother, Gail thought grimly. And hurt Jay, she realized, glancing at him. He had a sort of wistful look in his eyes.

"I'll help you look for it, honey.'' She got out of bed and went to her closet. "Let me get my robe.''

"Roxy," Mel called from the other room. "I found your silly old clip. It was in the bathroom, just like I told you.''

Roxy ran out. Gail tugged her robe around her and went to Jay, laying a hand on his arm. "Don't let it bother you. She just needs time.''

The wistful look cleared. "Yeah, I know. Come to

the kitchen with me and tell me what you're going to do today.''

She followed him out. ''I haven't forgotten about the puppies. I'll check on them throughout the day. Then I'm going to try to decide what furniture goes and what stays. We still need to talk about a few things. And I'm going to pack. And last,'' she said, shuddering, ''I'm going to go through the girls' rooms and throw out every broken toy they have. Not to mention, going through my stuff and getting rid of all the junk I've accumulated that I don't want to move.''

''Sounds exciting. Do something else for me today.''

''What's that?''

He cupped her cheek and smiled at her. ''Miss me.''

Her heart fluttered. When he said things like that she didn't feel as if he'd only married her for the baby's sake. ''I can manage that. Will you miss me?''

''Definitely.'' He kissed her just as the girls ran in.

''Yuck,'' Roxy said.

Mel giggled. ''Mommy's kissing Jay.''

Gail held out her hand. ''That's what people do when they're married. I need kisses from my girls, too. Come give me a kiss and then go get in the car. You're all going to be late if you don't hurry.''

After she saw them off she thought about going back to bed, but with a mountain of work staring her in the face, she knew she shouldn't. Thankfully, her boss had given her the whole week off, but if she didn't get organized, moving day would be a disaster. She pulled out several sturdy black trash sacks and took them with her to the girls' rooms. Might as well start with the worst job first, and get it out of the way.

Besides, if she made a lot of progress, she could justify a nap later.

Late that morning, when she thought she'd go crazy if she had to fill any more trash sacks, she went to Jay's to check on Fudge and Fluffy. They were ecstatically happy to see her, as if they hadn't seen a human in weeks, not hours. They jumped, slobbered, quivered with excitement. Luckily, they'd only managed to dig up one new flowerbed since Gail and Jay's return. It's a good thing they're so cute, she thought, remembering how pretty the back yard had been before puppies. Now it looked more like the site of a train wreck.

Indulging herself, and the dogs, she threw the ball several times, then filled their water bowl with fresh water and went inside. She and Jay hadn't had much chance to talk about combining their households. Or maybe, she thought with a smile, remembering the honeymoon, they'd had better things to talk about. Better things to do.

Jay's furniture was sparse, but she liked what he had. His bedroom suite was a beautiful dark wood that was the only thing he'd brought from California, so she knew he liked it. He'd just bought his couch, which gave Gail the chance to get rid of the one she'd been using for years, an ancient hand-me-down of her mother's. She loved her dining room set, fortunately, since Jay didn't have any furniture at all for that room.

She was trying to figure paint quantities in Mel's room when the phone rang. A little breathless from running to the kitchen to get it, she answered. "Hello?"

"Who is this?" a woman's voice asked sharply.

Gail rolled her eyes at the rude tone. "Who do you want?"

"I'm looking for Jay Kincaid. Is he there?"

"No. He's at work. Can I take a message?" She glanced around for a piece of paper, spying a note pad on the counter.

"I've tried his office and couldn't get through." She sounded irritated and impatient. "Are you the maid?"

Gail stifled a giggle as it dawned on her who the caller might be. "No. But I'll be glad to take a message," she repeated.

The woman huffed out an angry breath. "Tell him to call Carla. His fiancée." She waited a moment and added, "And if you're not the maid, who the hell are you and what are you doing in Jay's house?"

The back door opened just then and Jay came in.

"I think I'll let him tell you about that," Gail said. "He just walked in." She held the phone out to Jay. "It's for you."

"Who is it?" he asked, tossing his keys down on the kitchen table.

"Your fiancée," she said, and handed him the receiver. "Obviously, one of us is confused."

CHAPTER FOURTEEN

HIS FIANCÉE? Great, that could only be Carla. He didn't know anyone else running around calling themselves that. Jay had come home for lunch for a couple of reasons. The clinic's phones were out since the phone company had cut the regular lines while trying to install a new DSL line for the computers. He had wanted to check on Gail but mostly, though, he'd just wanted to see her. Hold her. Kiss her.

The last thing he wanted was to have another scene with Carla. And this one should be a doozy, since she didn't have a clue he was married. He took the phone from Gail and held it to his ear. "Hello, Carla."

"Hello, darling. I had some good news and I couldn't wait to share it with you."

"Yeah, I've got some news of my own." He glanced at Gail, who was leaning against the kitchen table with her arms crossed. He couldn't quite read her expression.

"I made partner in the law firm," Carla said. "It's going to be announced next week. Can you believe it?"

"Congratulations." He knew how hard she'd worked for the position. "You deserve it."

"Oh, Jay, you can't imagine how exciting it was. But there was one thing missing. One thing would make it perfect."

"Carla—"

"Jay, what do I have to do? Come back. Please. I'll do whatever you want. I swear I won't so much as mention the word marriage. Just come back to me."

"I can't." He started walking, wishing the conversation was over. Wishing he didn't have to hurt her, more than he already had.

She didn't speak for a moment and when she did her voice was strained. "You're involved with someone, aren't you? That woman who answered the phone. Who is she, Jay?"

"Her name is Gail. You've met her."

"Oh, please," she said, and laughed. "That drab little thing? She won't keep your interest for a week."

"Carla, I'm married." He could feel her astonishment over the phone line.

"Married?"

"Gail and I were married last weekend."

"You're lying. Or making a very unfunny joke. You walked out on me because you didn't want to get married. You swore you had no intention of marrying anyone."

He pinched the bridge of his nose. "Things…changed. I changed."

"You can't have changed that much. I don't believe you. There must be another reason. Something you're not telling me."

"I'm not discussing my marriage with you." Jay glanced over at Gail, but sometime during the conversation she'd left the room.

"How could you marry another woman? When you swore up and down you'd never marry?" Her voice was shrill, yet he could hear tears trembling in it. "Oh, my God, she's pregnant, isn't she? And you believe her? That's the oldest trick in the book."

"Carla, leave it alone."

"Fine, don't talk. But if she is pregnant, I recommend a paternity test. You might just find out you married her for nothing. Or another man's child."

He wasn't about to confirm her suspicions, and her comments didn't deserve an answer. "Are you through?"

"No, I'm not through! You could have called me. I deserved to know, not to find out like this. You weren't planning to tell me at all, were you?"

"We haven't been together for months. It didn't occur to me to call you. Why would it?"

"We lived together for two years. Did I mean so little to you that you didn't even think to tell me you were marrying another woman?"

He felt a flash of guilt. But he still didn't know if it would have been any kinder if he had told her before now. "Carla, don't do this. Whether I should have told you or not, the fact remains I'm married now."

Carla laughed harshly. "I always thought you were so smart, but you're a fool, Jay. Don't think you can come crawling back to me when this farce of a marriage is over.''

''I won't.'' If he'd ever been sure of anything, he was sure of that. ''And, Carla, I married Gail because I wanted to.''

''Bastard,'' she said, and the line went dead.

NOT WANTING TO torture herself any longer by hearing Jay talk to his ex-girlfriend, Gail had left the room shortly after giving him the phone. Unfortunately, she'd already heard more than she wanted.

Standing by the den window, the one that looked out into the back yard, she watched the puppies gleefully digging yet another hole. She knew she ought to go out and scold them, but she couldn't summon the energy. Instead, she replayed the brief snatches of conversation she'd overheard.

I can't, Jay had said. Had that been regret in his voice? She was nearly certain it had been. Regret that now he couldn't go back to Carla, even if he'd wanted? He had a wife now, and a baby on the way. And two stepdaughters, one of whom was probably making him regret he'd ever convinced Gail to marry him.

Things have changed. I've changed, he'd said. Because he'd had no choice. He'd done the right thing, he'd married her. Was he regretting it now? Part of him was bound to resent her. Barry had. Barry had resented being forced into marriage so much, he'd eventually left her. Would it come to that with Jay?

And what would she do if it did?

Sensing his presence, she turned to see Jay standing in the kitchen doorway. He gave her a rueful smile.

"I'm going to fix some lunch before I head back to the office. Want something?"

"Okay. There's not much food over here."

"I know. I think I can scrounge up a can of soup, though. Come keep me company."

She followed him into the kitchen and watched as he dumped soup into a pan and set it on the stove. His phone conversation with Carla sat like the proverbial elephant in the living room between them, until Gail finally grew frustrated enough to say something. "So, can we expect a wedding gift from Carla?"

His mouth lifted at one side and he shook his head. "I wouldn't hold my breath waiting for it."

"You look upset. Was it that bad?"

He shrugged and stirred the soup. "Pretty bad. At the end she called me a bastard and hung up. And that was the good part."

"You'd have to expect her to be upset." She took out a couple of bowls and set them beside the stove.

Jay transferred the soup to the bowls. "I should have told her. She shouldn't have had to find out the way she did."

"Why would you have told her? You broke up months ago."

He waited until they were seated before speaking again. "You told Barry. She was right, I should have told her."

"Barry is my children's father and lives in the same town. I see him every other weekend, for heaven's sake. It's hardly the same thing."

He looked a little annoyed. "It wasn't just some casual fling, Gail. Carla and I lived together for two years. I owed her the courtesy of telling her. But I didn't, because I didn't want to deal with her reaction."

"Maybe that's not the only reason you didn't tell her," she said, unable to stop herself. "You still have feelings for her, don't you?"

He set his spoon down and stared at her. "Not the way you seem to be implying. I don't want to hurt her, Gail, and I did."

"Fine." She could hardly speak because of the lump in her throat. Damn those pregnancy hormones! She always cried more easily when she was pregnant. "I don't want to talk about it anymore."

"Gail." He covered her hand with his. "I'm married to you. I'm committed to you. And to Roxy and Mel and the new baby. I don't want you to doubt that our marriage is important to me. I want it to work."

"I know," she managed to say. "I do, too."

He leaned forward and kissed her. "Good. Why don't we forget about Carla? I think she's caused enough trouble for one day."

They talked of other things until he went back to work. Her heart heavy, she watched him go. She believed he wanted their marriage to work. But the fact remained, if there hadn't been a baby, there wouldn't have been a wedding. And sooner or later, that reality was going to hit home. Then how would Jay feel?

Trapped. And forced to make the best of the situation.

GAIL AND JAY SETTLED into married life quickly once they all moved into one house. Roxy still hadn't warmed up to Jay, but Mel seemed perfectly happy with her mother's marriage and her new stepfather. Jay was surprised at how quickly he grew accustomed to the near-constant noise level of life with two little girls. Living with one woman was nothing like living with three. Most of the time, he enjoyed it, though he did like the weekends the girls spent with Barry, when he had Gail to himself.

One Saturday afternoon a few weeks after Gail and the girls moved in, Jay attempted to watch a ball game on TV. Attempted being the operative word. Mel sat beside him, chattering and asking him so many questions he couldn't concentrate on the game. Then she got up and started running around, which was even worse. But the final straw came when he missed a Longhorn touchdown because Mel was doing a cartwheel in front of the TV. And he couldn't even cuss.

"Mel, honey, why don't you go see what your mom is doing?" he asked through gritted teeth. And leave him in peace to watch what precious little was left of the game.

A blood-curdling shriek came from the bedroom.

Afraid Gail had fallen, Jay raced in there, closely followed by Mel.

"Good God, Gail, I thought you were dying," he said, relieved to see her standing and apparently, unhurt.

She stood in the doorway of her walk-in closet, clutching a mangled piece of something—maybe leather?—in one hand. Her cheeks bloomed with color, her chest heaved, and he could swear sparks of fire shot from her eyes. She looked magnificent.

"Do you know what this is?" she demanded, thrusting the scrap beneath his nose.

Yips and growls could be heard, coming from the closet behind her. "Part of a shoe?" he hazarded.

"Exactly. To be more specific, this is all that's left—" she thrust it toward him again "—of my best pair of heels."

Her eyes shimmered with anger, the blue as deep and dangerous as the ocean. She sucked in a deep breath, which caught his attention because her shirt stretched much tighter across her breasts than normal. He dragged his gaze from that mesmerizing chest up to her eyes again.

"Do you know how much high heels cost?" She shook her fist at him. "Do you?"

He had a pretty good idea. "I'll buy you another pair."

"Don't even start with me. I can buy my own shoes. I don't need or want your money. But I'll tell you what you can do. Take a good look at that." She stood aside and gestured dramatically to her closet floor. Completely unrepentant, or possibly unaware,

Fudge and Fluffy played tug-of-war with yet another shoe.

The closet was a shambles, half-eaten shoes lay everywhere, and if the smell was any indication, at least one of the dogs had pooped as well.

"Uh-oh," Mel said, as Roxy came in behind her. "Somebody's in big trouble."

Jay swallowed. There was always Mastercard. Surely she'd let him pay for the shoes, once she calmed down. "Listen, Gail, I know you're upset but—"

"Upset?" she yelled. "Upset doesn't even begin to describe my feelings." Eyes blazing, she took a step toward him. "They've destroyed every single pair of shoes I own, except the ones on my feet. Did you let those furry fiends from hell into my closet?"

He started to deny it, but he happened to glance at Roxy. Her eyes were huge, her face white as a sheet. Her gaze met his. Defenseless against the plea in those eyes, he sighed and prepared to immolate himself.

"I watered earlier." He glanced at the French doors, open to the backyard. Muddy paw prints marched across the beige carpet, disappearing into the closet. "I might have left the doors open. I was watching the game, so I might not have noticed."

Roxy and Mel watched them, wide-eyed, fascinated and utterly silent.

"You *might* have left them open or you *did* leave them open?"

He shifted, stuck his hands in his pockets. "Well,

I doubt the puppies could open them, so it must have been me.''

"You were watching the game,'' Gail repeated, her tone ominously calm. "So naturally, you allowed your two miserable, misbegotten, horribly trained mongrels full run of the house. You couldn't be bothered to even close the damn door,'' she said, her voice rising with each word.

He rubbed the back of his neck. "Gail, it's football. The Longhorns are playing.''

She let out a strangled scream and stepped forward until she stood nose to nose with him. Her index finger jabbed firmly into his chest. "Let me tell you what's going to happen. I'm going to the mall and I'm going to replace my shoes.'' She glanced at the closet, then back at him. "I have to get at least one pair for work, even if I can't afford to replace all of them. And when I come back—'' she punctuated her words with another jab of the finger ''—there won't be a sign, not a trace, not even a dog hair, to indicate that those canine criminals were ever anywhere near my closet. Got that?''

He bit the inside of his cheek to keep from laughing. After all, he didn't have a death wish. "Absolutely. Are you sure you won't let me pay—''

"I said, don't start.'' Her gaze narrowed. "The subject is closed. The only thing I need from you is for you to clean out my closet!'' she yelled, her voice rising on the last words.

She stalked off and a few minutes later, he heard the back door slam.

Jay let out a breath and shook his head admiringly.

"Wow, what a woman. Does she get that mad often?"

"Nuh-uh," Mel said, blond curls dancing, eyes still wide. "Last time was when Roxy and me spilled purple paint on the living room carpet and we had to get new carpet. But she's always sorry after she yells." Mel reached out a pudgy arm and gave him a hug. "Don't feel bad, Jay. You didn't do it on purpose."

"He didn't do it," Roxy said, speaking for the first time, her lip quivering. "It's my fault. I let the puppies in. Not on purpose, but I came in to get a drink of water and I forgot. Jay told Mommy he let them in, so I wouldn't get in trouble."

"She had more fun yelling at me," he said, hoping to avert the tears that trembled in her eyes. "Don't worry about it. Your mom will forgive me." I hope, he added silently. "But we better get this cleaned up. How about some help? First, we toss the puppies outside."

Even with both the girls helping it took them a while. Finally, Jay decided it wouldn't get any better. The ruined shoes were in the trash, the closet and bedroom carpet cleaned and vacuumed, and a generous dose of air deodorizer followed by cologne had neutralized the smell.

"What's your mom's favorite meal?" he asked the girls as they left the room, carefully shutting the door behind them. "Something I can pick up, not cook."

"Uncle Wang's," they said in unison.

"She likes the chicken in black bean sauce," Roxy added. "But you have to go to Corpus to get it."

"Why don't we run over there?" He thought about what else Gail liked. "And while we're out, let's pick up some Rocky Road ice cream."

"Are you trying to bribe Mommy?" Roxy asked, her eyes big.

"Not bribe. Just trying to do something nice for her." To soften her up. Not a bribe, exactly.

On the way to the car, Roxy slipped her hand into his. "Thank you, Jay."

"You're welcome." He ruffled her hair with his other hand. "But you know, your mom would have forgiven you. She loves you and Mel a lot."

"I know. And she loves you, too, so she'll forgive you. Right?"

"Sure," he said, though he wasn't certain of any such thing. Oh, he knew Gail would forgive him. But love him? That he didn't know.

WHEN GAIL WALKED IN that evening, she thought she'd entered the wrong house. The kitchen was spotless and dimly lit. A delicious smell, that of her favorite Chinese dish, permeated the air. Curious, she dropped the shopping bag and her keys and followed the low hum of music into the other room.

The dining room table was set for two with her good china and crystal. A huge vase of yellow roses dominated the center of the mahogany table, flanked by a pair of crystal candelabras with white candles burning in each arm. Her lips twitched as she recognized the music—the same song she and Jay had danced to the night they made love for the first time.

"I had the devil of a time finding that CD." She turned to see Jay standing in the doorway, a champagne glass in one hand and a single red rose in the other. "I thought about a white flag, but I figured you'd like flowers better."

Not quite ready to let him off the hook, she clamped down on her lips to keep from smiling. "What's in the glass?" she asked when she had control.

"The grocery store's best brand of sparkling grape juice. Four bucks a bottle." He handed her the glass, along with the rose.

She took a sip. "Where are the kids?"

"In Roxy's room. They've already eaten and have promised to play a game and go to bed early."

"How did you manage that?" she asked, taking another sip. "This is good, by the way."

He spread his hands. "I bribed them."

"You do that well, I see. Is that smell what I think it is?"

He nodded. "Chicken with black bean sauce from Uncle Wang's."

Gail sighed. "You're making it really difficult for me to stay mad at you."

He smiled, his dimples deepening. "That's the idea. We have Rocky Road ice cream for dessert. A lot of ice cream. It's what I used with the girls."

"You're a wicked man, Jay."

"A guy's gotta do what a guy's gotta do." He set her glass on the table, and the rose beside it. Then he put his arms around her and tugged her close. "Your closet is as spotless as I could get it. I don't think it smells anymore, but if it does, I'll switch with you, and I'll move everything." He nuzzled her neck, then kissed it. "Am I forgiven or am I still in the doghouse?"

"Speaking of dogs—"

He raised his head and looked at her. "Fudge and Fluffy have been severely chastised and are now contemplating their sins in the back yard. Roxy and Mel are taking them to obedience classes starting Monday."

"I like a man who thinks of everything," she said, her lips curving upward.

"Not quite everything," he said and kissed her mouth slowly and thoroughly.

His arms tightened around her. She let herself relax and return his kiss. Her knees had started to turn boneless when he released her. "Let's eat. Can't have a perfectly good bribe going to waste."

They fed each other bites of chicken, vegetables and rice, and sipped the sparkling grape juice from the same glass while the candles gutted and the music wailed a sexy saxophone. They talked, of everything and nothing. Gail had to clutch her stomach from laughing so hard when he described how both girls had run shrieking from the room and refused to help until he cleaned up the smelly part of the mess.

"I'll explode if I eat another bite," Gail said finally some time later, taking a last lick of ice cream. She put her spoon down, crossed her arms on the table, and looked at Jay. "You worry me."

Jay lounged back in his chair, long legs stretched before him, a smile curving that perfect mouth. "Why's that?"

He wore a green dress shirt with the sleeves rolled up over his forearms. Her eyes traced the by-now familiar features, the honey-blond hair, strong jaw, straight nose. The deep green eyes, now shaded by candlelight. She wanted to lick her lips. He looked, she thought, every bit as delicious as the meal they'd just consumed. "No man should know how to get around a woman so easily."

The smile deepened, as did the dimples. "I'll tell you a secret. It wasn't easy."

"Mommy?"

Roxy and Mel stood in the doorway. Mel was holding a piece of paper. Roxy looked scared, but determined. Gail had an inkling of what had really happened earlier.

"Here, Mommy," Mel said, handing her what turned out to be a crayon drawing. "It's Fudge and Fluffy," she explained. Two brown and white blobs were holding a banner in their mouths that read: We're sorry. We love you Mommy.

"It's beautiful, honey. Thank you," she said and kissed her.

"You're not gonna make us get rid of the puppies, are you, Mommy?" Mel asked anxiously.

"No, I wouldn't do that."

Mel smiled sunnily and ran off. Gail looked at her oldest daughter and held out her arms. Roxy ran into them and immediately burst into tears.

"I'm sorry, Mommy," she said when she'd mastered her tears. "It's all my fault. I let Fudge and Fluffy in by accident. Jay told you he did it so you wouldn't be mad with me."

"Oh, honey, I wish you'd told me." Swamped with love, and remorse, she patted her daughter's back. "I know I was angry, but I would have forgiven you."

Roxy nodded against Gail's chest, her arms clinging around her mother's neck. "That's what Jay said. 'Cause you love me. And he said you'd forgive him, 'cause you love him, too."

She glanced at Jay, who looked a little alarmed at that statement. Wonderful. It made him nervous to think she might love him.

"Ah, that wasn't exactly how the conversation went," Jay said after Roxy left. "Hey, what's wrong?"

Gail got up, sniffling. "I need a tissue."

He jumped up, taking her arms to detain her. "You're crying. Why are you crying?"

"Because you were so sweet to me." She waved a hand at the table, and wiped at her cheeks. "And you took the blame for Roxy," she said, struggling to quit crying.

"Oh, that." He relaxed and slipped his arms around her. "I had to. She was looking at me with those big baby blues, scared to death, and I didn't have the heart to let her take the heat."

"I'm a monster to have scared her so badly. And over shoes. Something so unimportant."

"Imelda Marcos would argue that."

Gail laughed, her tears drying. "Yes, I would have, too, earlier. But I shouldn't have lost my temper."

"Look at it this way, if Roxy thought you were such a terrible mother, she'd never have confessed."

"That still doesn't make it right. And I was awful to you. I yelled at you."

"Yeah, you sure did." He grinned. "As long as we're coming clean, I have a confession to make."

"What?" she asked suspiciously.

"You know when you were so mad, standing there just furious and ripping my head off?" Gail nodded. "You looked so damn sexy, I thought my heart was going to stop beating."

She stared at him. "It turned you on? Me being mad?"

"Oh, yeah. Big time."

"Is this like the strawberries? A guy thing?"

He laughed. "Yeah, it's a guy thing." His arms tightened around her and he bent to murmur in her ear. "If you're really sorry, you can make it up to me."

His lips laid a trail of liquid heat along her neck. Her heart rate sped up, her breathing quickened. "How?"

His hand slipped down to caress her rear. "Model your new shoes for me. The ones with those skinny high heels."

"How do you know what I bought."

"I've seen the kind of shoes you wear."

"Okay, you're right. I did buy a couple of pairs like that. Is that it?"

"Not quite." He put both hands on her rear and looked at her, smiling as he brought her closer against him. "I want you to wear the shoes, and those thigh-high hose you have. And nothing else."

Her lips curved. "And then we'll be even?"

"You'll be even. I'll be in heaven."

Gail laughed. "You are so easy. When did you want this to happen?"

"Now seems like a good time to me."

"I think that could be arranged," she said, and kissed him.

GAIL WOKE in the night, still wrapped in Jay's arms. She got out of bed to take care of business, smiling as she passed the trail of hose and shoes leading to the bed. He'd taken them off her, but not until after he'd made spectacular, mind-blowing love to her.

Chilled, she pulled on a nightgown before she crawled back into bed. "Are you okay?" Jay asked.

"I'm fine. Just cold. I thought you were asleep."

"Was. Now I'm awake." He smiled at her, his eyes at half mast. "Come here and I'll keep you warm," he offered, his voice thick with sleep.

So she let him wrap her in his arms again. Sighing, she snuggled against him and kissed his chest, listening to his breathing even out.

She'd fallen in love with her husband. And she had no idea if he was in love with her, or was only staying with her for the baby's sake.

CHAPTER FIFTEEN

ONE EVENING, Gail took Mel with her grocery shopping, while Jay stayed home with Roxy, who was supposed to be doing her homework. While Jay sat on the couch reading the newspaper, Roxy lay on her stomach on the floor in front of the TV, staring at a piece of paper, desultorily flipping it over, and then back. It only took three deep, bone-rattling sighs before he realized something was up and she wanted his attention.

"Need some help?" he asked, laying aside the paper.

She sat up and crossed her legs, tailor fashion. "It's spelling. Mommy always asks me the words, and then I spell them."

"Do you want me to ask you the words?" Although their relationship had greatly improved since the puppy incident, Jay still never knew if his offers of help would be rejected or accepted.

"'Kay," she said morosely, holding the paper out.

Jay took it from her and looked it over. "These are fifth-grade words?" He'd be depressed, too. They looked hard to him. Too hard for a ten-year-old, but what did he know?

Roxy nodded, a smile now tugging at her mouth. "They're for the spelling bee. My teacher says if I study hard, I can win. She thinks I'm the best speller in my grade."

"Spelling bee, huh? Sounds exciting. When is it?"

"Tomorrow night." Her head bobbed and she grew more animated. "It's gonna be in the auditorium, and Mrs. Beasley said we'll be *famous,* 'cause even the newspaper will be there."

"Wow, sounds like a big deal."

"Uh-huh." She played with her shoelace and shot Jay a look beneath her lashes. "Mommy's coming. And Daddy said he'd come. And maybe Gramma Randolph, too." She paused, fiddled with her shoelace again. "My teacher said we could ask whoever we wanted. And um, well..." Earnest eyes lifted to fix on his. "Will you come, Jay?"

His breath clogged in his throat as he stared at her. She wanted him to come to her spelling bee? Funny how a little girl could take your heart and wrap it around her finger. He cleared his throat and managed to speak. "I wouldn't miss it for anything."

If he hadn't been choked up before, the way her face lit up when he answered would have done it.

"So, will you ask me my words?" she said.

"Yeah." He cleared his throat. "I'll be glad to."

Some time later, they finished. While Roxy had been letter perfect on the words, she still seemed a little unhappy. "Is something else wrong, Rox?"

She shook her head, then sent him a calculating look. "Mommy said I wasn't supposed to bother you about it.'' Legs crossed, she sat up straighter. "But if I just *tell* you, because you *asked* me, that's not the same as bothering you. Is it?'' she added innocently.

"No,'' he said, thinking he might be on slippery ground.

Clasping her arms around her drawn-up knees, she sighed dramatically. "Dance lessons,'' she breathed, starry-eyed.

"Dance lessons?'' he echoed, confused.

Roxy nodded vigorously. "Mommy said I could have them. Well, she promised we'd try, this year, and that means yes,'' she explained with perfect seriousness. "But then she said she couldn't afford it. She said me and Mel are already doin' lots of things, and she can't add one more.'' Her expression clouded. "All my friends are taking them, and they want me to come, too.'' Her lower lip trembled. "So then I asked Daddy. And he said it was silly, and he couldn't afford it, neither.''

So now she was asking him. Why the hell hadn't Gail come to him? But he knew the answer to that. Gail wouldn't ask him for anything, least of all money for her daughters' activities. Hell, she hadn't even mentioned the spelling bee, and that cost nothing.

"Let me talk to your mom, Roxy. Maybe we can work something out.'' He knew better than to promise anything, before he talked to Gail. But that didn't stop him wanting to ruffle Roxy's hair and promise her anything her little heart desired.

"You're not gonna tell Mommy I bothered you, are you?''

"You didn't bother me. You talked to me, and there's nothing wrong with that."

"Thanks, Jay." The back door slammed and she got up. "There's Mommy! Can you talk to her now?"

He smiled. "I think I can manage that. Hey, Rox," he said, before she left the room. "I want you to know, you can talk to me whenever you need to. Don't ever think you're bothering me. Okay?"

"Okay." She flashed him a brilliant smile and left the room skipping.

Jay only wished he felt as good.

GAIL DIDN'T MIND the shopping part, but she hated to unload groceries. It always surprised her when Jay helped her. Barry never had, of course, but Jay seemed to take it for granted that if he were around, he should help. He did that with the laundry, too, she thought smiling. Though he'd been known to get confused with some of the girly things a time or two.

"You're awfully quiet," she said, stuffing the meat in the freezer. "Did something happen with Roxy while I was gone?"

"Nothing bad." He put the milk in the refrigerator. "Roxy tells me she's going to be in a spelling bee tomorrow night."

Gail went to the pantry, stretching to put up a can of soup. "Oh, that's right. I meant to mention it." She glanced at him over her shoulder and smiled. "I hope you didn't have plans for the two of us, because I need to be there. But don't worry, you don't have to go."

His expression blank, he stared at her a minute. "Roxy asked me to come."

"Oh." A bit surprised, she opened the refrigerator and began putting away vegetables. "Well, I'm sure we can think of a way to explain it if you don't want to come."

"Why wouldn't I want to be there?"

Baffled, she glanced at him. He'd quit putting away groceries and leaned against the counter, staring at her. She shrugged. "I don't know. It's a spelling bee. Not the most exciting thing on earth."

"Roxy specifically asked me to be there. Do you think I'd say no?"

Becoming a little exasperated by his attitude, she said, "Not if she made such a point of asking you. I didn't realize she had."

"Even if she hadn't, has it occurred to you that I might be interested in what the girls are doing?"

What bug has gotten up his nose? Gail wondered. Hands on hips, she tilted her head and considered him. "I'm not sure why I'm the bad guy here. For heaven's sake, Jay, it's a spelling bee. I forgot to mention it. What's the big deal?"

He shook his head, put his hands in his pockets. "Nothing. Absolutely nothing."

Gail returned to putting away the groceries. What was going on with him? What had she missed?

Long moments later, Jay spoke, breaking the silence. "My father left us on my eighth birthday. I doubt he knew it was my birthday." He gave a humorless laugh. "If he had, he wouldn't have cared."

Gail stopped and waited for him to go on. He'd never told her about his father. He talked about his mother occasionally, but never, ever his father.

"I was only in second grade, but I remember things. I remember him. He never came to any school play, or program, or even a lousy open house. Never came to the Little League games, or showed up at anything I can remember." His gaze, grim and decisive, locked on hers. "I'm not going to be that kind of a father."

Her heart aching for him, she walked over to him and put her hand on his arm. "Of course you're not. You'll be a wonderful father."

"Yeah, to the baby." His eyes lifted to hers. "But what about Mel and Roxy? I'm not their father, am I? I'm only a stepfather, and one you obviously aren't interested in including."

"Don't you think you're overreacting? I haven't not included you. Not purposely, at any rate." Or did he have a point? Perhaps she had been hesitant to ask him to do things with them. She didn't want the girls hurt, and she wasn't sure of Jay's willingness to be involved.

"If this was the first time I'd been excluded I'd agree you have a point. But it's far from the first. Before Roxy asked me, I thought they didn't want me there. I can deal with that, with them making an adjustment. I know it's going to take time. But tonight made me wonder if maybe you're the one who doesn't want me there."

Guilt and temper fought for dominance. "Jay,

that's ridiculous. I didn't realize you'd be interested. I have to beg Barry to come to these things, so it just doesn't ever occur to me—"

"That I'm not like your goddamn ex-husband?" The words cracked like a whip.

Again, she struggled with temper. "I don't think you're like Barry. And you're blowing this situation way out of proportion."

"Am I?" He moved away from her, to pace the length of the kitchen. "Maybe you're right. But I intend to be involved in my child's life. How are Roxy and Mel going to feel if I can find time for my own child, but never any for them?"

Oh, God, she'd never really thought about it that way. She felt like a total heel. "You're right. They'd feel terrible. I hadn't even considered that." Or that she'd obviously hurt Jay by excluding him. "I'm sorry. I hurt you, and I didn't mean to."

He rolled his shoulders. "I know. Forget it."

He didn't look as if he would forget it any time soon, though.

A few minutes after that, Roxy came in, asking for a cookie. Gail opened the package of chocolate sandwich cookies, noticing that Jay and Roxy seemed to be having some kind of wordless conversation. "How many?" Gail asked.

Roxy looked away from Jay to her mother. "Can I take them to my room?"

"No food in your room. You know that, Rox."

"'Kay. I just want one."

Now she knew something was going on. Roxy

could eat a dozen cookies if given the chance. However, Gail gave her the cookie, watched her stuff it in her mouth, and then run out.

"That was weird. What was that about?" Absentmindedly, she took a cookie herself and munched on it.

"Roxy mentioned something else tonight."

"What's that?'

"She told me about wanting to take dance lessons."

Frowning, Gail finished the cookie and dusted off her hands. "I specifically told her not to pester you about that."

"Yeah, I know. She told me that, too. I asked her what was wrong. She shouldn't get in trouble for telling me."

He still had his hands in his pockets, still leaning back against the counter as if relaxed. But she felt the tension between them wind tighter and tighter.

"So, Gail, what are you going to do about the dance lessons?"

To busy her hands, she stuffed the open package into a plastic sack. "Obviously, she told you both Barry and I said no."

He nodded. "She said neither of you could afford it."

"That's right. Did she happen to mention that both girls are in Brownies, both of them are taking art lessons, and she's also been asking me about joining the soccer league?"

"She mentioned something about other activities.

But knowing you, Gail, I don't think that's the end of it. When your daughters want something that badly, you'll move heaven and earth to get it for them. And Roxy's a hundred percent set on this. You got her the lessons, didn't you?''

Her heart sinking, she nodded.

''How did you get the money?''

He said it so quietly, so calmly, and she knew the storm would hit like a hurricane when she told him. Bracing herself, she spoke. ''I borrowed it from my mother.''

His eyes flashed, sharp green and angry, but he spoke calmly enough. ''You didn't consider asking me? You knew I'd be happy to pay for the lessons, didn't you, Gail?''

How to explain it to him? Especially with him looking at her as if she were some kind of criminal? ''I—well—I didn't—I didn't think it was your responsibility. And I've borrowed money from my mother before. It's not a problem, even though I don't like to do it unless—'' Horrified at what she'd nearly said, she broke off.

''Unless you have no other choice,'' he finished for her, his voice devoid of emotion. ''I wasn't an option. You couldn't ask me. Your husband.''

''Jay, I didn't think about it that way,'' she said, beginning to feel desperate. ''It's just a habit, to go to my mother. I should have asked you, but I didn't— I simply didn't think about it.''

''Bull.'' He straightened and took a step toward her.

Shocked, she put her hands on her hips. "What do you mean, bull?"

"Just what I said. That's bullshit. You thought about it. And you decided you didn't want me involved. You don't want me to be involved in your daughters' lives. Not monetarily, or in any other way."

He turned his back and started toward the door.

"Jay, wait! That isn't true."

He halted, turned around and looked at her. "Yes, it is. What I don't really understand is why. If you thought I'd interfere with how you're raising them, I could see it. But hell, I haven't said a word, and don't intend to unless I'm asked. And it's clear as crystal I'm the last person you'd ask. For anything."

He jerked open the back door. The look he sent her was as cold as she'd ever seen from him. "I'm going for a drive."

"Don't go. Can't we talk about this?"

"No," he said, and shut the door behind him.

Her heart in her throat, Gail stared after him, listened to the roar of his engine, and the squeal of tires as he left the driveway. She pulled out a chair, sat down at the kitchen table, buried her face in her arms and wept.

JAY DIDN'T HAVE a destination in mind when he left, but he wound up at the beach. It was cold, windy and deserted, which suited his mood perfectly.

He grabbed a jacket from his car and began walking, stuffing his hands in his pockets. Maybe Gail was right and he'd blown the whole situation out of proportion. But he didn't believe he had. Damn it, they were never going to make it as a family if Gail refused to allow him to share in her daughters' lives. And whether she meant to or not, she cut him out of the equation continually. He didn't enjoy feeling like an outsider, especially not in his own home.

But if a home meant a family, working together, then it wasn't much of a home. And apparently, he and Gail didn't have much of a marriage.

He halted and stared out at the ocean, watching the crash of waves against the sand, smelling the salt tang of the air. Usually, the ocean soothed him, but tonight it seemed as moody as he was. He stooped to pick up a shell, gleaming white in the moonlight. It reminded him of his and Gail's honeymoon, when they'd walked the beach and talked for hours. They weren't talking any longer. Depressed, he tossed the shell aside.

Why couldn't Gail ask him for anything? Ask him for help, of any sort? Why did she have an almost obsessive need for independence? He didn't have the answers, but he'd bet his last penny it had something to do with her first marriage. It hadn't escaped his notice that while Gail had told him of the beginning of her marriage, she'd said nothing of the end.

Did she think he was going to leave her, after the baby came? That he was just marking time until he could leave her? Or maybe, he thought with a sick feeling in his gut, maybe she was the one who wanted out. He'd talked her into marrying him, after all. Had it been a mistake? Maybe she'd seen it as the logical solution, and then after she had the baby, they could call it quits.

Except he'd be damned if he would let her end their marriage so easily. Not without a fight. Because Jay had a very good reason for wanting their marriage to work. Tonight, when Gail had told him she hadn't thought to come to him, he'd finally realized why it hurt so badly.

He'd fallen in love with his wife. Hell, he'd probably been in love with her for weeks. A blind man could have seen it, yet he hadn't. Not until it clubbed him over the head in his kitchen tonight.

The wind whipped at him and he pulled his jacket closer around him. Yeah, this is perfect, he thought, beginning to walk again. He'd finally fallen in love, and with his own wife yet, and she very clearly wasn't the least bit in love with him. Because if Gail loved him, how could she continue to cut him out of her life, and her daughters' lives?

He wasn't ready to concede defeat, though. He'd approach his problem logically. He had a way with women, knew what they liked, knew how to treat them. And with Gail, he had a big advantage, because they were living together. She liked him, she loved the sex, so how hard could it be to make his own wife fall in love with him?

CHAPTER SIXTEEN

THE ANNUAL ARANSAS BAY Area Spelling Bee, which several area schools combined to host, always drew a large crowd. This year it took place at Roxy's school, but unfortunately, someone had been overly optimistic about the auditorium's capacity. Mel sat on the floor up front with a group of her friends. Gail couldn't find her mother in the crowd, though knowing Meredith, she'd found a seat somewhere.

Leaning back against a partition, Gail counted herself lucky to have its meager support. Too bad she'd been standing and walking all day at work, and her feet were killing her. She'd kill for a chair.

"Do you want me to try to scare up a chair? I thought I saw some folding metal ones over by one of the doors," Jay said, as if reading her thoughts.

She smiled at him and shook her head. "Thanks, but I'm sure it's impossible. I'm fine here."

Gail hadn't seen Jay until he'd walked in that evening, shortly before they left for the spelling bee. The night before, she'd tried to wait up for him, but finally, around midnight, she'd fallen asleep. When she woke in the morning, he'd already left for work. So she'd been apprehensive, to say the least, about his mood when she finally did see him.

And here he was, acting as if they had never exchanged a harsh word. She should be glad, she supposed, but instead it ticked her off. How dare he act as if nothing had happened when she'd spent half the night and the entire next day worrying that he was angry? Or hurt. Or didn't care about her anymore. The jerk.

Still, he'd had reason to be upset with her. At first she'd dismissed what he'd said about her not wanting him involved in the girls' lives as an exaggeration. But throughout the long night and even longer day, she'd been forced to do a lot of thinking. And she had to admit, she had excluded Jay. Oh, not consciously, but subconsciously, she'd been afraid to share her daughters. With Barry, she had no choice. With Jay, she did. And she'd chosen wrong. It was past time for her to admit it.

"About last night," she began. "I'm sorry."

She couldn't read his expression when he looked at her, but then he smiled. "Yeah, I am, too. But I don't think now is the time to go into it."

"No, I know. I just wanted—"

"Well, if it isn't the happy couple," Barry said sarcastically, halting in front of them. "What are you doing here, Kincaid? Shouldn't you be off saving lives?"

Jay glanced at Barry. "Roxy asked me."

That had Barry frowning and Gail, in turn, smiling. Barry must have seen, because he turned to her with a smarmy smile. "You're looking a little bilious, Gail. But then, pregnancy never agreed with you, did it? At least, it never did much for your looks." The smile changing to a sneer, he glanced at Jay and added, "Did Gail tell you she trapped me the same way? Or did she forget to mention that little news item before she forced you down the aisle?"

Slightly nauseated, Gail sucked in a deep breath. Barry always had known how to hit her dead in her insecurities.

Jay looked at him a minute before he spoke. "I didn't think you could possibly be as stupid as you seemed, Summers, but I see I was wrong. You're even more stupid. As for Gail," he reached for her hand and smiled at her, intimately, then glanced back at Barry. "I'm smart enough to know a jewel when I see her. And to hang onto her."

"If you're through making an ass of yourself, Barry," Gail said, "you can go now. I'll get the girls' bags to you after the program."

He started to speak but the lights dimmed, and people began shushing each other, so he left without saying anything else. But the damage had been done, Gail knew.

Because next to Jay, where she couldn't help but overhear every juicy detail, stood Letty Mason, arguably the biggest gossip in Aransas City. By the end of the program it would be all over town that Gail Kincaid was pregnant and that nice young doctor had married her because of it.

Jay spoke in her ear. "Don't give him the power to upset you."

"I'll try," she said, looking up at him and giving him a wan smile. "Thank you. That was really sweet, what you said to him."

The backs of his fingers brushed her cheek. "I meant it," he said.

Their gazes met and held, his serious, compelling. The program started, breaking the connection. Gail drew in a shaky breath, and put a hand on her stomach to calm her jumping nerves. What had just happened?

"DID YOU SEE Roxy's face when they took the picture for the newspaper?" Gail asked Jay on the way home. "She had a death grip on that trophy. I'm not sure I've ever seen her so excited. I'm so proud of her."

"You should be," Jay said. "She had some stiff competition." He glanced over at her, glad to see that though she still looked tired, the pinched exhaustion seemed to have faded since she'd finally gotten off her feet. "Obviously, she gets her brains from your side of the family."

Gail laughed. "Barry actually did quite well in school. That's why it was so funny when you told him he was stupid tonight. I'm not sure anyone ever has."

"It's time someone did." He knew she might not answer, but he asked the question, anyway. "Why did you tell him you were pregnant?"

They pulled into the driveway just then and Jay hit the garage door opener.

Gail sighed. "I didn't tell him. He guessed when I told him we were getting married."

Cheered that she hadn't confided in her ex, Jay got out of the car and opened the kitchen door. "Do you think he'll tell Mel and Roxy?"

Gail shook her head. "Not directly. But since Letty Mason was standing beside you tonight when Barry was talking to us, I'm sure the news is going to be all over town. We're going to have to tell the girls sooner than I'd wanted to. I want them to hear it from me."

"Letty Mason?" He couldn't quite place her, then he remembered last week she'd been in the clinic. "Oh, yeah, the woman who never shuts her mouth. Luckily, she's Tim's patient, not mine."

"Unfortunately, she knows everyone in Aransas City. And she'll tell everyone, too."

He put his hand on her arm. "Does it bother you so much that people will know you're pregnant with my baby?"

"It bothers me that like Barry, they'll think I tricked you into marrying me. I know I shouldn't let it matter, but it does."

He smiled, then leaned down and kissed her mouth lightly. "Then don't worry. Because all they have to do is see us together, and they'll know that's not the case."

She looked as if she wanted to argue the point. She was also pale and exhausted again, so rather than keep her standing, he simply scooped her into his arms. "Come on, you need to go to bed."

"No, I don't. Put me down. We need to talk."

He glanced at her. "On one condition. You lie on the couch and let me get you something for your headache."

Those pretty lips pursed. "How did you know I had a headache?"

"I'm a doctor, remember?" he said, and put her on the couch. "Plus, you've been rubbing your temples every few minutes," he added as he left the room.

A few minutes later, he came back and gave her the medicine and a glass of water, then pulled her feet up and into his lap and started to massage them.

Her eyes closed and she gave a heartfelt groan. "That feels like heaven. Oh, God, I think I love you."

What would it be like if she said those words to him and meant them? But he answered in kind. "Yeah? If I'd known that's all it took, I'd have rubbed your feet a long time ago."

She opened her eyes and stared into his. He wasn't sure what to make of her expression. Surprise, uncertainty, apprehension. Nerves. He smiled, realizing he was making her nervous.

"Your ankles are swollen. Did you sit down at all today at work?" Gail had pretty feet, small and delicate, even if her ankles were swollen to twice their normal size.

Bemused, she gazed at him. "Not really. It's not usually so busy."

"If you can put your feet up, even for half an hour at lunch, it will help you."

"Yes, Doctor." She gave him a cheeky salute.

He smiled and shrugged. "Sorry, occupational hazard. But you need to take better care of yourself."

He began on her legs, his fingers loosening the tight muscles of her calves. Just that little bit of pampering and she already looked much better.

"Jay, about last night." She leaned forward and laid her hand over his. "I'm sorry. You were right, I should have come to you for the money. I just—have a hard time with the money issue. It's important to me to know I can support myself and my daughters."

"I'm not sure what one has to do with the other. I don't want you to quit your job. I just want to help. To share."

"It's hard for me to take money from anyone."

"Even your husband?" he asked softly.

"Even you. I'm sorry."

At least she was talking, even if she wasn't saying exactly what he wanted to hear. "After I cooled off, I got to thinking you might have been right. I might have overreacted." He shot her a sideways glance. "A little."

Her lips quirked, then she sobered. "When you left, I thought you might not come back."

"Why? Is that what Barry did?" he asked quietly. He knew there was something important she wouldn't tell him.

Her eyes closed. "I don't want to talk about Barry. Can we talk about it another time?"

Or never? Would she ever trust him enough to tell him? It cost him, but he didn't press her. Instead, he said, "I left because I didn't want to say things I'd regret. And I knew if I stayed, I would. But it never crossed my mind not to come back."

She leaned forward and kissed him. Placed her hand on his cheek and looked deep into his eyes. "I'm glad you were there tonight."

"Gail." He hesitated, wondering if he were making a mistake, but he asked anyway. "Will you let me pay for Roxy's dance lessons?"

She smiled. "Yes."

"And if you need something in the future, will you let me help you?"

She studied him for a long moment. "What if I promise I'll talk it over with you, and we can decide together."

It wasn't the answer he wanted, but it was a hell of a lot better than having her go to her mother to borrow money. "Sounds like a deal," he said. "And now, let's get you to bed." He got up and picked her up to carry her to the bedroom.

"What if I'm not sleepy?" she asked with a sly smile, winding her arms around his neck.

He laughed. "Good. Because I'm not sleepy, either," he said, and kissed her.

THE NEXT MORNING, Gail went shopping with her mother. Since he didn't work Saturdays this left Jay at loose ends. He decided to go see his brother and maybe talk him into doing a little fishing.

He knocked on the door and hearing Mark call out, entered a scene of bedlam. His brother stood with his back to him, holding the baby while looking up at his son, who perched on top of the refrigerator, brown eyes sparkling with devilment.

"Thank God," Mark said, thrusting the squalling baby into his arms. "I've got to get Max down and I need both hands to do it." He turned back to the refrigerator. "You've got two seconds to come down from there, Max," he said sternly. "I mean it."

The voice that struck fear in the hearts of animal smugglers everywhere didn't seem to have the same effect on Mark's son. Max shook his head. "Don't wanna."

Jay looked down into the little red face of the infant in his arms. "She's got your temper," he told Mark. Sniffing, he detected one reason Miranda wasn't happy. "I think she's dirty."

"Well, change her," his exasperated brother said, hauling his now hysterically screaming son down off the refrigerator and stuffing him under his arm. "Don't just stand there like a moron. I'm going to have a talk with Max."

"But..." Jay gulped. "She's dirty. You know, not just wet." He'd changed a diaper before. He was almost certain he'd changed Max when he was little. Hadn't he?

Mark halted at the door and shot him an evil grin. "Get used to it. Babies are always wet, dirty or hungry." With that, he went out with Max.

Miranda had tuned up to full volume now, shrieking and wailing, her face growing redder by the minute. How could such a tiny thing make such a huge amount of noise? "How hard can it be?" Jay asked her. "Come on, Princess. Uncle Jay will take care of you."

Fifteen minutes later, Miranda rewarded him with a beaming smile. It had only taken him four diapers and half a box of wet wipes, but he had succeeded, by God. He felt pretty good about the whole thing, too. He put the baby in her crib and went to wash his hands.

When he returned, Miranda was kicking her feet in the air and cooing, just as though she hadn't been throwing a walleyed fit only moments before. Marveling at the lightning-quick changes of mood, Jay scooped her up and went into the living room.

Sitting in the rocker, he settled his niece in the crook of his arm. Buddy, Cat's parrot, greeted him with a raucous, "Hello, sucker!"

"You may be right," Jay said, looking down at the gurgling baby. If holding his niece turned his heart to mush, what would it be like to hold his own child in his arms? He suspected he might be even more of a soft touch than Mark.

"That child is going to kill me," Mark said, entering the room a few minutes later. "I'm having a heart attack." He put his hand to his chest. "I'm sure of it."

Jay grinned. "You look healthy enough to me. I take it you left Max contemplating his sins?"

"Hah. I'm sure he's plotting something even more diabolical." Mark shuddered and took a seat on the couch. "But he's in his room, and I think, safe for the moment."

"Where's Cat? Out with the birds?"

Mark frowned. "Getting her hair cut. I told her it looked fine, but she laughed at me. Told me to have fun," he added glumly.

"Too bad. I came by to see if you wanted to go fishing. The redfish are running."

"Fat chance. If I know my wife, she's going to take full advantage of me being home with the kids. God knows what she'll do after the hair thing." He glanced over at Jay and the baby. "I see you figured it out."

"No problem. Did you think I wouldn't?" Miranda grabbed his finger and began gumming it.

"Right. How many diapers did you ruin?"

"Only four."

They both laughed. "So, how's married life treating you?" Mark asked.

"Good." He thought about that and frowned. "Most of the time."

Mark lifted an eyebrow. "Yeah? Trouble in paradise?"

Jay shrugged. If he couldn't talk to his brother, who could he talk to? "Is Cat stubborn about money? I mean, is it a family trait I need to be aware of?"

"Stubborn how? Cat's an accountant." He looked at the parrot, who was playing with his bells. "When she's not rehabbing birds, anyway. She's careful with money."

"No, it's not that. It's—" He broke off, rocking a

bit and thinking how to put it into words. "I don't know, it's like Gail is obsessed with supporting herself, and Mel and Roxy. Hell, I had to twist her arm to get her to let me pay for the household expenses." Remembering that conversation, he snorted. "She actually wanted to split the expenses."

"Oh, I get it." Mark nodded. "It probably has something to do with the way that son of a bitch Barry left them high and dry. After that, anyone would be obsessed with supporting themselves. I know Cat said Gail had hell for a couple of years, until she got her real estate license."

Left them high and dry? "What are you talking about?" Jay asked sharply.

Mark looked surprised. "You know. How he walked out with all the money. Gail had to borrow from her mother until she got on her feet." Mark stared at him, his expression clouding. "You didn't know."

Grimly, Jay shook his head. "No. Gail forgot to mention that little detail. You want to fill me in? Since my wife didn't see fit to."

"Oh, man." Mark shoved his hands through his hair. "Why hasn't she told you?"

"That's easy. Because she doesn't trust me." So that's what she'd been hiding. "Go on, Mark."

"I don't know much more than that. She came home one day and bam—he'd left with damn near everything they had. She didn't see a dime from the bastard until he moved back to town, two years after he'd left."

That explained a lot. "Thanks for the info. Too bad my wife didn't consider telling me this."

"Maybe she thought you already knew. I did."

"Believe me, she doesn't think that." He shook his head. "I asked her point-blank, last night. No, she kept it from me deliberately." Because, once again, she didn't trust him. At least now he had a better idea why she found it hard to trust. Or maybe impossible to trust.

Miranda began fussing. Jay put her on his shoulder and patted her back.

"Do you want me to take her?"

"No, I'm fine." He rubbed her back and she quieted. "But if she dirties another diaper, she's all yours."

Mark laughed. "Like I said, you need to get used to it." They were quiet a moment, then he asked, "What are you going to do?"

"I don't know. Hope I can get Gail to trust me enough to tell me. Confronting her wouldn't do any good."

"Probably not." He paused a moment. "Have you told her you're in love with her?"

"No." He glanced at his brother, now smiling at him sympathetically. "I just figured it out the other night. How did you know?"

"Been there, done that. I know the symptoms." Mark got up and walked over to the rocking chair. "Come here, sweetheart," he said, taking the baby from Jay.

He cuddled her a minute, then looked at his

brother. "Go home and tell her, Jay. Women really go nuts over that kind of thing."

"I'll think about it," he said. "Thanks, Mark."

Could it be that simple? Jay wondered as he drove home. Would telling Gail he loved her solve the problem? Somehow, he couldn't imagine that it would, regardless of what his brother said.

It might even make things worse.

CHAPTER SEVENTEEN

GAIL HELPED MEL back into bed following another episode of dry heaves. "Are you sure you didn't get sick over at your Daddy's, honey?" It seemed odd to Gail that the child had yet to actually throw up.

"No," Mel wailed. "I told you I didn't. It hurts, Mommy. Make it stop." She rolled her small body into a ball and began to cry again.

That's it, Gail decided. She was married to a doctor, for heaven's sake. It would be stupid not to call him. She passed her hand over Mel's forehead. Hotter than just a few minutes before, she thought. "I'll be right back, sweetie. You just rest a minute."

She had just punched in the number when Jay walked in. "Oh, good," she said with relief, hanging up. "I was just about to call your cell phone."

"What's wrong? Are you okay?" He tossed his keys down and crossed swiftly to her side.

"I'm fine. But Mel's not feeling well. I just brought her back from Barry's. He said she's been complaining of a stomachache off and on since last night."

She'd asked Barry why he hadn't called her the night before. She knew full well that if Barry thought the kids had any kind of communicable disease, he'd send them back to her as quickly as possible.

As usual, he'd shrugged her concern aside. "It's a stomachache, Gail, not the bubonic plague," he'd said. "She'll get over it."

"Do you want me to take a look at her?" Jay asked her.

"Would you mind?"

Apparently, he didn't think that worth commenting. "I'll get my bag. Hang on, it's in the car."

When he returned he asked, "Where is she, in her room?"

Nodding, Gail followed him. "Thanks. I know it's probably nothing, but her stomachaches don't usually last this long. She's been having dry heaves, but she hasn't thrown up. She says she didn't get sick at Barry's either." Except for one time with the flu, Gail couldn't remember another stomach problem so severe.

"Did you take her temperature?"

They could hear Mel crying as they approached the room. "Yes. It's a hundred and one."

"Could be the flu," he said, entering the room. "Hi, Mel. Your mom says you have a stomachache." He sat beside her and put a hand to her forehead. "Are you sick to your stomach?"

Mel nodded, her breath catching, tears trembling on her eyelashes. "Wanna throw up. Only I can't."

"Will you let me feel your tummy?"

Mel remained curled in a fetal ball. "It hurts."

"I know, baby." He managed to get her to raise

her head enough so he could put his fingers on the glands of her throat. "Glands aren't swollen. How about letting me look in your throat?"

Mel allowed that, and also let him listen to her chest with his stethoscope. With a good deal of coaxing and persuading on both Gail's and Jay's part, they finally managed to get her stretched out on her back so he could examine her thoroughly.

Jay pressed gently on her stomach in various places, asking each time if it hurt. She complained that it did during the entire procedure. Gail didn't really see that it was getting them anywhere. Then he pressed on her lower right abdomen and she screamed.

Gail's heart almost stopped at Mel's cry of pain.

Jay's eyes lifted to meet hers. "Right lower quadrant abdominal pain is a classic symptom of appendicitis. So is the nausea she's been experiencing." He began putting away his instruments and continued talking. "We need to get her to the hospital, get a white count, and have a surgeon examine her. I know a good surgeon over at Varner Memorial. I'll call him and let him know we're coming."

His glance fell to Mel's face and he smiled reassuringly. "Your mom and I are taking you to the hospital, Mel. They'll make you feel better real soon."

"Okay," Mel said in a tiny voice. Then she closed her eyes and curled up again.

"Appendicitis?" Gail repeated.

"I think it's likely." Jay rose and took her arm,

walking her toward the door. "Throw some stuff together and get Mel ready to go."

"We're going to the hospital? You're calling a surgeon?" Stunned, Gail put a hand to her throat as his words finally started to sink in. "Do you really think she needs surgery?" Neither of her girls had ever had an operation. Or anything significant wrong with them.

"It's a possibility." His arm came around her and he gave her a brief, bracing hug. "But it's not a certainty by any means. There are other things that can cause similar symptoms. The flu, for one. We'll know more once we get her to the hospital and run some tests."

"Are you calling an ambulance?" She marveled that she could speak at all, much less calmly. Maybe it was the surreal feel to the situation that enabled her to. She felt as if she were wading through mud. She couldn't think, couldn't seem to function. Surgery. That was the only thought that registered. Her baby might need an appendectomy.

Jay glanced back at Mel, frowned, then shook his head. "No, we'll get there much sooner driving. Remember when Cat went into labor?"

Gail stood there, staring at him. He took hold of her upper arms and squeezed gently, his gaze calm and reassuring. "She's going to be fine, Gail. But the sooner we get her to the hospital, the better we'll all feel."

She gave a jerky nod and sucked in her breath. Her

spine straightened. Mel needed her now. If she had to, she'd fall apart later.

GAIL STOOD just outside the hospital entrance, talking to Barry on her cell phone. "Yes, we're at the hospital. Yes, the close one." Not that she could remember the name of the damn place right now. She looked on the wall. "Varner Memorial, that's the one. The surgeon says it's appendicitis and they want to operate as soon as possible. I can't talk any more, Barry. I have to get back to Mel while they prep her for surgery."

"Surgery? Are they sure? This is Kincaid's doing, isn't it?"

Gail squeezed her eyes shut and prayed for patience. "Jay thought we should bring her in. And according to the surgeon, he was right. Doctor McGuire himself told me Mel needs an emergency appendectomy. I'll call you as soon as the operation is over. Tell Roxy I love her."

"I'm coming to the hospital. I'll take Roxy to your mother's place."

Barry, coming to the hospital? The thought boggled her mind. "Since when do you show up at hospitals?" she couldn't help asking.

"She's my child, too, Gail. I'll be there as soon as I can."

We'll see, Gail thought cynically.

Forty-five minutes later, Gail sat in the hospital waiting room, anxiously awaiting word of the operation's progress. Since they had taken Mel in only minutes before, she knew it would be a while. Jay sat beside her, holding her hand. She took comfort from that, and also from his calm manner.

Intellectually, she knew an appendectomy was a common operation and most people recovered quite easily. Emotionally, what she knew didn't matter squat. Her baby was in there, having surgery. She was a wreck.

"Dr. McGuire seems awfully young," she finally ventured, trying to do something to break the cycle of *what ifs* going on in her mind. The baby-faced surgeon had talked to them both, though he'd spoken to Jay in more technical terms. "Very nice. But so...young."

Jay smiled. "He's not as young as he looks, and he's had a lot of experience. No telling how many appendectomies he's performed." He brought her hand to his lips and kissed it. "If I had to have surgery, he's who I'd want to do it. Mel is in good hands, Gail. I promise you that."

"I know." If Jay hadn't trusted the man, she knew he wouldn't have put Mel in his care. "I'm just scared. She's never had surgery before. Neither of the girls have had anything major wrong. And Mel's so...little. She looked so young, lying on that gurney."

Jay put his arm around her and hugged her, rubbing his hand up and down her arm. "She'll be fine, Gail. But I guess it's useless to tell you to try not to worry. You will, until the operation is over."

She looked at him, trying to gauge his mood. "You're not worried? Not at all?"

"Sure, I'm concerned, because it's Mel. I wish she didn't need the operation, but since she does, I'm glad she's in good hands." He hugged her again. "McGuire's good, Gail. It helps me to know that."

Barry entered the waiting room a few minutes after that. Even though he'd said he was coming, Gail hadn't quite believed it. But it was Barry, even if he didn't look like himself. His normally perfectly groomed hair stood up in spikes, as if he'd run his hands through it, and his eyes were wild with emotion. Gail had grown so accustomed to his expression of boredom, she hadn't realized he could look, or be, so rattled. It was certainly outside her experience with her ex-husband.

"I've been looking all over the damn hospital for you. Is Mel in surgery yet?"

"They started a few minutes ago," Jay said. "We'll get periodic calls from the OR updating us on their progress."

Barry sat down heavily in the chair on the other side of Gail. Elbows on knees, he put his head in his hands. "My God, surgery. I just thought she had a stomachache. How can she need surgery?"

Gail felt a stirring of pity, surprising herself. "A stomachache is one of the symptoms."

"In a lot of cases, appendicitis mimics the flu," Jay added.

Barry raised his head and met Gail's gaze, his own guilt-ridden. "I should have brought her in last night.

I told her to quit whining. If I'd known it was this serious—'' He broke off, apparently overcome.

Tentatively, Gail reached out and patted his arm. "I didn't know it was, either, until Jay looked at her." Of course, she'd suspected, but there was no need to rub that in to Barry. For once, she honestly believed Barry loved his daughters.

"If you'd brought her in last night, it's most likely they would have sent her home," Jay said. "The pain probably didn't localize to her right side until this morning. Appendicitis takes a while to confirm. Sometimes you end up with several trips to the hospital before they can confirm the diagnosis."

Barry looked at Jay, his eyes pleading for reassurance. "She's not—I didn't make it worse by not bringing her to the hospital?"

"No. Now, if her appendix had ruptured, it would have been much more serious, but we got her here before that happened. And she would have been in more severe pain if that had been the case." He paused a moment, then squeezed Gail's hand. "They should be calling soon with an update. We would have heard by now if there had been a complication of that magnitude."

"Thank God," Barry said, getting up and walking over to the window. He stood there a moment, his back to them.

Gail stared at him, then looked at Jay. "Who would have ever thought?" she murmured. "He really does love her."

"It's impossible not to," Jay said. "Both of them."

Gail smiled and squeezed his hand. "It is, isn't it?"

"Call for you, Dr. Kincaid," the volunteer manning the phones said some time later.

Barry came to stand by Gail while Jay took the call.

"Everything's going smoothly," Jay told them on his return. "The appendix did need to come out, but there are no complications. They said they'd call again when they're nearing the end."

"Did they say how much longer?" Gail asked.

"Half an hour or so. Then she'll go to recovery. It will be an hour and a half or two hours before you can see her."

"But it's looking good," Gail said.

He smiled at her. "It's looking great," he agreed.

Barry put his hands in his pockets. "Kincaid, I—" Shifting uncomfortably, he broke off, then started again. "Thanks for getting her here. I appreciate it." He held out a hand.

Jay shook hands easily. "You don't have to thank me. I care about Mel and Roxy, too. They're great kids."

Barry didn't seem to know how to respond to that. He cleared his throat and said, "I'm going for a cup of coffee. Either of you want anything?"

"No, thanks," Jay said.

Gail declined, as well, waiting until Barry had left before turning to Jay. "I had to see it to believe it.

Barry, thanking you for bringing Mel in.'' She shook her head in wonder.

"Yeah, it was a bit weird." He rubbed a hand over his chin and smiled.

"That was a nice thing you did."

"What?"

"Not making him feel worse about Mel. Was it true, what you said?"

"Yes." He shrugged. "Most parents would have done the same thing he did. I didn't see the point in making him feel worse than he already did. He obviously loves Mel, and is worried about her." He was silent a moment, then added, "But I still think he's a jerk."

Gail laughed, surprised she could. "I do, too. And I doubt the change of heart is permanent." Closing her eyes, she sighed and leaned her head back against the wall. After a moment she opened them to look at Jay. "I'm so glad you're here with me. You've helped me stay sane."

"I'm glad, too." He smiled, then cupped her cheek, his gaze turning solemn as he looked at her. "Gail—" He started to speak, then apparently thought better of it. "Never mind. It will keep."

JAY HADN'T THOUGHT it would be so hard to find the right time to tell Gail he loved her. But clearly, when she was totally consumed with her sick child wouldn't have been the ideal time. And a week later, after Mel had been home for days and life was getting back to normal, he still hadn't found a good time.

Barry had been coming around a lot more than Jay was comfortable with. He wasn't sure what to think about the "new" Barry—the one who loved his daughters and was nice to Gail and even pleasant to Jay. But Jay did know one thing.

He didn't trust him. The man obviously still wanted Gail back, and had no compunction about using his daughters to help him achieve that goal. He might have been grateful to Jay for taking care of his daughter, but that didn't mean Barry liked Jay any more than Jay liked him. They were rivals, pure and simple.

The problem was, Barry being around more made Mel and Roxy happy, and at this point, Jay would do anything to make the girls happy. Mel's operation had brought home to him how much he loved Gail's daughters. He'd fallen for them as quickly and strongly as he had for their mother. So he endured Barry, and told himself Gail had too much sense to go back to a man who'd made her so unhappy.

Especially not when she had a husband who treated her right. And who loved her, even though she didn't know it.

Not that Gail seemed interested in going back to Barry. Still, the whole situation made him uneasy.

Jay walked into their bedroom after work one day shortly before Thanksgiving, and heard Gail in her closet, cussing. A wry smile twisted his mouth. Tonight didn't look like the perfect night, either.

As he neared the closet, a pair of jeans came hurtling out and hit him in the face. "Damn it! Nothing fits!"

"I think that's why they invented maternity clothes," he said, leaning in the doorway and watching her with a grin. "Good aim, by the way." He dangled the jeans from his hand. "What should I do with these?"

"Burn them," she said, hands on hips. "I can't believe I'm so fat." She glanced down at herself and grimaced. "I'm only three months along. What will I look like at six months if I look like this now?"

"You're not fat. You look great," he said, eyeing her appreciatively. She wore only a white lacy bra which barely contained her breasts and a tiny pair of turquoise bikini panties. So maybe her stomach wasn't flat like it had been before the pregnancy, and her waist was definitely thicker, but Jay didn't think it hurt her looks at all. In fact, he was getting hard just looking at her.

"But maybe I should make a closer examination. To put your mind at rest." He stepped inside and closed the closet door behind him. "You haven't kissed me hello," he said softly.

Gail tilted her head, considering him. "Somehow I don't think kissing is all you have in mind."

He pulled her into his arms. "You're a very smart woman. I like that about you," he said, and lowered his mouth to hers.

Her lips met his, her tongue slipped into his mouth with a slow, sensuous rhythm. Against his mouth she murmured, "The girls are home. And awake."

"I'll be quick," he promised, popping her bra

open. Her breasts spilled out and he groaned, filling his hands with them. "Real quick."

She laughed and wrapped herself around him.

"Mommy." Mel knocked on the closet door. "Are you in there?"

Jay gave another, even more heartfelt groan. He wanted to yell. The child had perfect timing. To demolish his sex life, that is.

Gail met his gaze, her eyes dancing. "What do you need, honey?" she asked, a tremor in her voice.

"Nothing. I was just looking for you."

Why me, God? he asked silently, closing his eyes.

"Is Jay in there, too?"

"Yes," he said, opening his eyes and gritting his teeth. Gail was stifling giggles, making her body vibrate against his. It didn't help cool his raging libido one little bit. "Mel, do me a favor and scram."

"What are you doing, Mel?" he heard Roxy say. "Why are you standing in front of Mommy's closet?"

Great. Now both of the little angels were out there. This just wasn't his day.

"Mommy and Jay are in there," Mel said. "And they won't come out. Mommy, what are you doing?"

"Silly," Roxy scoffed with the superiority of a ten-year-old. "They're kissing, of course."

Now giggling uncontrollably, Gail leaned against him. Jay touched his forehead to hers. "I'm cursed," he murmured. "I must have been an ax murderer in a previous life."

Gail laughed out loud.

"Girls," he said, raising his voice so they could hear above their mother's laughter. "Scram."

After much giggling and whispering, the noise faded away and the bedroom door slammed shut.

"Kind of a mood killer, aren't they?" Gail asked, her eyes still bright with humor.

He unbuckled and unzipped his pants, shoved them down over his hips, taking his briefs along with them. "I'm alone in a closet with a nearly naked, beautiful woman who happens to be my wife. Nothing less than a hurricane is going to kill my mood."

She looked down at his throbbing erection and smiled. "I can see that."

"So. What about your mood?"

In answer, she wiggled out of her panties, wrapped her arms around his neck and kissed him. He lifted her up, sank inside of her in one fluid drive, groaning at the feel of her, warm, wet and pulsing around him. He braced them against the door, pushing inside of her and withdrawing, as slow as he could make it.

Her legs tightened around him, her arms clung tightly, twined around his neck. Her head fell back against the door, but her eyes stayed open and locked on his as he took them both deeper with each plunge. She started to convulse, and all hope of control or taking it slowly fled. With her muscles squeezing him, his vision darkening, he gave a last solid thrust and came as her eyes went blind and her orgasm ripped through her.

He didn't know how long it was before he started breathing again. He could barely stand, probably couldn't have at all if they hadn't been supported by the door. "Gail."

Her eyes opened, blue and dreamy. "Hmm. That was really, really nice."

"I know this isn't the most romantic place in the world—" he began. *You're in a closet, for God's sake,* the rational part of his brain lectured him. *Don't do it now. Women like romance, soft music, candlelight. You're in a damn closet.* "But I'm really tired of waiting."

"Waiting for what?" She looked puzzled. "Do you want to let me down?"

He shook his head. "Not yet." He wanted to be inside her when he told her for the first time. "I love you, Gail."

Her eyes widened. Beautiful, deep blue and filling with tears.

"Why are you crying?" Not the reaction he'd hoped for.

"Oh, Jay." She kissed him, then drew back to look at him, smiling through her tears. "Because I love you, too."

CHAPTER EIGHTEEN

"I THINK IT'S TIME to tell the girls about the baby," Gail said, later that evening.

Jay and Gail were sitting together on the couch, ostensibly watching TV, but in reality just cuddling. He couldn't remember ever being as content.

"It's up to you," he said, brushing a hand over her hair. "But I thought you wanted to wait a little longer." He certainly did. It made him nervous to think about their reaction. Especially Roxy's. Things were good between them now. Why risk her getting upset?

"Well, I did, but Letty Mason made that impossible. Remember I told you she'd spread the news?"

"Yeah." Still playing with her hair, he added, "I take it she did."

"Oh, yeah, big time. Today at the grocery store, four people asked me if I'm pregnant. The girls are bound to hear it, and I'd rather they hear the news from us."

"You're right." Unfortunately. "Are you going to tell them now? Do you want me to take a drive or something?"

"No, silly." She pressed her cheek to his, then

drew back and smiled at him. "I want to tell them together."

If he hadn't already loved her, he'd have fallen for her right then and there. "You told them about the marriage by yourself."

"This is different. We're a family now. We should tell them together."

It was true, he realized. Sometime in the past few weeks, they'd become a family. A different kind of family than he'd ever had before. He'd never had what Gail and the girls had given him. He didn't feel excluded any longer. He felt as if they really belonged together now. All four of them.

But he was still nervous as hell about how Mel and Roxy would take the news.

Gail left the room to call the girls in. When she returned, she took one look at Jay and said, "It's not an execution."

He recognized what he'd said to her at their wedding. His lips twitched when he answered. "Then why does it feel like one?"

The girls tripped in and sat on the couch beside their mother. Jay elected to stand by the fireplace. And sweat. If he'd been wearing a collared shirt, he'd have been loosening it. As it was, there was nothing he could do to ease the tightness in his throat.

"Jay and I have something to tell you," Gail said. She gave him an encouraging smile, then looked at the girls. "We're going to have a baby."

They both stared at her. After a long moment, Mel spoke. "How come you're not fat, Mommy? When

Aunt Cat was pregnant she was humongous,'' she said, holding her little arms out to demonstrate a huge belly.

Gail laughed. "That won't happen until later. The baby isn't coming until June."

They digested that news for a moment. "Will we get to play with it? Like we do Max and Miranda?" Mel persisted.

"Of course. Only the baby will be your brother or sister, instead of your cousin."

Roxy had yet to speak. Jay cleared his throat and took the plunge. "What do you think, Roxy?"

She turned to him. When she smiled, his heart tripped. "It's okay, I guess. I like babies. Aunt Cat lets me help her with Miranda. It's fun."

"Yeah, but you gotta learn to change poopy diapers," practical-minded Mel said. "That's not fun."

They all laughed at that.

"Do we still get our own rooms?" Roxy asked suspiciously. "Because if we don't, I think Mel should share with the baby. I'm the oldest, so I should have a room of my own."

Naturally, Mel protested loudly against that idea until Gail hushed them both. "We're going to turn the guest room into a nursery for the baby. So yes, you'll both still have your own rooms."

"I think this calls for a celebration," Jay said. "How does ice cream sound?"

Roxy's and Mel's eyes lit up. "Chocolate chip!" Roxy said.

"Chocolate," Mel said. "I want chocolate."

They began arguing over which flavor was best. Gail got up and walked over to him, slid her arm around his waist and leaned her head against his shoulder. "See, that wasn't so bad." She turned laughing eyes up to his. "And the ice cream bribe didn't hurt a bit, either."

"I'm a firm believer that ice cream could solve a lot of the world's problems."

Life is good, Jay thought. And sometimes it's damn near perfect.

THE FOLLOWING MONDAY, Gail was late getting home from work, so she chose to make her standby quickie meal, macaroni and cheese. As she put the ingredients together, she thought of that first meal Jay had eaten with her and the girls, when she'd also made macaroni and cheese. She hadn't dreamed then that in a few months she and Jay would be married, expecting a baby, and unbelievably happy.

Jay came in a little while later. "Dinner will be ready in about twenty minutes," she said, and smiled at him. "It's macaroni and cheese, I'm afraid. I was running late."

"Fine." He tossed his keys on the counter. "I'm going to change."

Puzzled, she stared after him. For the first time since they'd been married, he hadn't kissed her when he came home from work.

A short while later, they all sat down to dinner. Excited about their upcoming vacation for Thanksgiving, the girls chattered about school. Jay didn't talk, but ate his meal in silence. Gail didn't think he heard a word the girls said, which wasn't like him. What had happened to make him so distant?

"I sold a great property today," Gail said after the girls had run down. "The commission is my largest yet."

Jay finally looked up, his gaze flat and lifeless. "That's good."

A little miffed at his lack of interest, she tried again. "I'm taking the Friday after Thanksgiving off. What about you? Do you have to work?"

"Yes."

Something was definitely going on with him. "Did something happen at work today?"

He shot her an irritated glance. "It was work. Something always happens."

"Is it anything you want to talk about?"

"No," he said abruptly and got to his feet. He carried his plate over to the sink, rinsed it off and put it in the dishwasher. Then he left the room without another word.

Surprised, Gail and the girls looked at each other. "Well," she said, for lack of anything better.

"Do you think Jay's in a bad mood, Mommy?" Roxy asked, turning questioning eyes to her. "I think he is. He was kind of grumpy."

"Yes, he was."

"I've never seen him be grumpy like that."

"Neither have I," Gail admitted.

"You should go talk to him, Mommy," Mel said.

"You always make us feel better when we're in bad moods."

Roxy nodded agreement.

"I think you're right. Something's obviously bothering him. Will you two do the dishes?" Gail asked, rising.

"Can we have cookies?" Roxy asked.

"After you do the dishes, Cookie Monster."

Gail didn't have far to go to find him. He'd gone out back, but instead of playing with the puppies, he was sitting in a chair, doing nothing. Except brooding, she thought.

She crossed her arms and hugged herself. "It's chilly out here."

"Then go back inside."

Insulted, she stared at him. Then her sense of humor kicked in. He certainly knew how to stop conversation. "I will. To get a coat. I'll be back."

When she returned a few minutes later, he hadn't moved a muscle. She took the other chair and said, "What happened at work today?"

He turned his head and glared at her. Really, she thought, there was no other word for it.

"I don't want to talk about it."

Gail nodded. "Yes, I sort of got that idea when you stomped out of the kitchen."

"Then accept it. Go back in, Gail."

"I can't," she said simply.

"Why are you nagging me about this?"

She put her hand on his arm. "Because I love you

and I'm not going to let you close yourself off when you're hurting. Talk to me, Jay.''

For a moment he looked at her. She recognized the expression in his eyes with a start of surprise. Not anger. Grief. He was grieving something, or someone. ''Tell me,'' she said again. ''Please, Jay, talk to me.''

He shook his head, then fell silent, apparently gathering his thoughts. ''I diagnosed one of my patients with a glioblastoma today.'' He glanced at her and added, ''That's a malignant brain tumor.''

''Is it fatal?'' she asked hesitantly. But she knew the answer. Why else would he be so upset?

He nodded. ''Virtually always. He'll go to MD Anderson Cancer Center in Houston and they'll treat him, but unless a miracle happens, he'll die.''

''I'm sorry. I can't imagine having to tell someone he's dying.''

''It's part of being a doctor. Something you have to learn to accept. And you do, because you tell yourself for every patient you lose, you'll save one, too.''

He paused, closed his eyes and added, very quietly, ''But some of them get to you more than others.''

Obviously, this one had gotten to him. ''Do you know why this one is bothering you so much?''

''Yeah.'' His expression grim, he looked at her. ''He's thirty-two years old, Gail. He came in today hoping and praying I'd tell him his symptoms were nothing, or at least, something minor we could treat. Instead, I as good as gave him a death sentence.''

She squeezed his hand and waited for him to continue.

"I asked him to bring his wife, so he brought her and their baby with him. His wife's a pretty little thing. Reminds me of Cat. The baby looks like his father. He's a year old."

Silently, she held his hand.

"The two of them sat there, holding hands, the baby in his lap, while I explained what he had and recommended they go to Houston right away. I'd already talked to the specialist there, and I knew he'd make time for him. They asked a lot of questions. Some patients do, some of them don't want to know anything."

"I would want to know as much as I could," Gail said.

He nodded. "This couple did, too. Then he asked me his odds of surviving. I knew he would ask me. You can tell which ones need to know. Just like I knew if I didn't tell him, he'd go look it up on the Internet, and God knows, that would be worse. Besides, as his doctor it's my responsibility to tell him. So I told him the truth. The mean survival length after diagnosis is eight to ten months."

"Less than a year?"

He nodded grimly. "After two years, the survival rate is ten percent. So there are survivors, but damn few of them. The doctors will operate, they'll give him radiation and chemo, but the odds are overwhelming the tumor will come back."

"Why did you send them to Houston, instead of Corpus Christi? Wouldn't it be easier on them to be closer to home?"

"Because MD Anderson has a neurosurgeon who's the best in the state. If there's going to be a miracle, this is the man who'll make it happen. It's also got one of the best cancer centers in the country. I want him to have the best possible care."

"He already does. He has you."

He smiled a little and shook his head. "I can't do anything for him except diagnose him and send him to a specialist. The neurosurgeon's the one who has a chance of saving him."

"But thanks to you, he's going to have the best shot at living." She got up, put her arms around him and hugged him. "That poor couple. I can't imagine what they must be feeling. What do you think they'll do?"

"I know what I'd do. I'd go home and play with the baby and then put the baby to sleep so I could make love to my wife. And I'd do my best to forget the whole thing. At least for one night."

"I can make you forget," Gail said softly. "If you'll let me."

He smiled at her and pulled her into his lap. Wrapping his arms around her, he sighed when she laid her head against his shoulder. "We're so lucky," he said. "We have each other. The girls." He placed his hand on her stomach. "The baby."

"I know. Are you feeling guilty about that?"

"Not guilty." he shook his head. "It's just hard, when it's someone so young. Someone with so much to live for."

She kissed him.

"You were right," he said, after a moment. "I needed to talk."

"I know." She smiled. "Mel and Roxy told me to come talk to you."

"Smart girls."

"Come inside with me. Make love with me."

"An even smarter mother," he said, and kissed her.

THEY SPENT THANKSGIVING day with Gail's family, over at her mother's, since it was the only place large enough to hold the entire clan. The day after that, a cold, rainy, dismal November day, Barry took the girls, since he had the day off. With Jay working, that left Gail free to do some serious planning for the nursery.

Early morning found her checking out books of wallpaper from a home improvement store in Corpus Christi, making it back home just before the storm really loosened up. By midmorning, her head was whirling. She sat in the floor of the soon-to-be nursery, leafing through book after book and listening to the crash of thunder outside. Too many choices, she thought. How would she ever decide? Jay would just have to help her. He didn't have any problems being decisive.

The doorbell rang. Thankfully, she closed the book and went to answer it. She opened it to a blast of cold, wet air. "Barry? What in the world are you doing out in this weather? Are the girls all right?"

He walked inside, stripping off his drenched raincoat and handing it to Gail. "Yeah, it's a real monsoon. Believe me, if I didn't have to be out, I wouldn't be. The streets aren't flooding yet, but the water's rising.''

Gail hung his coat on the rack and he continued. ''Mel's pitching a fit about some damn PlayStation game or other. Why she can't play with the ones we have at my place, I don't know.''

''You're spoiling her, Barry.'' Something she'd never really thought to see, but Barry had changed since Mel's illness. It seemed to have awakened in him feelings she hadn't realized he had.

''I know.'' He looked a little sheepish. ''But it's not that big a deal to come get it. I left them with Lee Anne,'' he said, referring to his neighbor's teenage daughter, one of the girls' favorite sitters.

Gail sighed. ''You should have brought Mel. Her games are strung out all over the house, but I guess we can start in her room. Which one did you say she wanted?''

Barry told her and followed her into Mel's room. ''Start there,'' Gail told him, pointing at the TV stand. ''Maybe we'll get lucky.'' She looked under the bed and pulled a large box out, filled with a variety of things, including video games.

''So, where's Kincaid?''

''He had to work.'' She dug around in the box and pulled out one of her own shoes. Now what was her shoe doing under Mel's bed? she wondered, before she saw the teeth marks on it. Ah, this one had survived the puppy assault.

''Good.'' Barry abandoned the TV stand and came

to sit on the bed. "I've been wanting to see you alone."

Alarmed, Gail glanced up at him. "Why?" Surely he wouldn't bring up them getting back together again. Hadn't she been clear enough the last time?

He leaned forward, forearms on his knees and caught her gaze with his. "Because I had something to say to you I can't say in front of your husband."

"Barry, I don't think—"

"Just let me say it. I'm still in love with you, Gail."

She stared at him, realizing he believed it. "You were never in love with me. But that's beside the point," she added when he protested. "We've been through this. You and I are never going to get back together. I'm married to another man. I'm happy with him."

He laced his fingers together and looked at his hands. "I thought—I thought you married him because of the baby. So there could still be a chance for me." His eyes lifted to hers. "We have two daughters together, Gail. Don't they count for something?"

"The girls aren't enough to make a marriage, Barry. That's all we have. And I'm not in love with you."

"I know I screwed up, Gail, but I've changed a lot since then."

Maybe, Gail thought, but she would never trust him. "For your sake, I hope that's true. Because I don't think you're ever going to be happy until you do change." She got up, stood looking at him a moment. She wanted their relationship to be better, not combative, because it would be easier on all of them, especially Roxy and Mel. She did not, however, want to go through this scene whenever she happened to be alone with him. "It doesn't matter, Barry. I'm in love with Jay. And he's in love with me."

He nodded heavily. "I was afraid of that. When I saw you two together at the spelling bee, I think I knew. That's why I said what I did."

"Barry, you have to accept that I'm married, and that you and I are over. I don't want to go through this again. Not ever."

He closed his eyes, passed a hand over his forehead before he opened them and looked at her. "All right. I've had my say. I won't bother you again."

Knowing Barry, she wasn't sure she believed him. But she might as well pretend she did. "Good. That's settled, then. Now, I'm going to check in the den closet for Mel's game. You look in the closet here, okay?"

She didn't think she'd tell Jay about that conversation. He wasn't likely to be happy about it, and besides, she'd handled it. No reason to upset him and make things even more strained between him and her ex-husband.

Opening the closet door, she glanced around. She thought she remembered packing a box of games. Sure enough, she spied it on the top shelf, perched on top of another box. She dragged a step stool over to the closet and by standing on her tiptoes, managed to wedge the box out. Arms full, she stepped backwards, her foot missing the bottom rung. The cardboard box went flying and she landed flat on her back on the hard wood floor.

Stunned, she lay there a moment, trying to catch her breath.

"Gail?" Barry called out. "What happened? I heard a crash."

She tried to answer, but couldn't get the words out. *You're okay,* she told herself. *Just a little spill. Nothing major.*

"Gail?" Barry stood over her. "My God, are you all right? What happened?" He squatted beside her and continued asking questions, though she couldn't speak for some minutes.

Finally, she was able to say, "I—missed the step. I'm okay."

"Here, let me help you," he said, giving her a hand and pulling her into a sitting position. "Why didn't you call me? You shouldn't be climbing on ladders when you're pregnant."

"I know." And Jay had said the same thing. But she hadn't even thought about it, she'd just done it automatically. Besides, dizziness hadn't caused the fall. General klutziness had. Gingerly, she got to her feet. "No harm done." Her leg, where it had tangled in the stool throbbed, and her butt still smarted, but at least she hadn't broken anything.

"I'm not usually so clumsy. I'm going to sit down for a minute. Why don't you look in that box I pulled down? There should be some video games in it."

Barry did as she suggested. A short search produced what he'd come for. "Here it is." He shot her an irritable glance. "If you'd keep those games in some kind of order, it would be a lot easier to find them."

Since Gail had never been neat enough to suit him, it was an old refrain, but she didn't rise to the bait. "You're welcome," she said acerbically. "Let yourself out, okay?"

Barry went to the coat rack, pulled his raincoat off and shrugged into it. "You're all right, aren't you?" he asked with obvious reluctance.

Gail smiled, knowing the last thing he wanted was to be around an ailing, pregnant woman. Self-centered to the end, she thought. "I'm fine. Tell the girls I love them."

After Barry left, she debated whether to call Jay or not. On the one hand, she didn't seem any the worse for her tumble. But she knew talking to him would make her feel better. That decided her. She got up to get the phone. Midway to the kitchen a sharp cramp hit her in the stomach. Gasping with pain, she doubled over. Her arm crossed protectively over her stomach as she waited. An endless time later, the pain eased and she was able to straighten.

Oh, God, no. Please, don't let it be the baby.

CHAPTER NINETEEN

OH, MY GOD, I'M LOSING THE BABY. The very idea paralyzed Gail with fear and panic.

With a major effort, she forced herself to calm down. One pain didn't mean anything, she told herself. Surely the cramp had been a fluke. People didn't miscarry from a fall like the one she'd had. That happened only on soap operas, didn't it?

Still shaky, but feeling a little better, she walked into the kitchen. If she could just talk to Jay, he would help her calm down. He'd know what to do. Grabbing the cordless phone, she punched in the number and discovered the line was dead. Swearing, she took her cell phone out of her purse, only to find it wasn't working either.

Neither of these events should have been a surprise, because the phones often went out during storms. A tremendous crack of thunder sounded, and Gail glanced out the window, watching the wind blow a huge plastic trash can down the street. The storm might not carry hurricane force winds with it, but it was no gentle shower, either.

Knowing Jay was likely to come home for lunch, she decided to wait and tell him what had happened then. There was no sense getting all bent out of shape over nothing. She started for the nursery and had almost reached it when another cramp hit. Tears, as much from fear as pain, filled her eyes. She could do nothing but wait it out, and though it only lasted a minute or less, the wait seemed endless.

Finally, the pain eased, and she was left gasping and frightened. The second cramp had decided her. If she couldn't reach Jay by phone, she'd just go to the clinic. Without much hope, she tried the phones again, and when that failed, grabbed her coat, purse and keys and left the house. She gave a fleeting thought to the puppies, locked in the laundry room because of the weather, but decided they'd be all right.

Once in her van and on the road, she discovered the storm was even worse than she'd thought. She crept along, dodging branches and debris, hardly able to see through the torrential downpour. A nerve-racking fifteen minutes later, she pulled up to the clinic.

Only to find it shut up tighter than a drum.

She got back in the car and pressed her fingers to her eyes, fighting back tears. Obviously, they were either at lunch, or closed because of the storm. Either way, she couldn't afford to sit around waiting for someone to come back. If she went back home on the chance Jay was there, she only put herself farther away from the hospital. And if he wasn't there, she'd have wasted that much more time.

She felt another twinge in her stomach. Not a pain,

but a definite twinge of discomfort. It dawned on her in horror that she might be starting premature labor. Drawing in a deep breath, she started the car.

SHE DROVE TO THE HOSPITAL in the teeth of the storm. The rain hurtled down, dumping massive sheets of water she could barely see through. Howling wind buffeted the car, causing it to shake as she crawled along the highway. Even before she'd reached the highway, she'd begun to regret her choice, but by then she knew she'd come too far to go back.

The drive to the clinic had been bad, but the one to the hospital was indescribable. Fingers clenched tightly on the steering wheel, Gail leaned forward, peering blindly through the windshield. She didn't know how long the drive took, being too occupied trying not to get killed to check the clock, but it seemed like forever. Finally, the exit for the hospital came into sight.

The reddish glare of taillights registered even as she swerved to avoid them. She heard a crash, a sound of shattering glass and shrieking metal, and fought to escape, missing the car's rear end by inches. She stomped on the brakes, harder than she should have, and the car fishtailed, going off the shoulder into a ditch, and heading straight for a concrete piling. Again, she hit the brakes, pumping them before she applied more pressure. The car jerked to an abrupt halt, not twenty feet from the piling, and her head banged sharply against the steering wheel.

Her head swam and she saw stars, but she didn't

lose consciousness. Sick, shaking with nerves and fear, she managed to get the car into park. She touched her head, then looked at her fingers, relieved to find no blood. But a lump had sprung up immediately and seemed to be growing larger by the second.

Turning around, she squinted, trying to make out the accident through the rain. In a brief slackening of force, she saw a Mack truck and two cars twisted together in a tangled mass of metal and glass. Her stomach roiled. If she'd been in the middle of that mess, her van would have crumpled like an aluminum can.

And she and her baby could have been dead.

AT FIRST, JAY WASN'T too concerned not to find Gail at home. He figured she'd gone to see a friend, or possibly one of her brothers, though she hadn't mentioned she planned to. He didn't think she'd go much farther, not in this storm. And she wouldn't be at Cat's, since Mark had taken the family to Dallas to see their mother.

By late afternoon when she still hadn't shown up, though, he began to get worried. The phones were out, and had been for hours. The storm grew worse by the minute. Gail wouldn't voluntarily stay out in this kind of weather. Not when she couldn't reach him and she would know he'd be worried.

Although his cell phone worked intermittently, it didn't do him a lot of good with the land lines still out. Especially since he couldn't reach Gail's cell phone either. He did get hold of Gail's mother, who hadn't seen her either. That's when he decided to go look for her, and got in his car.

He checked everywhere he could think of. The clinic, a couple of friends, Gabe's house, and didn't find her anywhere. Surely she hadn't gone to Corpus in this kind of weather, he thought. But if she had, there was nothing he could do about it. He drove to the Scarlet Parrot, his last shot.

Not surprisingly, the restaurant was closed, so he went upstairs to Cam's quarters and beat on the door. It took several tries, but eventually Cam opened it, wearing jeans, no shirt, and an expression of extreme irritation.

"What the hell do you want?" his brother-in-law said.

"I'm looking for Gail." He glanced over Cam's shoulder, into the living room. A trail of clothes led to the hall doorway, among them a lacy pair of panties and a bra. In spite of his concern, he smiled. "But something tells me she's not here."

"Brilliant observation," Cam said, but he moved aside to let him in. "Ever hear of a telephone? Call her. She should have her cell phone with her."

Since he was soaked and dripping an ocean, Jay didn't go any farther than the entryway. "The lines are down, but I guess you wouldn't know that."

Cameron grinned. "Nope. Mine's been off the hook since last night. Okay, why would Gail be out in this storm?"

"I can't think of a good reason. That's why I'm

worried. I came home at lunch and she wasn't there then.''

Cam frowned and scrubbed his hands over his face. ''I haven't seen her or heard from her since yesterday, at Mom's.'' He thought a moment and said, ''Gabe's gone and so are Mark and Cat.''

''Yeah, I know. I went by Gabe's. In fact, I've looked for her car all over town. No luck.''

''Who has the girls?''

''They're at Barry's.''

''Did you try his house?''

''No.'' That was the only place he hadn't tried. Maybe the girls had gotten through to her earlier, and she'd gone over there to do something for them. But if so, why wasn't she back? She'd been gone for hours.

Just then a sultry redhead came to the hall doorway, wrapped in a sheet. ''Cameron, honey, you said you'd be right back.'' She leaned against the doorjamb and asked, ''Who's your friend?''

Cam smiled at her. ''Jay, meet Rita. Rita, this is my brother-in-law, Jay. I'll be there in a minute, baby. We've got kind of a problem here.''

''So do I,'' she said in a Georgia drawl, her lips pursed and pouting.

''Let me handle this and I'll be right back,'' he told Jay, and went to the redhead. Sliding his arm around her, he led her away.

Jay's cell phone rang. He snatched it up eagerly, but when he checked caller ID, his stomach plummeted. ''Kincaid.''

"Dr. Kincaid, this is Varner Memorial Hospital."

"Yes. Is this about my wife?"

"Yes, sir," the woman said, sounding surprised. "She's just arrived at the emergency room by ambulance. She's been involved in a car accident."

His heart literally stopped. He sucked in a breath, managed to say, "Her condition?"

"She hasn't been examined yet, but I can tell you she's conscious, and doesn't appear to be badly injured. She gave me your cell phone number and asked me to call you. And she said to tell you not to worry, that she's fine."

He was vaguely aware of Cameron, standing next to him now. "Did she tell you she's pregnant?"

"Yes. Her OB has been alerted."

"Good. I'll be there as soon as I can."

"What is it? You look terrible," Cameron said. "Was that about Gail?"

Jay stared at him blindly for a moment, then nodded. "She's at Varner Memorial." He looked into Cam's concerned eyes. "She was in a car accident."

Alarm flooded his eyes. "An accident? Oh, God, Jay. Is she—did they say how she is?"

"They don't know yet, but the nurse said she's conscious and doesn't appear to be badly hurt." That still didn't give him any clue as to the baby's condition, but at least Gail was alive and conscious.

"I've got to go," he said, turning toward the door.

"Wait, I'll come with you. Give me five minutes."

"Hurry," Jay called after him.

CAM HAD TAKEN ONE LOOK at him and refused to let him drive, so they went in his brother-in-law's four-wheel-drive truck. Probably a good thing, Jay thought, partly because the truck would handle the weather better and whoever drove needed to keep his mind on the road. For him that was clearly impossible. Jay spent the drive remembering every harrowing vehicular trauma that had ever come through the ER during his time there. What if Gail had internal injuries? What if she lost the baby as a result? Worse, what if— With a strong effort of will, he forced those thoughts away.

Normally, he wasn't so pessimistic. But he'd never had a wife and unborn child to worry about before. To try to get his mind off what he could do nothing about, he spoke to Cam. ''Rita didn't look too happy with you.'' Cam had bundled her up and made her leave when they did. She'd been half dressed and spitting mad when they drove away.

Concentrating on driving, Cam hadn't said much, either, but he grinned at that. ''She'll get over it. And if she doesn't—'' He shrugged. ''It was fun while it lasted. I don't know her well enough to leave her there, especially with access to the restaurant.''

As they neared Varner Memorial, Jay called, trying to get an update, but he struck out. He hung up and spoke to Cam. ''Still no news. The doctor hasn't seen her yet.''

''Is that a good sign or a bad sign?''

Jay hesitated, then decided to tell the truth. ''Could be either. She might be low on the list because she doesn't have a life-threatening injury. Or they could just be so busy that no one's been able to see her yet." In which case she could have internal injuries no one was aware of. He glanced out the window at the driving rain. He had a hunch the ER was a madhouse. Most of them were during storms like this one.

"Here's the exit," Cam said. "We'll know soon enough."

"And there's her car," Jay said hollowly, staring at the green van, crushed against the concrete piling with the driver's side completely smashed in.

"Oh, my God," Cam said, his hands gripping the steering wheel tightly. "And they said she's conscious and not hurt badly? How can that be when the car is totaled?"

Jay's stomach rolled as images of the van flashed in his mind. "I don't know. But she had to be conscious or they wouldn't have had my cell phone number to call. Besides, I don't believe the nurse would have lied to me."

"I hope to God you're right," Cam said.

Cameron dropped him off at the emergency room entrance and went to park the car, saying he'd catch up with him later. Jay stopped at the desk, where one of the nurses recognized him.

"Hello, Dr. Kincaid. I'm the one who called you earlier. Would you like me to take you to your wife?"

"Yes, thank you. Has anyone seen her yet?"

The nurse shook her head. "I think her OB may be in with her now."

"Why the hell hasn't the ER doc seen her?"

She looked surprised. "Well, all she had was a bump on the head. With the storm—" she gestured outside "—everyone's seeing the more severe trauma."

"A bump on the head? I passed her car on the way here. It's totaled."

She looked puzzled. "I don't know, Dr. Kincaid, but she said herself she was fine. She was anxious to see her OB, though."

Realizing he'd gain nothing more from her, he abandoned the nurse. "Never mind. Where is she?"

She pointed to a cubicle. Gail wasn't in it, but he tracked her to ultrasound. She was lying on the gurney while the nurse spread gel over her stomach and her doctor held the transducer, ready to begin the procedure.

Dr. Fletcher looked up, the annoyance on her face changing to pleasure when she recognized him. "Well, look who just walked in. I know someone who'll be thrilled to see you. Your wife's been asking for you every five minutes."

"Jay?" She turned her head to look at him and promptly burst into tears.

He reached her side in seconds, grasping the hand she held out to him. "Shh, baby, I'm here." She sobbed louder and said something incoherent. He soothed her again, dropping a kiss on her forehead, all the while checking her out. Just as the nurse had said, she had a bruise on her forehead, but he couldn't see a drop of blood anywhere. He didn't understand it, but he was sure as hell thankful for it.

"How is she, Merrilee?" he asked the doctor. "Has one of the ER docs seen her?"

"No, but I don't think it's necessary. I examined her before I did the pelvic and aside from a bump on the head, she seems fine. She's not dilated, or having contractions. She's no longer cramping, so I think we're safe in assuming the baby is fine, too. But we'll do an ultrasound, just to make sure. Let's get started," she said to the nurse.

Gail had quit crying, though she still held his hand as if she'd never let go. "I'm so glad you're here."

He smoothed his hand over her hair and smiled reassuringly at her. "Yeah, me too."

Dr. Fletcher began rubbing the transducer over Gail's stomach. "Plenty of movement," she said, pointing to the baby on the ultrasound screen. "See? The baby is very active. There's the heart beating." The nurse made an adjustment and the sound of the baby's heartbeat filled the room. "Strong heartbeat," she murmured. "I'm afraid it's a little early to tell the sex."

"That's all right." Gail smiled, tears welling in her eyes. "As long as the baby is healthy, we don't care what it is."

"Everything looks good, Gail. Your pregnancy is progressing just as it should." She handed the transducer to the nurse and smiled at Gail while the nurse wiped her stomach. "In a healthy pregnancy, a fall such as the one you described shouldn't cause you to miscarry. It's possible, but unlikely."

"What fall?" Jay asked the doctor sharply. Looking at Gail he said, "Aren't you here because of the wreck?"

"What wreck?" Gail asked, turning puzzled eyes to his. "I didn't have a wreck."

Not have a wreck? Then what the hell would she call it? A fender bender? "Gail, your car was totaled. Cam and I saw it on the side of the road."

"Cam? What's he doing here?"

"Never mind that. Your car is totaled and you don't even remember the accident?"

She still looked confused. "When I got out there wasn't a scratch on it. There was a pileup, but I managed to avoid that. Someone must have run into it after I left."

"Your wife had a fall earlier, Jay," Dr. Fletcher put in. "She experienced some cramping and decided to come in. Obviously, you didn't know about it."

"No, I had no idea," he said slowly. "The hospital called me and said she'd been in an accident."

"I'm sorry, Jay. I tried to reach you, but you weren't at the clinic and the phones were out."

He stared at her, trying to take it in. "You fell? What happened?"

"I was looking for something of Mel's and I fell off the stepstool. I had a couple of cramps." She glanced at the doctor, who smiled reassuringly at her. "I guess I panicked, thinking I might be going into premature labor, but Dr. Fletcher doesn't think there's anything to worry about."

He gazed at her incredulously as he took in what she was saying. She'd been afraid she was losing the baby, so she'd gone to the clinic, but hadn't found him there. So instead of coming home—where she was bound to know he'd be—she'd driven herself to the hospital. Alone. In the middle of a goddamn hurricane, yet. That was carrying independence a damn sight too far.

Dr. Fletcher's beeper went off. She glanced at it and frowned. "I have to go in a minute. Patient in labor." She looked at Gail. "Any more questions?"

"Why did I have those cramps? That's what scared me."

"They could have been caused by any number of things. Certainly, anxiety might have played a part." She scribbled on Gail's chart, then glanced at both of them. "As I said, I think you and the baby are fine, but I do think you should take it easy for a few days. If anything happens, if you have any symptoms, especially any bleeding or any more cramps, then, of course, call me."

"Do I have to stay in bed?"

"No, but I wouldn't do anything strenuous. No aerobics, for instance." She smiled and added, "And I'd refrain from sex for a few days, to be cautious."

Gail frowned and the doctor laughed. "Just for a few days," she repeated. "Don't worry, it's not for the duration. Make an appointment in a week, and we'll see how you're doing then."

"Thank you, Dr. Fletcher."

"I'll walk out with you," Jay said. "I'll be back in a minute, Gail." He needed some time to pull himself together, as well as speak to the doctor in private.

"She's fine, Jay. Really," Dr. Fletcher said.

"When you told her to take it easy, what exactly did you mean?"

"Just what I said. No heavy physical activity. No sex. She should rest more." She considered him a moment. "I'm not quite sure what's going on, but I get the idea you're not pleased about something. I'd think twice before I picked a fight with Gail. She doesn't need the emotional upset right now, either. She's already very emotional from the fall and the drive over through the storm."

Yeah, so was he. Jay nodded. "Don't worry. I won't do anything to upset her."

Gail had done it again, was all he could think. Cut him out one more time, this time with his own child. He'd been deluding himself that she was ready to share her life with him. All the progress he thought they'd made had disappeared the instant she drove off without him. But he wouldn't say a damn word about it. Even if it killed him to bottle up his feelings, he would do it. The baby's health, and Gail's health, were more important than his pain or hurt or anger.

He fought an overwhelming urge to put his fist through a wall. Instead, he took a deep breath, squared his shoulders and went back in the exam room to take care of his wife and unborn child. He wouldn't allow her to lock him totally out of their lives, no matter how much she might want to.

CHAPTER TWENTY

ON THE WAY HOME, Jay hardly said a word. Cam and Gail talked, Cam asking her what had happened. But Jay didn't make a comment or even ask a question. Gail put it down to the fact that he'd been worried about her and the baby, but his silence still bothered her.

She'd been scared to death to realize how very much she'd needed him. Physically, and more, emotionally. The drive to the hospital, alone in the storm, had only reinforced those feelings. When he'd walked in the door, she'd never been so glad to see anyone in her life.

Once they were home, he didn't become much more talkative, though. "What do you think I should do about the van?" she asked him. "It looks pretty bad." Again, she suffered a pang of guilt. Though it hadn't been her fault, since she hadn't even known about it, she realized the sight of the crushed van must have made Jay wild with worry.

"I'll arrange to have it towed to the shop. You can decide what you're going to do after you talk to them."

"Okay." She waited, but he didn't say anything

else. "Jay, are you upset with me?" she finally asked him.

He didn't answer directly. "Why don't you get in bed and I'll bring you some dinner."

Go to bed like a good girl, she thought. "Thanks, but the doctor said I didn't need to go to bed."

The look he gave her made her feel like a recalcitrant child. "It won't hurt you to rest, Gail. You've had a rough day."

"Fine," she said, exasperated. "But I asked you a question."

"You need to rest. We'll talk later," he said, and left her in the bedroom.

But they didn't. Not that evening, and not during any of the following days or evenings. Oh, they talked. But not about Gail's fall or her trip to the hospital. And while Jay was the same with the girls as he'd always been, with her he couldn't be called anything but chilly. He wasn't mean to her, he didn't act angry, but living with him was like living with a stranger.

The only reason Gail could think of for his behavior was that he was upset about her accident. She tried several times to get him to talk about it, but he simply refused. Once, he even left the house rather than talk to her. Gail thought that was carrying things a bit too far, but she couldn't figure out what to do about it.

The following Friday Gail met Cat for lunch at the Scarlet Parrot. Brooding about her troubles, she listened to Cat with half an ear until her sister rapped her hand on the table and said, "Gail, what is with you? I asked you the same question three times and you haven't answered me yet.''

''I'm sorry. I was thinking about something else.'' She picked up a French fry and munched on it without much enthusiasm. ''What did you say?''

''Never mind that. Is something wrong?''

''Why do you ask?''

''Gee, I don't know. You've hardly spoken a word.'' She tapped Gail's plate. ''And you've hardly touched your lunch. That's not like you.''

Gail sighed. ''I'm just not hungry.''

A frown creased Cat's brow. ''Now you've really got me worried. You're always hungry. Spill it,'' her sister commanded.

''There's nothing to spill,'' she said, frustrated. ''If I knew, I'd tell you.''

''Is it you and Jay? Are you two having problems?''

Gail nodded miserably. ''Something's going on, but I can't figure out what it is. I think Jay's mad at me, except he won't talk to me enough for me to figure it out.''

Cat took a sip of tea and settled down to listen. ''Why would he be mad at you?''

''The obvious answer is last weekend. But he won't discuss it. At all.''

Cat frowned. ''That doesn't sound like Jay. Do you really think he's that unreasonable? I mean, it isn't like you fell on purpose.'' She regarded Gail for a long moment, then said, ''You're feeling guilty, aren't you?''

Gail started to deny it, but found she couldn't. "Yes, but not about the fall." Her gaze met Cat's and she continued. "It was the accident. I'm telling you, Cat, when I saw that wreck and realized how close I'd come to being in the middle of it—" She shivered. "Both the baby and I could have been killed."

Cat covered her hand and squeezed comfortingly. "But you weren't."

"No, but I'm afraid that's what Jay is thinking, too. Remember, he saw my totaled van on the way over, and I'm sure that scared him to death. He didn't know I hadn't been in the car when that happened."

"Yeah, that was bound to have revved him up, and fear generally makes people mad. Especially men," she said reflectively. "Have you ever noticed the more scared they are the madder they get? And if they're scared about someone they love, it's even worse."

Gail nodded. "I know. And I think he was really scared by the time he got to the hospital. He knew I'd given the nurse his number, but he didn't know anything about the baby."

"But why hasn't he said anything? Is that how he usually reacts when he's mad?"

Gail laughed and shoved her plate away. "No way. Usually, he blows up and yells, and if he's really ticked off, he leaves. Then he comes back and acts as if nothing happened."

Cat tapped her fingers on the table, frowning. "Maybe he's afraid to upset you. He's worried about you and the baby.'' She picked up her sandwich and took a bite.

"Maybe." She shrugged. "I just don't know. He's not acting like himself at all. He won't talk. He won't kiss me, unless I kiss him first. Since last weekend, he's hardly touched me."

"Your doctor said no hanky-panky," Cat reminded her. "Could be he just doesn't want to tempt himself."

"It's possible, but I don't think so." Thinking hard, she frowned. "He's nice. He's polite." She slapped her fist on the table. "And he's so damn distant it's like living with a stranger."

"Sounds like you're just going to have to force him to talk to you."

"Don't worry, I intend to," she said. "And tonight's the night."

GAIL PLANNED THE EVENING carefully. First, she would seduce him. Then, while he was recovering from that, she'd sneak in under his defenses and get him to talk. If he would just tell her what was bothering him, she knew they could fix it. His stubborn refusal to talk wasn't helping either of them.

He wouldn't get the chance to leave, not if she had to flush his keys down the toilet and throw herself bodily in front of the door.

Like a general placing his troops, she set the scene. Mel and Roxy had gone to Barry's. A tomato basil pesto sauce, one of Jay's favorites, simmered on the stove. She lit candles, put on soft music, chilled a bottle of wine for him and one of sparkling grape juice for herself. She wore a soft pink cashmere sweater that made the most of her new curves and a short skirt that she probably wouldn't be able to fit into in a week.

After stirring the sauce, she tasted it, and hummed her approval. Pretty good, if she did say so herself. She heard his car drive up. When the door opened she turned around and gave him a welcoming smile. "Dinner should be ready soon. Why don't I pour you a glass of wine?"

His expression wary, he tossed his keys and brief-case down on the kitchen table. "All right. I'm going to change."

He didn't stop by the stove to kiss her, which didn't surprise her, since he hadn't kissed her hello in a week. In fact, he hadn't kissed her voluntarily, period, in a week. She pushed that thought—and the hurt it brought with it—out of her mind. Now wasn't the time for grievances, but for action.

A short time later, he returned, wearing soft, faded jeans and a long-sleeve knit shirt. Looking, she thought, good enough to eat. "Your wine is on the table," she told him, and bent to pull another pan out to cook the pasta in.

"Thanks." He picked up his wineglass and took a sip.

"What happened to the music?" she asked him.

"I turned it off."

She stared at him a minute. "Why?"

He didn't answer, just shrugged and took another

sip of wine. He glanced at the bare kitchen table. "Do you want me to set the table?"

"It's set." She glanced at him and forced a smile. "In the other room."

Again, that wary look came into his eyes. "So what's the occasion?"

"No occasion. I just wanted to make a nice meal for the two of us." She tamped down on her irritation. Was he being deliberately obtuse? It sure seemed like it. She wanted to seduce him, not bop him over the head, but he was making it difficult to remember that.

He took a seat at the kitchen table and began reading the newspaper. Gail gritted her teeth, counted to ten, then put the water for the pasta on to boil and popped the French bread in the oven.

A little while later, she told him dinner was ready. He filled his plate and went into the dining room ahead of her. When she came in after him she noticed he'd turned on the overhead lights and was in the act of blowing out the candles.

She stopped in midstride and bit her cheek to keep from screaming. She sat down and started to eat, even though by now everything tasted like ashes.

They ate in silence until she finally broke it. "I had an appointment with Dr. Fletcher today."

Jay looked up from his plate. "What did she say?"

She set her fork down and looked at him. "The baby and I are both fine. Dr. Fletcher said we're healthy as could be, and that I can resume normal activity." She paused and added, "*All* normal activity.'' Surely she didn't need to spell it out more than that.

His expression became hooded. "That's good news," he said, but his voice was flat. He returned his attention to his food, not saying anything more.

"Yes, isn't it?" she said sarcastically, her temper snapping. "Not that you give a good damn."

He glanced at her irritably. "Don't be ridiculous, Gail. Of course I'm glad you and the baby are doing well."

"Just like you're glad we can make love again? Because if you are, you have a damn funny way of showing it." Tears of frustration sprang to her eyes, but she wouldn't let them fall. He'd already ruined the evening she had planned. She didn't intend to let him make her cry as well.

He didn't answer, but finished his pasta and took his plate into the kitchen. Infuriated, Gail followed him. He'd blown her idea of seduction, but she'd be damned if he got away with ignoring her any longer.

"If you think you're going to get out of talking about this, think again. I've had it up to here—" she put her hand under her chin to illustrate "—with your attitude."

He said nothing, just continued to rinse off his dishes and put them in the dishwasher.

"What's the matter with you? You won't talk to me, you won't touch me..." Her voice trailed away as a sudden realization hit her. She put her hand on his arm, and to her mortification, her voice broke.

"Jay, what is it? Tell me, please. Do you just not want me anymore?"

"Not want you?" His eyes were bleak, his tone, almost desperate. "I'll always want you. I want you so much I'm almost willing to—" He broke off, shook his head, turned away from her. "I can't do this."

"Oh, yes you can." She put her hand on his arm and jerked on it until he turned to face her. "Don't you dare leave. We're talking this out, whether you want to or not."

His gaze met hers, his eyes sharp, and hard as diamonds. "All right."

He jerked her into his arms and crushed his mouth to hers, kissing her with a greedy desperation she'd never felt from him before. Her head swam, her blood heated. She flung an arm around his neck and kissed him back, though a part of her hated that he could wreck her defenses with a kiss, make her forget how he'd treated her the past week and even that very evening in a burst of passion and fierce longing.

He raised his head, still holding her crushed against his chest. "I want you, Gail. So much that I conned myself into believing that what we have is a marriage, instead of mutual lust and fantastic sex."

Shock shook her to the core. "That's not all we have. You know it isn't."

He released her. Walked away from her, then turned to face her again. "Isn't it? I don't deny you're willing—happy—to share your body with me, but I've had to twist your arm to get you to share anything else. The girls, our living expenses, every single thing you've shared, you've only done it because I forced the issue.''

''If this is about last weekend—'' she began.

He laughed, though he didn't sound amused. ''Yes, Gail, this is about last weekend.''

''You're angry because I fell—''

Again, he cut her off. ''Give me some credit. I'm not angry because you had an accident.''

''Then why are you so upset? I told you I tried to reach you. I went to the clinic. You weren't there.''

''No, I was heading home. Which you knew.''

She had known, but she brushed his words aside impatiently. ''I was afraid if I went home I'd lose time. It's on the opposite side of town, Jay. I couldn't be positive you would be there,'' she said, knowing she sounded defensive and hating it. ''I thought it was more important to get to the hospital.'' She'd done what she thought best. If he couldn't see that, to hell with him.

''So instead of coming to me, you drove to the hospital in the middle of a goddamn hurricane. By yourself.''

''I didn't have a choice! I was afraid I was losing the baby!''

His gaze hardened, as did his jawline. ''You did have a choice. And you made it. Alone. Just like you make all your choices. All your decisions. You value your independence so much you put your life and our baby's life at risk rather than ask someone for help. Rather than ask me, your husband, for help.''

"If you'd been at the clinic, I would have asked you. But you weren't there for me. Just like—" Horrified, she bit her lip at what she'd been about to say.

"Go ahead and finish it. Just like Barry. Isn't that what you were about to say?" He took a step, standing right in front of her, though he didn't touch her. His eyes flashed, his mouth tightened into a grim line. "It doesn't matter that I've been there for you every other time, whenever you needed me. And I would have been there for you this time, if you'd only trusted me. But you can't do that, can you, Gail? You're never going to let yourself trust me. No matter what I do, how many hoops I jump through, you won't trust me. Because you don't *want* to trust me."

"Trust has nothing to do with this. You're angry because I made a decision without you." She'd been alone, and she'd learned her lesson well from her first marriage. She could only depend on herself. "I did what I thought was best. Who are you to second-guess me?"

"Nobody important. Just your husband."

They stared at each other in silence for a long moment, then he turned his back and walked out of the room.

She stood there a moment, quivering with fury, with guilt, with desperation. A seething mass of contradictory emotions. Tears stung at her eyes, but she brushed them away impatiently. She had no time for tears. How had they gone from deliriously happy and in love one week to shouting such hurtful things at each other the next? Had Jay always felt this way?

Or was he just reacting to the accident, and this is what came of it?

She found him in the bedroom, sitting on the side of the bed. She was sick and tired of taking all the heat for a decision she still believed had been the right one. "You're condemning me for making a choice, and you have no idea what I felt like when I made that choice."

He glanced at her. "I'm not condemning you. I'm finally admitting that you're never going to trust me, no matter what I do. I kept thinking the trust would grow. That if I just loved you enough, you'd trust me, eventually." He laughed without humor. "Last weekend proved to me that was never going to happen."

Anger spiked in her bloodstream. "According to you this is all my fault. Well, I've got news for you, Jay. If you think it's been easy living with you for the past week, you're wrong. Your way of solving the problem is to avoid it, and guess what? It doesn't work."

"Oh, and this does?" He got up and stood glaring at her. "I can't see that we've accomplished anything by talking. Besides, your doctor said not to upset you. I didn't think a scene like this would be good for you or the baby." He turned away.

Her heart constricted. "It's always the baby, isn't it? We wouldn't be married, hell, we probably wouldn't even still be together if not for the baby. Tell me something, Jay." She paused until he looked at her. "If I had lost the baby would you have stayed married to me?"

"You didn't lose the baby. Besides, the baby isn't the issue here. Our marriage—or lack of it—is."

"You don't love me at all, do you?" she whispered, suddenly struck by the truth. "You love the baby. It's always been the baby, and I've just been too stupid to see it."

"You're wrong. If I didn't love you why would I care if you trusted me, or shared your life with me?"

She couldn't answer.

"This is pointless," he said after a moment. "I'm going to sleep in the spare room." He started gathering his things, his pillow, the book on the beside table.

The baby's room, Gail thought. "No." She shook her head. "No, don't."

"Gail—"

"I want you to leave." Unable to stop them, the words burst from her. She'd never imagined saying those words to Jay. Never imagined the pain it would cause her to speak them.

He stopped gathering his stuff and stared at her incredulously. "You're kicking me out?"

"You need to leave," she repeated, barely able to speak past the tightness in her throat.

"Is that really what you want? You want us to break up?"

"I...don't know. I know I need to be alone."

"Fine. You want your goddamn independence so much, you've got it."

He went to his closet, returned a moment later with a duffel bag he threw on the bed. In silence, he began to pack. Gail watched him, unable to speak. She felt as if she were in a dream. No, a nightmare.

He finished packing, zipped the bag, and looked at her, as if waiting to see what she would say.

"Where are you going to stay?"

"The Palm Tree motel," he said, naming the only hotel actually in Aransas City.

She winced, knowing the place was only a step above a dive. "You can stay at my house. Since it hasn't sold, there's no reason for you not to."

"No. I can't stay two doors down from you." He shook his head. "I'm going to the Palm Tree. I'll call you about picking up the rest of my stuff."

The rest of his stuff? It sounded so final. How could he be so calm when she felt as if her world was coming apart? "I'm not talking about divorce," she said, hating the sound of the word. "I just think we need some time…to think. To consider our problems."

"Right." He stopped at the bedroom door and looked at her. "You let me know what you decide, Gail."

He's furious, she realized, looking into those sharp green eyes. "This isn't over," she said, desperately hoping that was true.

"Isn't it? It feels pretty damn final to me," he said, and left.

CHAPTER TWENTY-ONE

JAY HAD KNOWN the Palm Tree wouldn't be the most luxurious place to stay, but the reality of it exceeded even his worst expectations. The night before he'd been too mad and upset to notice much, but the light of day brought the realization that he'd be suicidal if he stayed more than a night or two in the dump.

It wasn't dirty, but that was the best you could say about it. The room boasted a kitchenette with cracked Formica countertops, an ancient stove and an equally ancient refrigerator. A battered, stainless steel drip coffeepot stood on the stove along with a few equally hammered pots and pans. The cupboards and drawers held a set of four mismatched dishes, glasses, silverware, a can opener and a broken corkscrew.

Home sweet home, Jay thought. The rest of the room was no better, with dirt-colored carpet, grimy dark walls, a broken-down couch, a TV that only got one channel, and a bed whose sagging springs were covered with the ugliest bedspread he'd ever seen.

He would have to find an apartment. He'd spoken the truth when he said he couldn't live two doors down from Gail. How could he stand seeing her daily, not to mention Mel and Roxy, and know he couldn't be with them? No, an apartment it would have to be. Gail would keep the dogs, he knew. The girls loved them and she was fond of them too. Hell, maybe he could have visiting rights to the dogs, along with his child and the girls.

Visiting rights. The thought made his chest hurt. Gail had said she didn't want a divorce, but he could see what way they were heading and it wasn't getting back together.

He admitted the whole fiasco last night had been partly his fault. Before he knew it, he'd found himself yelling about everything that bothered him or worried him in their relationship. More, everything he'd kept bottled up for the past week had gushed out of his mouth like a damn flood. And Gail had been right. He'd blamed everything on her. Hell, no wonder she'd kicked him out.

He'd overreacted, and he knew it. But damn it, that's why he knew talking things out never solved anything. What had talking done but get them to this point? he thought, looking around at his dismal surroundings. On the verge of divorce with no way to fix it.

Someone pounded on his door. His heart leapt as he rose. It had to be Gail. She was the only person who knew where he was.

He opened the door to his brother. *Stupid,* he thought. *Of course it's not Gail. Haven't you gotten it through your thick head that she doesn't want you?*

"What the hell is your problem?" Mark asked, striding inside.

"The only person who knows where I am is Gail. So obviously, you know what my problem is." He took a seat on the couch, propped his feet on the rickety coffee table and watched his brother pace the room.

"What the hell are you doing? How could you leave Gail? She's pregnant with your kid, for God's sake."

"I didn't leave her. Gail kicked me out."

That stopped Mark. "She said you left."

"I did. When she asked me to."

"Oh, man." Mark took a seat beside him on the couch. "I'm sorry, Jay. I didn't know."

Jay shrugged. "Forget it."

"Do you have any coffee?" Mark asked.

"On the stove. It's drinkable. Barely."

"This place is disgusting," Mark said as he came back with his mug. "Come stay with us."

"Thanks, but no. I won't be here long. I'll find an apartment soon."

Mark sat down again. "What happened?" he asked after a moment. "Why did she kick you out?"

Jay shot him an irritable look. "Talking's what got me into this mess in the first place. Nothing good ever comes from talking. That's a female myth."

"You have a point," Mark said, and was quiet a moment. "Do you still love her? Do you want to get back together with her?"

"Yeah." More than he could say. "Not that it matters."

Mark frowned. "That's a defeatist attitude. You

had a fight. So what? Everyone has fights. Why don't you try to fix it? You know, grovel if you have to.''

Jay's laugh held no humor. ''Groveling won't help. I don't think anything will. It wasn't just the fight. Gail's finally figured out she doesn't really want to be married to me.'' His gaze met Mark's. ''I've had to talk her into everything, starting with marriage, from the get-go. I can't do it anymore. It isn't working. It never worked. I was just too stupid to see the failure.''

''So you're going to give up on your marriage? Just like that? Without even a fight?''

Jay stood up, shoved his hands in the pockets of his jeans and began to pace. ''What else can I do, Mark? Gail asked me to leave. She doesn't want me there anymore. She doesn't want *me* anymore.'' Did she ever, he wondered. Or had it all been him?

''Bull. She's crazy in love with you.''

''No, she's not.'' He shook his head, realizing it was true. ''She might think she is, but she isn't.'' She was crazy about the sex, but love was a whole different story. Too bad he hadn't figured that out until now.

''What are you going to do?''

''I'm going to give her what she wants,'' Jay said. And if she wanted a divorce, he'd give it to her.

He would survive. He'd survived when his father left. When his mother deserted them. He would live through Gail divorcing him.

But damn it, he didn't want to live through it. He wanted to live with Gail, and Mel and Roxy and the new baby. He wanted to keep the family he'd found. So he had a choice. Give up, or fight for what he wanted.

GAIL KNEW she was being irrational, but she couldn't believe Jay had left so easily. He hadn't even tried to talk her out of it. Maybe he'd wanted to leave her, but his conscience wouldn't let him. His sense of obligation. So she'd given him the perfect opening when she'd asked him to leave.

She'd slept, finally, but badly, her dreams tortured and jumbled. And always with the one image of Jay walking out the door with his duffel bag slung over his shoulder. She'd awakened that morning reaching for him. Of course, he hadn't been there. He would never be there again, unless she asked him to come back. But did he even want to come back to her?

She went through the motions of her day. Alone. Knowing Jay wouldn't be walking in the door. Knowing she wouldn't have him to tell about the latest crazy thing the puppies had done. Or what Mel or Roxy had said when they called. Knowing he wouldn't touch her, hold her, kiss her. How could she miss him so much when he hadn't even been gone a day?

Cat had called and wanted to come over, clearly after talking to Mark. Gail had put her off, unwilling to talk to anyone about what had happened. She wanted to wallow in her misery alone.

God, she was an idiot. Why had she asked him to leave? So what if he'd been wrong to blame everything on her? That didn't mean she had to kick him out of the house. Besides, though it hurt to admit it, he'd had a point. She'd known ever since she looked at that wreck, that if she and the baby had been hurt or injured it would have been her fault and hers alone.

Was Jay right? Did she just not want to trust him? No, she wanted to, but she was afraid to trust him. Afraid to let him in that last part of her heart. Because of Barry, she realized. When Barry had left her, he'd destroyed her ability to trust again. She was allowing him—by her reaction to his leaving—to wreck her marriage with Jay just as he'd wrecked their own marriage.

She had a choice. Watch her marriage crumble, or fight for it.

AFTER PICKING UP a pizza and a six-pack of beer, Jay returned to his motel room. He'd thought about eating it at the pizza place, but since he had no desire to talk to anyone he knew, he took it back with him. As he'd discovered earlier, the door stuck, so he had to put down everything and ram his shoulder into it to get it to open.

He picked up the pizza and beer and walked in, then stopped dead in his tracks when he saw who sat on his couch.

"Hi," Gail said, getting up. "I hope you don't mind, but I got the clerk to let me in."

Mind? She stood there, her blond hair feathering around her face, her voice soft and inviting. He wanted to eat her alive. Instead he set his dinner down on the coffee table. "No, I'm glad to see you."

Her hands twisted together nervously. He couldn't decide if that was a good or a bad sign.

"This place is awful," she said, glancing around. "I told the clerk we were married, but I don't think he believed me." She shuddered. "He told me to have fun and gave me the nastiest wink when he let me in."

"I don't imagine he gets a lot of married couples here. At least, people who are married to each other." He wanted to take her in his arms, kiss her, make love to her. He tucked his hands in his pockets so he wouldn't touch her. "Why don't you sit down? Have you eaten? There's pizza."

"No, thanks. I'm not very hungry."

"Are you sick?" he asked, concerned. He'd never known Gail not to be hungry.

She smiled reluctantly. "No. But my heart is."

Relief swept over him like the tide. If she could admit that so easily, then they still had a chance. "I didn't think it was possible to miss you so much. It's only been one night and a day."

"Oh, Jay," she said, her voice breaking. "The minute you left I wanted to kick myself. I love you. I missed you, too."

He closed the distance between them and took her in his arms. "Thank God. I love you, too," he said, and kissed her. She wrapped her arms around him, holding him as tightly as he held her. He kissed her again. Her lips were warm, her mouth soft, welcoming. He felt as if he'd come home and wanted to kiss her forever.

Finally, she turned her head and gave a breathless laugh. "I need to catch my breath."

So did he. He was so happy to be holding her in his arms again that he ignored the voice in his mind reminding him that they still hadn't solved anything.

"I was a jerk," he said, and kissed her head where it rested beneath his chin.

She looked up at him and smiled. "Yes, you were. But you were right, too."

He took the few steps to the couch and pulled her down beside him, putting his arm around her. "What was I right about?"

"I should have come home instead of driving to the hospital by myself. It wasn't a good decision, but at the time, I thought I was making the right one."

"You were right, too," he told her. "I should have respected your decision. When I saw your car, though, I went ballistic. And it didn't help that I couldn't really say anything to you."

"We were both wrong. But you were wrong about something else, too," she said, and smiled. "I do trust you, Jay."

He couldn't help looking skeptical, but he didn't say anything.

"I came over here to tell you a story. About Barry and me. And when he left me."

"Mark told me. Some, anyway."

"I wondered if he hadn't. But Mark doesn't know the whole story. Neither does Cat. No one does."

But she was telling him. Maybe she did trust him, at least a little. He pulled her close against his side. "What happened?"

"You know the short version. I came home one day from visiting my mother with the girls and found a note from Barry. He said he had an opportunity in another city. Something big, something that could be great. But he couldn't take us with him, and he knew I'd understand. He didn't ask for a divorce, but after that, I couldn't see any other option." Her eyes met Jay's and she smiled ruefully. "Especially when the next day I discovered that he'd cleaned out our bank accounts. He left me with a hundred dollars."

He'd known it was bad, but he hadn't realized quite how bad. "I'm surprised your brothers let him live."

"They wouldn't have, if they could have found him. But we didn't know where he'd gone. I didn't hear from him for two years, when he moved back to town and decided he did want his daughters after all."

"A lot of women wouldn't have given him that chance."

"He's their father. Even if I think he's a pig, he's still their father." She shifted, rubbed her cheek on his shoulder. "When he left, I wasn't sorry. Shocked, that he'd left like he did, but not really sorry. We'd had problems from the beginning."

She shook her head, gave a wry smile. "He had affairs. I pretended he didn't. He never was there for me. I pretended that didn't matter either. Even when he didn't show up at the hospital when I had my babies, I let it go. Do you know why?'' she asked and looked up at him.

He shook his head. ''Because you loved him?''

''No, not by the time he left. No, I let him treat me like he did because I was scared. Of being alone, of having to support myself and the girls.'' She sighed and shook her head. ''I hadn't worked since I had Roxy. I had a marketing degree, but I didn't like my job. So after I had Roxy, I quit. I liked staying home with the girls. I didn't want to go back to work and leave them.''

He took her hand and squeezed it. ''Wanting to stay home with your kids isn't a bad thing, either.''

''No, except that it made me too dependent on Barry.'' She straightened and met his gaze. ''When Barry left, I panicked. I had no real job skills. Believe me, nobody wanted a marketing major who'd been out of the game for nearly five years. And I had no choice that time, I had to support myself and the girls.''

''Anyone in your position would have been scared. That's a lot of responsibility to shoulder alone.''

''I was a spineless, gutless fool,'' she said flatly.

He frowned, not liking to hear her run herself down. ''Don't say that. You weren't.''

''Yes, I was. I let Barry treat me like dirt, because I was afraid. But I changed. After he left, I knew I could never, ever put myself in a position like that again. I found work. Not a career, but a job. For a long time, I worked two jobs and Mom took care of the girls. I decided I'd better find a career, because working the two jobs was killing me and I never saw my children. That's when I decided to get my real estate license.''

"You'd just taken the test when we met,'' he remembered.

She nodded. "That's right. I was celebrating that night. Getting my license was one of the best things I've ever done. I love my job.'' She faced him, gazing at him intently. "And I need it. For more than just the money. Do you understand that?''

"Yes.'' He touched his fingers to her cheek. "Gail, I've never even considered talking you into quitting your job. Why would I?''

She reached up to take his hand. "I know you wouldn't. But you want to take care of me.''

He opened his mouth to deny it, but he couldn't. She was right, he did want to take care of her. And the baby and the girls and the dogs. He liked taking care of people. It was one reason he'd become a doctor. "I can't help that. It's what I do.''

"It scared me,'' she said. "I was afraid that if I let you take care of me, I'd become that clingy, dependent woman I had promised myself I'd never be again. I didn't realize it consciously, but subconsciously it made me all the more determined to be independent.''

"And I didn't help matters. Because what I saw as sharing, you saw as being dependent.''

Her eyes on his, she nodded. "And I'm sure I'll do it again and we'll fight about it again. Because that's my nature as much as taking care of people is in yours. But it doesn't mean I don't trust you, Jay.''

This time he believed her. "I understand that now. I didn't before." He smoothed his hand over her hair and smiled at her. "I'm glad you told me."

"I was afraid to tell you. Afraid you'd be disgusted."

"Never." He kissed her. "You're a lot harder on yourself than anyone else would be. You didn't do anything wrong, Gail. You simply depended on the wrong person. Don't forget, Barry was as much, or more at fault than you were."

She sighed, and snuggled against him. "I never wanted to tell anyone before. I didn't think I *could* tell anyone about it. But now that I have I feel—" She hesitated a moment. "I feel good."

"Me, too." He kissed the top of her head and held her tight. "There's one thing that could make us feel even better."

"Really?" She drew back and gave him a sultry smile. Put her hand on his leg, and slid it slowly up his thigh. "Now, what would that be, I wonder?"

"Keep going," he said, and sucked in a breath as her hand continued its journey and her lips locked on his. "I'm sure we'll figure it out."

EPILOGUE

Five months later

GAIL CLUNG to Jay's hand, squeezing it as hard as she could as pain rippled through her.

"You're doing great, sweetheart," he said, and used his other hand to brush her hair out of her face. "Just a little bit longer."

"What do you know?" she asked, gasping as the pain ebbed. But another pain swamped her, even as the last one passed.

"All right, Gail," Dr. Fletcher said. "I want you to push with this next contraction."

"You—go—" she gasped out to Jay. "I want you to—deliver it."

"Are you sure?"

She could see his eyes light up even as he asked. She managed a smile. "Yes."

He kissed her, then moved to join her doctor. Gail concentrated on pushing, and trying to breathe through the pain. She pushed and panted, until exhausted, she lay back. "I can't do any more," she wheezed.

"Yes, you can," Jay said. "The head is crowning. You're almost there, honey."

The words worked like a tonic. She gathered herself one more time, and bore down, digging her hands into the sheet and straining with everything she was worth. Jay and the doctor were both talking, encouraging her, she thought, but she couldn't make sense of it. And then, miraculously, she heard a thin wail, rapidly turning to a full-bodied cry.

She pushed herself up on her elbows. "What is it? I want to see my baby."

"It's a boy," Jay said. Gail lay back and he put the baby in her arms. "We have a son, Gail."

"Oh, he's beautiful." Tears ran down her cheeks as she gazed at her baby, tracing her fingers over his cheek, his nose, his damply curling blond hair.

"Yeah, he is. And so are you," Jay said and kissed her. "Thank you for my son."

She smiled through her tears. "You had something to do with it, too."

"Yeah, but you did all the hard work."

"Oh, Jay, look. Isn't he perfect?" She marveled at the small fingers and toes, the tiny nose and rosebud mouth. She'd forgotten how tiny, how precious newborn babies were.

"Perfect," Jay said, and kissed her again, long and lovingly. "Funny how things turn out that way sometimes."

Later, when Gail watched Jay put his new son into Roxy's waiting arms, she thought her cup had overflowed. Even Mel was awed, leaning over Roxy's shoulder and stroking the baby's hair. A promise that she could hold him next had pacified her.

"What are you going to name him, Mommy?" Roxy asked.

Her eyes met Jay's and she smiled. "Jason. After his father."

"Jason Randolph Kincaid," Jay said. "My son."

"My brother," Mel said. "And it's my turn to hold him."

Roxy and Mel began to argue.

"Remember what we talked about," Gail said. "No fighting over the baby. You'll get your turn, Mel." She looked at Jay, beaming down at the children. "He's going to be hopelessly spoiled before he's a week old."

"That's all right," Jay said, dropping a kiss on his son's head. "What are families for?"

If you enjoyed what you just read,
then we've got an offer you can't resist!

Take 2 bestselling love stories FREE!

Plus get a FREE surprise gift!

Clip this page and mail it to Harlequin Reader Service®

IN U.S.A.	IN CANADA
3010 Walden Ave.	P.O. Box 609
P.O. Box 1867	Fort Erie, Ontario
Buffalo, N.Y. 14240-1867	L2A 5X3

YES! Please send me 2 free Harlequin Superromance® novels and my free surprise gift. After receiving them, if I don't wish to receive anymore, I can return the shipping statement marked cancel. If I don't cancel, I will receive 6 brand-new novels every month, before they're available in stores. In the U.S.A., bill me at the bargain price of $4.47 plus 25¢ shipping and handling per book and applicable sales tax, if any*. In Canada, bill me at the bargain price of $4.99 plus 25¢ shipping and handling per book and applicable taxes**. That's the complete price, and a savings of at least 10% off the cover prices—what a great deal! I understand that accepting the 2 free books and gift places me under no obligation ever to buy any books. I can always return a shipment and cancel at any time. Even if I never buy another book from Harlequin, the 2 free books and gift are mine to keep forever.

135 HDN DNT3
336 HDN DNT4

Name	(PLEASE PRINT)	
Address	Apt.#	
City	State/Prov.	Zip/Postal Code

* Terms and prices subject to change without notice. Sales tax applicable in N.Y.
** Canadian residents will be charged applicable provincial taxes and GST.
All orders subject to approval. Offer limited to one per household and not valid to current Harlequin Superromance® subscribers.
® is a registered trademark of Harlequin Enterprises Limited.

SUP02   ©1998 Harlequin Enterprises Limited

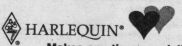
HINTBB

Saving Money Has Never Been This Easy!

Just fill out and send in this form from any October, November and December 2002 books and we will send you a coupon booklet worth a total savings of $20.00 off future purchases of Harlequin and Silhouette books in 2003.

Yes! It's that easy!

I accept your incredible offer!
Please send me a coupon booklet:

Name (PLEASE PRINT)

Address   Apt. #

City   State/Prov.   Zip/Postal Code

In a typical month, how many
Harlequin and Silhouette novels do you read?

❏ 0-2   ❏ 3+

097KJKDNC7   097KJKDNDP

Please send this form to:
    In the U.S.: Harlequin Books, P.O. Box 9071, Buffalo, NY 14269-9071
    In Canada: Harlequin Books, P.O. Box 609, Fort Erie, Ontario L2A 5X3

Allow 4-6 weeks for delivery. Limit one coupon booklet per household. Must be postmarked no later than January 15, 2003.

PHQ402